No Time To Waste

Written by Martin P. Frenette

Legal Deposit: First Quarter 2024
Bibliothèque et Archives nationales du Québec
Library and Archives Canada

Part One

Chapter 1.1—Lily Murdered

Steven Clark murdered his wife in 2002, Elizabeth, and hid her body. At least, that's what the public firmly believes. A court of law failed to condemn him, nor even see him arrested. Steven didn't actually kill his beloved. She apparently vanished into thin air one day, leaving her belongings behind, and never returned.

Steven adored Lily. In fact, he still does. Time changed him tremendously. Well, not that his life felt much better before his wife's sudden departure.... But at least, while he was dating Lily, Steven considered himself happy. His own family provided no affection or comfort. When Lily came into his entourage, she opened his eyes to how oppressive they acted toward him.

"But they never abused me."

"That isn't just what an abuser did to you. It's what they didn't do that they should have done. They should have loved you, made you feel appreciated, welcomed. It shouldn't rest on my shoulder to remain the first one to provide care for you."

And like always, she hit the nail right on! Not just on their failures as parents and as siblings, but also about how she did a lot of good to him.In reality, Lily remained the person he knew the most, and yet, he saw her as the biggest mystery of his life, even before she disappeared.

His wonderful wife worked as a historian, specialized on the Industrial Revolution. Her job took her to observe events generations away. She would devour any fiction set in that era, usually chuckling at the anachronism and the mistakes. Oh, so many of them, so many laughs. How people spoke, how they dressed, how the streets looked. Steven wondered how she could visualize these elements from ancient tales and get a great big picture of how life was in the 19th century. And yet, her studies narrowly focused on the evolution of a single tool from the Industrial Revolution. Just one.

3

At parties with her colleagues, they would sit in a half-circle around her as she used her brilliant imagination to tell old stories in depth, describing even the smell of a factory and the children's names tolling away. Often only remembered from yellowing company ledgers miraculously found in a forgotten rusty safe.

Because Lily did have a vivid ingenuity, and not just for the past. As a hobby, she dabbled in quantum physics, pushing discoveries that felt at least a century in advance. "It's the same principle, Stevie, don't you see? Steam carried the industrial era, quantum physics will propel whatever comes after the information age."

Steven often humoured that she couldn't remain anchored in the present, that she was studying the old times, or imagining the future. She would joke, instead, that she saw herself as both a historian, examining the remnants of the past, and a reverse historian, investigating the insignificant breakthroughs that would bring the next one.

Still, whenever he jested, she would contradict him. "My now, Stevie, delves on you. My studies, my work, are only so we can have a comfortable existence together, and my future... ah, that's our tomorrow. I'm pondering about things you could construct to evade the boring life of maintaining equipment by building your own projects and earning revenues from them."

According to her, he rose as her inspiration for impending projects that without him, she would never have thought about electronics. Her passion previously invoked inventions prior to electricity. And yet, Steven didn't mind the monotony. Work suited him, kept him grounded, safe, sane. He didn't bother with Lily earning more money than he did, but he would worry if he found himself unable to contribute.

Lily worked as a historian. Her broad subject focused on the evolution of technology, how it changes people, industry and the world. It remained her job to interpolate between scant sources two hundred years ago to figure out how advancements gradually arose between those records. Yet, she found a hobby in extrapolating where they would reach in twenty years.

"Steven, most of the discoveries weren't seen as pivotal. Gregor Mendel experimented with peas, not understanding that he would be seen as the father of genetics. When I attempt something wild, I try to find the next peas. The humble trials that anyone could do, but whom the pioneers would get called weird by their contemporaries and a visionary by upcoming generations. Peas remained the perfect choice because their traits developed as binary and independent. He could easily see the results of his experiments. I want to find my own simple project to peak toward the future because my job is to study how those events occurred generations ago. I would like to be there for the sake of our own or the next."

And for projects for the future, she had plenty. Including many with components that didn't exist yet but would *probably* see the light in a few years. The best example consists of her quantum antenna, which would be remembered as her crowning achievement if it worked! Her one chance at an invention that could alter humanity, and which she could only build with Steven's help. Changing the world, nothing less, and yet, Lily stayed always humble about it. She didn't aspire to fame or glory. Becoming or not a visionary according to anyone else hardly mattered. Lily just desired to feel like one. Indeed, she just wanted to push her concepts along. In this case, a quantum antenna. It stood as an idea, strictly on paper. In fact, originally, not even premeditated, as Lily lacked the structure, the capacity to note it properly down.

That's what Steven's contributed. That and the reality check she got from him about how electronics functioned. Because Lily worked with steam engines, not microchips, and she was trying, as a hobby, to construct the most advanced device ever built!

"But it works on neutrinos, not electrons, Steven." She would say, never getting his objection.He would explain. "Lily, if electricity powers it, and if it sends a signal I can measure with a multimeter, it's electronics."Lily would dismiss him. And Steven would quit pushing. When Lily wanted to accomplish anything, it seemed better to follow along than to question her. If it proved a bad concept, she would figure it out and stop. Often, she had frightening but amazing ideas…

And, yet, that quantum antenna?

He felt it wasn't named properly. Anything considered "Antenna" would need a wire, a coil, something conducting, open. Anything conductive which isn't connected to the ground, and able to capture an electromagnetic signal.

Lily, had weird components in the core, which she had already built with his help, and was planning to wrap her parts in a Faraday cage. She aimed to isolate her antenna! "Of course, I want to get quantum signals, you know, like neutrinos, that don't respect the speed of light. I could gather data from the past, from the future, from far away! And from there, peek across the veil of time, but only if we ground it from the non-quantum signals."

He would look at her as if he found her crazy, but she wasn't. He saw Lily as the sanest person in his life. He knew the project would prove futile and useless. He absolutely understood that it would never function. But every task that Lily tackled, always worked. Everything. They claimed she couldn't make her thesis subject interesting, and they were captivated. They said she wouldn't gather enough artifacts, and she did. And kept finding them until she vanished.

This time, however, what was blocking her wasn't even the antenna part. The challenge rested in the amount of input. She could program just enough to get by, and had already written the software to analyze the outcome. The problem stayed the bandwidth required to extract the details and the speed of computers to process it.

Her antenna would have to supply close to four gigabytes per second of raw data that her code would need to parse. Sure, they could check the raw frequencies with a spectrum analyzer to get an idea of the result. To get an accurate "picture," the outbound signal needed to include some level of modulation, just as a radar had to turn. And to modulate properly, you had to do it as a feedback loop from the inbound signal. This is just like how cameras autofocus. For that, the raw data needed to be crunched in real time.

In 2002, with USB 2.0, since each instant of capture would create four gigabytes of information, it would require at least 8.3 seconds of transfer, and close to four hundred to analyze. And still, no computers possessed enough memory to allow it!

And that's every second. Lily thought it would take a lot more to tune properly and focus. So, to work, she needed hours of data! It persisted as an impossible idea. Then she vanished. USB3 that could help would remain a dream for her.

The project was thus shelved, she later disappeared, and Steven had to move to get away from the attention the police and the press gave him. Time, then, stood in the way. Weeks of loneliness and routine changed to months and years.

Chapter 1.2—Legacy

Twelve years after Lily's disappearance, in 2014, computers became so fast, and USB3 so superior that he found bandwidth to spare. He can hold a capture in memory and the several minutes of summarized information without needing to even write to the disk, a process magnitude slower. While receiving the next second, the program analyzes the previous one and once done, deletes the raw data to leave space by using a more memory efficient model.

In just twelve years, Lily's project went from impossible on three fronts: USB, CPU speed and RAM capacity, to being within the specs of ordinary computers. Even his current laptop would be able to do, now that he upgraded it to thirty-two gigabytes. So, alone, in 2014, he dug out the schematic and completed Lily's antenna. He would finally see what she was hoping to find. He remained with plenty of time to finish the build, and already had most of the parts.

The rest, he had ordered from AliExpress, something that didn't exist in 2002, or he got it made by a client. So, he booted up his emission program on his ancient laptop. She had guided its evolution and while neither of them knew how to really develop, they found the code simple enough to implement. Plus, they had the software construction kit for the interface they purchased Today, an Arduino would do the job better, but Steven hadn't kept up enough with the progress to allow him to replicate the old code on the new platform.

In short, the module would send massive pulses on a stable carrier. It would emit on a fixed frequency, while keeping Steven's spectrum analyzer in front of him to see if anything bounced back to him. Lily had conceived a frequency multiplier into the system itself. He had no idea how it worked, but if he gained a two-megahertz signal, it would actually mean he would have received a two-terahertz pulse.

It didn't seem possible to devise such a circuit, but once designed, he was able to build it, and for this, he could employ a normal cheap device he had bought second-hand when studying. A spectrum analyzer, even his low-cost one, would serve a very useful purpose. Most people use oscilloscopes for measuring amplitude over time. Usually, it measures in volts, so you can perceive the evolution of a repeating signal, synchronizing at a certain timing. But waves have a frequency, and they can overlap. When you tune your radio in the FM range, you select a specific channel, say 98.3 MHz, his local classic rock station, but that's the middle of their range.

The input of an FM station will move to transmit the music, something missed using an oscilloscope, which only displays the signal itself, not changes in its frequency. That's the job of the spectrum analyzer! It shows the amplitude of each peak, allowing us to clearly see the encoding of an FM radio, for example. With Lily's Quantum antenna design, however, she theorized that the signal would work marginally like the Doppler effect.

This means that any drift in the frequency of replies could reveal their relative speed and movement when compared to his own fixed location.   With the frequency multiplier in place, now used as a divisor when reading back, any close objects would stay invisible and only massive speed differences would show up. Perhaps Mars or Venus would show! Maybe even the Moon, but not a car down the street.

Nervous, Steven turned the system on.

As the emission program counted down to emanating a 2.2 MHz, he witnessed a series of weak signals appearing in the 2.3 MHz to 2.4 MHz range. Lily had explained that in theory, thanks to neutrinos' ability to travel faster than the light does, the first echoes would possibly show up before the antenna radiated and once again. She seemed right! At the moment the countdown ended, once the waves found themselves propelled, new signals surfaced in the two almost two point two megahertz range, including a peak nearby. He probably picked up his own wave. That one, being near, wouldn't appear before or after: the distance remained too close for any time distortion.

The stability of those signals fascinated Steven: it's as if the one he was emitting bounced back to him at new heights, with a few neutrinos arriving from the round trip, returning before they left. A spike appeared on his spectrum analyzer, but it wasn't so much a new carrier, but almost like a dancing signal. Several new peaks appeared on the display and seemed to drift left and right, as if someone was scanning the antenna. Almost like a fly buzzing around.

Worried, he turned it off and suddenly, a faint but clear smell of ozone filled the air. Thinking he had scorched his antenna, he swiftly turned it on again and witnessed that it remained functional: he could see the same signals he had previously gotten and no sign of the erratic one.He rose from his seat and hazarded quickly to touch the antenna to feel whether it felt hot. He knew he should use a thermometer. He burned himself quite a few times checking client's machinery, but despite buying a quite effective infrared sensor specifically for that, he always relied on his fingers to experience the warmth of an object.

Worried, he turned it off and suddenly, a faint but clear smell of ozone filled the air. Thinking he had scorched his antenna, he swiftly turned it on again and witnessed that it remained functional: he could see the same signals he had previously gotten and no sign of the erratic one.He rose from his seat and hazarded quickly to touch the antenna to feel whether it felt hot. He knew he should use a thermometer. He burned himself quite a few times checking client's machinery, but despite buying a quite effective infrared sensor specifically for that, he always relied on his fingers to experience the warmth of an object.

It seemed tepid, at best. Still not even close to the heat it would have gotten if an arc had formed when he turned it on. In his experience, this remains the usual source of ozone when working with electricity. He touched other parts of the antenna and circled it, looking at every square inch of surface for darkened spots, when he saw something in the corner of his eye…

It was, well, a box. A metallic one. The size made him think of those photo booths from the mall from his youth. Perhaps barely bigger. Faint red lights came out from inside. It made him think more of it as a machine than just a simple container.

The dim ozone smell dissipated. As he gently approached the cubic object... a thought unsettled him. He didn't hear it at first: it felt like the universe tore open silently. The next moment, the strange container solidified its apparition in his workshop, placed as if it had always been there.

The machine reminded him of a Faraday cage he had seen at one of his client's locations. It displayed a dull, grey metallic colour. What looked to be multiple panels invited him to open them. Various connectors seemed visible on the side, most of which he couldn't begin to guess at their purpose. One of them, however, looked like a male power plug in a socket which made him think that perhaps that apparatus could be recharged in a simple one-hundred-and-ten-volt electrical outlet, but otherwise ran on batteries.

He circled it and noticed an actual door in the middle, to the left. The bar handle gently turned when he tried it and allowed the small entrance to swing open, revealing inside the machine what Steven thought of as a cockpit. What surprised him the most wasn't that he found a gorgeous maiden sitting in the dark, wounded, in the pilot's seat. He found himself shocked to find Lily, his wife, as beautiful and as young as the last time he had laid eyes on her. Not Lily 12 years older. Not Lily from 2014. No, Lily from 2002.

Lily didn't vanish. She had travelled to the future in a time machine and failed to come back. Finally, Steven received some answers. But let's not walk ahead of ourselves. How did he get there? Let's go back to when it started.

Chapter 1.3—Life Destroyed

On that fateful day, Lily wasn't at her college. She took one of those stay-at-home periods in which boosted her productivity. Seriously. Her supervisor seemed skeptical, but each time she was allowed to perform teleworking, outputs would double, triple or even more! As a teaching historian, her duties are confusing. At the top, she has obligations to her pupils. They're graduate level students who want to learn. Her topics and the syllabus, well... she got two classes on the Industrial Revolution and one about research.

This covers her schooling responsibilities. She also commits as an academic, contributing to the field of knowledge. Her mentoring vocation linked her to the college. Her call to exploration kept her home, borrowing tons of books to cite.Gwen, her supervisor, often challenged her methodology, "Surely, it would be easier in the actual library." But the one thing that she never questioned remained the results Lily got. Already, two historical societies in Great Britain had issued grants to assist Lily with her research and they talked about lending her to Cambridge University for a semester so she would help revitalize their Industrial Revolution Department.

Considering they were at the centre of that revolution, that's no easy feat! But Steven, that day, installing a new machine in the morning and maintaining one for a different client in the afternoon, could picture his wife! She would still be in her pajamas, at home. She would profess: "comfort first, presentation last." The school has it the other way around. Her hair would be tied in a loose ponytail, with probably a pencil tucked in the elastic. While a student, she would always have one up there, as well as a pen, but when hired as a teacher, it demanded of her some time to have the courage to do it. A good three weeks.

Lily felt afraid of Gwen's judgment, as everyone considers her the acclaimed resident expert on abuse of slaves on cotton plantations, but it didn't take long for Gwen to slip a stylus in her dreads too! "Easy access," she admitted. Gwen actually resented that their male colleagues could simply put their writing instruments of choice in a breast pocket, and this makeshift solution seemed just... fun!

Granted, few things excited Steven more than when Lily used two pencils to wrap a bun, and she would remove them, letting her hair fall down in a cascade. Usually, such as when working at home, a scrunchie did the heavy lifting. The objects remained only stowed in her wrapped ponytail until needed. Lily loved manual calligraphy. She had a great style and enjoyed the feeling of dragging a pen on paper. Steven once gave her a quill, but Lily didn't like it as much.

Her favourite gift from him, however, remains a scanner with an OCR software package, which was able to actually understand her writing. A miracle for the end of the nineties, thanks to her excellent penmanship. Steven came back home a little earlier than expected. Despite the client describing the problem as serious, just some lubrication and percussive therapy handled the stuck mechanism. Lily laughed at "percussive therapy." It basically meant hitting the thing until it works once more. It seems brutal and primitive, but in the hands of an expert like Steven, it's precise and surgical.

In reality, it's not so much applying violence. It's gently nudging the immobile piece so it can move again. It's more like encouraging it to perform its job by pushing it softly but firmly, and less about punishing it for refusing to collaborate. Her car was at home. Her research spread across the table. A newspaper archive from a small Ohio town showed a page about a steam power plant destroyed by a landslide caused by massive rain.

A few of the floor plan's sketches, made by her hand, loitered the workspace, along with a few rolled into a ball in the trash can next to it. Another book showed building permits from the same area. It stayed opened to reveal some descriptive texts on that building. It included dimensions, paragraphs on the rooms, but no schematic. Instead, some fireman ripped them out for an escape contingent.

Steven smiled. Lily had mentioned this commission from the city. They wanted the college to figure out the floor plan so they could perform an archeological dig of the site. Next to the books, was a ground-penetrating radar report which basically said, "Large structure found, details unclear." Steven called out Lily's name. Her keys lay on the table, next to her wallet. He received no response, which felt weird.

12

The locked front door, and her things stayed in the house. How did she get out? He thought that, maybe, she was in the bathtub with her headphones on. This fully felt natural for her, but usually later in the evening and only after cleaning the kitchen table.

Nothing. It's not that big of a place. Soon enough, he realized that something amiss occurred. He called Lily's cellphone, expecting to locate it in the house, but it went straight to voicemail. That's not normal. Checking around, he found in the hamper her pajamas from last night, showing she put on clothes. Did she leave? How did she lock the door? Why is her car in the driveway? He had a thought about the third set of keys, with her family. He contacted Sandra, his mother-in-law.

Maybe her parent came home, discovered Lily listening to a podcast or music on her headphones, and got in with her key. Lily could have changed, left with her mom, who would have used her access to lock back. This thought calmed Steven. Sandra often dropped in on her girl and sometimes, they would go to the store together to assist Sandra in buying new clothes for herself.

Lily wouldn't need her wallet or keys, and she loved to help her mother refine her style. Sandra, however, didn't have a cellphone back then, so he contacted her home. She picked up on the second ring. "Hello?" she welcomed him, as they didn't have caller ID.

"Hi Sandra, it's Steven, did you see Lily today?"

"Oh no! Isn't she at home? She asked me not to bother her, she was conducting that research on the steam generator plan."

"Right, she isn't home, but I found her car, her things, her wallet... it's too weird..."

"She leaves for a stroll from the patio door, at times." She explained.

But Steven knew his wife. How she likes to part from the backyard, without her keys, to walk around the block and think. With the back entrance unchecked, and little chances of a robbery. She usually went for only fifteen to twenty minutes anyway. Yet, he found the patio door secured, tight, with the normal bar you pull down to prevent forcing it open.

"It's locked, I already verified."

"Then she should be in the house. Right?"

Of course, Steven had checked the basement, even the small, odd room that they never use. In fact, they rarely go downstairs, but it's where she stores some of her findings. Steven had examined it before even starting to panic. George, Lily's father, does have a cellphone and seemed surprised to get a call from Steven during the day.

"Sorry, Son, I haven't heard of Lily at all. Maybe check with my wife?"

But he already had. He now needed to contact Gwen. Steven didn't have her in his contacts, but her number was on the refrigerator. At first, she didn't answer. About two minutes later, she called back and confirmed herself as the last person to reach Lily, before lunch. Most of Lily's few friends worked during the day, so after checking with them, despair got to him. Almost an hour passed. She would have returned from a walk, by now. He did the only thing he had left to do.

"911, what is your emergency?"

"I don't know if I have one, ma'am, but it's my wife. I couldn't find her anywhere. She's supposed to work from home."

"Could she have left and not tell you?"

"Sure, she could have gone on an errand or something. Her car, her keys and her wallet stayed home when I arrived."

"Can she have been out?"

"With every door locked?"

14

"What's your name, sir?"

"Steven Clark. And my wife is Lily Connelly, sorry, Elizabeth Connelly."

"OK, we will send a unit."

"Don't you need my address?"

"Are you at 119 Brookline Avenue?" The dispatcher confirmed.

"Oh, yeah," Steven sighed, realizing that 911 probably had a much better caller ID system.

"Don't worry. We'll find her"

They didn't. Soon enough, Steven became the number one suspect.

Chapter 1.4—Law Enforcement

Of course, it wasn't just the fact that he had lost his wife that made Steven depressed. Most people couldn't stomach a false accusation of murder. Since Steven is a freelance electromechanical technician, his contracts dried up. Initially, Steven was able to endure the various police inspectors harassing him daily, especially when they slowly turned into weekly visits, and more recently, monthly. "You'll ALWAYS remain a person of interest." They regularly warned him. Some of the officers believed him, but most follow the maxim that when a wife suddenly disappears, it's usually the husband's fault.

Detective Kelley showed up in Steven's life the morning after that fated nine-one-one call. Uniformed police agents took his first statement, and an investigator from the local precinct, "Jennifer" as she wanted to be referred to, spent the evening with Steven to reassure him. She asked permission to search the house, and found a few photo albums, which she opened. She slowly looked at it while Steven was stunned on the couch.

The young detective stayed patient, kind. Steven was in shock and kept hoping his wife would show up at the door wondering what was going on, but it had been over six hours since the call, and the night fell outside. A new batch of police officers came and photographed the house in detail. Instead of wearing uniforms, they had white coveralls. Had Steven not been overwhelmed, he would have noticed their job as CSI technicians, but to him, everyone arrived to try to figure out what happened.

Steven was worried Lily was kidnapped or could be raped or tortured, but the nice young detective kept reassuring him. Most missing person cases were solved within 48 hours, and many before the end of the evening. Steven had already considered other possible reasons Lily vanished. None of her friends heard from her. Her parents didn't either. She wasn't in contact with his family much. Her work colleagues also remained in the dark. In no way could she have had an affair. They simply weren't apart from each other enough for her to even find the time for one.

And yet, the young detective kept inquiring about pictures taken months or years earlier. Evidence from their wedding, with every guest reviewed by the detective. He even talked about those absent from the memory, and name each one, focusing on one man in particular. They hoped to know more about Henry, one of her neighbours, growing up. Then, he dated Lily's cousin, who cheated on Henry. He married another woman, but Steven kept saying how he and Lily stayed close, how little they were apart from each other, how Henry stayed in her past. Jennifer gathered every bit of information as she pursued her quest for truth.

Soon enough, only Jennifer and Steven remained, with the rest of the house falling silent again. Just like the gap between the 911 call and the arrival of the first officers, only this time, the cavalry had come, and left. Now, the house now only held two occupants: just him, and this noisy nice lady who was just trying to get to know Lily. Favourite restaurants, movies, TV show, books, hobbies and even clothes. "Could I keep this picture for now?" and "Would you mind if we took this dress into evidence?" to which Steven always agreed. Especially since they promised to return everything.

16

But they never did. And he now suspected they never would. Not until the case would be closed. Only, he didn't know that at the time. His only priority consisted of finding Lily, and short of that, to gather some rest, once Jennifer would leave him alone. Steven did get to sleep, and Jennifer stayed. A new young detective, who didn't bother to make introductions, kept guard in the living room while Jennifer napped on the sofa in the basement. This fell outside of police norms, but Steven didn't understand that. Just as he didn't know that already, he represented the number one suspect. The next morning, a well-rested and happy Jennifer drove him to the main station.

"No need to keep you in your things, we'll just go over any questions our team has for you," she said. They stopped at the diner, and she paid for a decent breakfast for both of them, of which he only ate half.

At the station, Jennifer sat next to him, around a conference table. Various pictures of Lily and documents about her loitered their sight.

A map showed his previous travel, as per his recollection.

"Is this your approximate route?" casually inquired Jennifer.

"Pretty much"

An officer put weather radar photos on the wall, with a note indicating the moments of the day when it rained, between 10:32 AM and 4:54 PM, which was when he contacted 911.

"What happened at 10:32 AM?" Steven asked.

"When she hung up with a call from one of her colleagues," explained Jennifer.

Detective Paterson had entered the room without Steven noticing it. The endured veteran had thirty-one years of experience and had been controlling the investigation from the sidelines like a demented puppet master. With wild, scruffy, full salt and pepper hair, he showed pride in avoiding baldness.

17

"That's the last moment we can positively place your wife's location." He informed Steven, with his deep tenor voice.

"I texted her around noon, and she didn't reply." Steven confessed.

The detective didn't ask Steven to sit down. Instead, he simply pointed at the chair and waited long enough for Steven to get the message. Jennifer sided with Steven, almost offering him a safe presence. The young lady who had passed a few comments while browsing his picture books about his and Lily's evident happiness. She treated him for breakfast. She even encouraged him to shower. In this sad and depressing period, she represented the closest thing to a friend that Steven ever felt.

"Mr. Clark, do you know how a doctor performs a differential diagnosis?" began Detective Paterson.

"What?"

"He produces a hypothesis, the most likely one, and find the tests needed to dismiss or prove that hypothesis."

"If you say so." Steven sighed.

"A police investigation works the same way. But instead of searching for a disease, we're looking for a suspect. Do you understand that?"

"I guess."

"Now, people think we're supposed to snatch the criminal. Except we seldom pinpoint any, do you know why?"

"No?" says Steven, out of his depth.

"Because that's the jury's job. The police's responsibility is to find suspects and investigate them. They do so without any prejudice or preconceptions other than those provided in the case."

"That's good"

"Well, Mr. Clark, we have a one where your wife, Elizabeth Clark, has vanished into thin air in a locked house."

"Exactly." Steven's patience ran out.

"So, it's my job, as the lead investigator, to find out what happened to her."

"Thank you." Steven wished them to evaporate in the slender atmosphere.

"Oh, I wouldn't thank me yet, Mr. Clark. You see, currently, I suspect foul play, and the person who took your wife both knew her and had the key to your house."

"Right... her parents, myself and her"

"We retrieved her set in your place. We spoke to her family. That leaves your key."

"Which I had on me the whole day." At that point, Steven feared for unintentional self-incrimination.

"So, the first hypothesis I require to prove or not, is that you took your wife elsewhere, with or without her will."

"But I'm the one who contacted nine-one-one!"

Jennifer spoke gently, putting her hand on his arm: "Relax, Steven, we just need to follow the routine. Before we can look for other suspects, we need to know that we can trust you."

"But I called nine-one-one!" He nervously repeated.

The senior detective stood up and paced: "We seized over two hundred thousand dollars in small amounts, from a drug trafficker. It's in a box. My authority allows me to pull them out. I could, while I put some findings from your case, grab that money and hide it on me. In a few days, however, someone will spot the theft. When the inventory is listed, they will have the logs of everyone who went into the evidence locker and might have stolen it.

Now, I know this, so I might invite others to blur the trail, or perhaps report that some of the boxes were missing when I entered. I won't insult your intelligence and consider that should you have decided to harm your wife, you could have simply called nine-one-one to cover your guilt under a guise of innocence."

Before Steven could even respond, the senior officer continued: "Again, Steven, this is only to prove that you didn't do anything wrong, so we can focus on whoever did something. You get that?"

"Right, like when I repair a machine that no longer works. I need to first check if the breaker tripped," Steven concluded.

"Exactly. And in a way, we see you as the breaker. If innocent, you have nothing to fear." Jennifer smiled.

Steven could hardly escape this nonsense. Stress kept piling up. For the following few hours, he painfully detailed every minute of his previous day, in chronological order, from the moment he left in the morning to when he called nine-one-one.

Several times, Detective Paterson would ask for clarification and causality links in the chain of events. Questions like "Why did you park at that particular location for your lunch break?" or "why did you use Cedar Drive instead of Grove Avenue?" The red light at the intersection and in his experience showed Cedar Drive as a wrong option. But a green light on Grove Avenue makes his course easier. Some stupid details, such as the songs on the radio, and if it played a part in his impulsive decision to choose the latter route over the former alternative, made him smile.

Steven couldn't figure out how relevant this could have been, but he complied. Especially with Jennifer reassuring him. She left for a lunch break once they made it to the nine-one-one call. Detective Paterson pressed on, mainly going over the paper trail on the desk, browsing through pictures of Lily and Steven, and each document retrieved from their house. When Jennifer came back, Detective Paterson felt with certainty that Steven missed something crucial, so he decided to try a thought experiment. He asked him to narrate the day once again, but in reverse order, from the nine-one-one call to the moment he left.

"I'll help you." Jennifer smiled.

But Steven found it harder going backward, and Jennifer's assistance made it more confusing. So much, he begged her to stop. Hunger crammed him. He needed some water, and was offered a small conical paper cup barely filled. He wetter his lips than drank, and Detective Paterson reminded him that the sooner he would be convinced that Steven wouldn't have done it, the faster they could send him to a nice restaurant.

"I'll pay again, if you don't mind." Jennifer winked. "I can either keep you company, or go back to my husband. Anything to put you at ease."

It wasn't fast, and the more errors Steven made, the angrier detective Paterson became. His anger didn't show on the general timeline, but rather remained focused on the errors in the details, and on the delays. Steven found himself hungry, thirsty, and afraid about what was happening to Lily. Often, Steven had to reflect on how he ended up somewhere and to figure out why he left, which forced him to think chronologically and which introduced mistakes. Jennifer kept reassuring him, but at some point. Steven lost patience.

"We've wasted the whole day on me, instead of looking for whoever grabbed Lily."

Detective Paterson, calm, simply said a few words that Steven will always remember. "Oh, we've found who took Lily. Why do you think we've been questioning you at this time?" Suddenly, Steven realized something. He understood the interrogation technique, the good cop bad cop play which began the previous evening. He thought of Jenifer's wrinkled eyes, barely hidden by concealer makeup. Likewise, he acknowledged that, with her ponytail and her clothes, she looked like a junior detective. Yet, she most likely possessed years of professional experience.

He was in a trap! He felt alone against a cold, uncaring machine trying to pin Lily's disappearance on the most convenient suspect. Himself. After confirming that he wasn't under arrest and receiving the information that he could leave at any time, he did just that. He stood up and took a taxi back home.

Chapter 1.5—Landing in the Public Eye

Police officers kept dropping over to ask questions, including Detective Paterson. Jennifer, however, didn't show herself to Steven for almost a decade. She had served her purpose. She served as the good cop to Paterson's bad cop. Steven recollects having encountered her, early in a 2009 afternoon, on a Wednesday. He visited a hardware store to buy some lubricant for a contract. Jennifer stood in the aisle with a slightly older redhead woman. They argued about the paint colour for their new bedroom. Didn't Jennifer say she had a husband? Both women wore wedding rings.

Seeing the couple laughing hurt Steven. In front of his eyes stood the woman who could have truly assisted him to find Lily. Instead, she played a role in trying to… what? Frame him to close the case quickly. Did she lie on her marital state to a man to solicit compassion of some sort? Did she divorce and get remarried? Steven definitely couldn't tell. Not that he even cares. Just because she had tried to arrest him didn't mean she deserved misery herself. When in line at the cash register, Jennifer and her second half were behind him. He decided not to intervene, but Jennifer did.

"Steven Clark, right?" she says, holding the hand of her wife, as if to reassure the civilian in the presence of a suspected woman murderer.

"Jennifer." He simply replies.

"Paterson died last month."

"What?"

"The detective, my former partner. Heart attack"

"Sorry to hear that," says Steven, following customs.

"That's a lie. He acted like a completed jerk to you."

"And you helped him."

"Well, I did resign in protest." Steven looked at her.

"Does that mean you think I didn't do it?" He inquired, after paying for his lubricant. He could leave, but he hoped to get some closure.

"Oh, no. Just that he lacked diplomacy and tact. It's why I transferred myself to the Sheriff's department."

"I see. Well, good luck painting"

"Thank you. Our kids moved out, so we're heading into a smaller house more suited to our needs."

Steven nodded and left. Why should he have expected closure? Her role as a detective consisted of luring him into a false sense of security. Everyone, from the city police to the Sheriff's department, believed he killed his wife. Why would she change her mind? Would she do it just because he encountered her in her private life Steven didn't dislike the fact that others found happiness. He hated that he didn't. Well, that's not true. He did despise journalists Officers had a duty to follow the law. They couldn't harass him more than a tolerable minimum.

The city's papers caused more problems for him, as on every slow news date, articles on the "disappearance of Professor Elizabeth Connelly" would run. It took only a few days for the journalists to use her maiden name. Lily didn't mind becoming a Clark, especially since, as she would say, "It's the same initials anyway." But it annoyed Steven since they insisted on treating him as if he remained just a stranger, as if he didn't know her, like a stalker. A few even had the nerves to reiterate on their salary differences, and his debts from his equipment, to engage in his own freelance company. In reality, he had paid her way through college, and she was delighted to assist him in starting his venture when he had lost his first, and so far only, job. But what could he expect? He had seen previous sensationalistic newspapers in his town, and any unsolved atrocity usually fuelled the crowd's imagination for years, helping to drive publicity revenue in the various local media.

23

The ironic twist is that he found most of his former clients via advertisements he had placed during the investigation of Robert Finley's son's death. In the end, the coroner ruled it purely accidental despite the audience's taste for blood. Even rapes rarely capture the puritanical fabric of the gossipers, who preferred to talk about violent crimes rather than sexual ones... even a botched bank robbery failed to inspire the rumour mill since the felon was apprehended, just a drifter from out of state.

But a high school sweethearts couple? A glorified Romeo and Juliet pair mixed from two opposite families? An intellectual belle who falls for a manual simpleton who later kills her? That sold issue, even if many people knew that Steven was no dolt. He graduated from a very prestigious technical college and a fraction of a point behind the valedictorian. And yet, Steven read newspapers, not for updates on his case, but out of the twisted hope that some unexplained new fresh memory would propel the public away from his own situation. After those years, nothing really grabbed the population's eye like the tragic disappearance of a cute born local historical science University professor in her prime.

What complicated the ability of the community to grasp is that Elizabeth vanished without her usual pocket money, credit cards and other things normally found on herself. With her car parked in the driveway and keys still in the house. She didn't have classes that day. Her husband had several small repair gigs on the opposite side of the town. In theory, it granted him plenty of time to come back and see his wife, which he admits he didn't, but without being able to supply a clear explanation why. He just claimed that when she was home, she graded documents or prepared lectures and as such, he preferred not to bother her. He had packed a lunch and read machine schematic parked on a random street while waiting for the next gig to start.

Even Detective Paterson, in his forward in time and then backward retelling of the chronology, seemed to have accepted it during the interrogation. His complete lack of a demonstrable alibi showed up as a nefarious thing in the papers. Despite Steven explaining the daily life of a freelancer who must visit clients.

In turn, reporters would pressure the law department and Detective Paterson would be back on the incident. First reluctantly but slowly increasing the stress until he would reach the point where he would need more concrete proof to generate progress. That's usually when he would leak to the journalists that fresh information has surfaced with a renewed call for witnesses, creating a new press cycle to put strain on the police to solve the case. Only a three-day weekend, busy media or apathy at the absence of original details would kill the buzz. Inevitably, on an anniversary linked with the event, the hype would resume.

Never mind the complete lack of motive: Elizabeth made the most wealth currently in the relationship, they were madly in love with each other. Even her own parents often admitted that. More importantly, apart from a mortgage and a small life insurance, Steven gained nothing from her death. In fact, the police seized the money from their shared bank account and didn't actually reinstitute it. Steven, almost ended up penniless.

On the day of her disappearance, none of their neighbours saw anything. It was raining that day and Elizabeth didn't take any of her coats or umbrellas. It's as if she had, simply, dissipated into thin air from within their house! His own siblings pushed him apart ever further than usual. His friends had given up on him as soon as the news of Lily's disappearance reached them. The only social contact left consisted of Lily's parents, who had gladly accepted him into the family and probably remained the only two individuals in town who believed in his innocence.

They knew him. They heard from their daughter of their love, of their successes and their hardship. Also, they understood how much Lily trusted Steven, and they did as well. Just as she consisted of his rock, they saw him as her foundation. The one person that was able to take her crazy ideas and convert them into tangible projects without killing her enthusiasm. Growing up, her parents explained, Lily kept talking about the type of man she wanted, and as it turns out, that was him!

Initially, he thought he would only count on them to help him shelter the storm brewed from his grief, but Steven quickly realized something. He had lost his wife, the person he had adored the most for many years. The whole of their adulthood and the last few years of their teenage years. But her parents gave birth to her. They had loved her for her entire life! She became his bride. Yet, to them, she would remain first, and foremost, their daughter. While they accepted him, they were confronting their own grief.

Chapter 1.6—Living Cheaply

After years of isolation, solitude no longer meant loneliness. He kept himself occupied with his projects when he didn't have to help his dwindling number of customers. Before Lily's disappearance, he had a series of reasons to wake up every morning and leave the bed: spending time with her, seeing his friends, going to his job. He would execute most of his task, well, right there. In his current workshop. This is where he fabricates certain parts required by his clients and repairs those that need extensive maintenance.

Presently, he has three DC motors to rewire, none of which he thought urgent or paying enough to prioritize, a protection plate to adjust and a bearing to unjam. A substitute was installed, and the goal of the customer was to have these original items as a replacement. Well, except for the protection plate. This comes from an automatic bolting machine. The operator places the two pieces of metal to be latched, and presses two buttons that activated the press which positions a rivet.

Presently, he has three DC motors to rewire, none of which he thought urgent or paying enough to prioritize, a protection plate to adjust and a bearing to unjam. A substitute was installed, and the goal of the customer was to have these original items as a replacement. Well, except for the protection plate. This comes from an automatic bolting machine. The operator places the two pieces of metal to be latched, and presses two buttons that activated the press which positions a rivet.

He had removed it the previous day and would get it soon enough, but his heavy instruments are in his atelier, where he does most of his machining. Well, only most, since his space only offers a portion of his former work area and sometimes, he just can't move a device in due to the lack of room. He had found years earlier a job that combined two of his passions: music and electromechanical repairs. He received a salary as a part-time technician in charge of the maintenance of the apparatus which printed the CDs for a record label. While idle the rest of the day, he worked in the shipping dock, half of which remains his current workshop, shipping the CDs to record stores and distribution companies.

One of the perks of labouring for the disk industry was being able to function with music blasting over the sound of the machinery. Not necessarily the tunes he loved, but always ones he kind of liked. It also pretty much fitted the description of how he felt when busying himself. This paradigm shifted since the birth of MP3 players, iPods, satellite radio, and streaming services, replacing physical CDs. As a firm located in an industrial park which allowed nearby businesses to employ him part-time. His opportunities ramped up. His bosses let him use a portion of the shipping dock as a base of operation for his other commitments. That's how he decided, with the help of his loving wife, to start his freelancing company.

He could even split the wide dual door in two halves, so that he could have his own separate workspace. In this manner, an ambitious Steven managed to please more than one leader. Whenever free, with fewer and fewer hours labouring for the music firm, until laid off and propelled to focus on his outside career, full time. Instead of a severance package, Steven salvaged his atelier gratuitously from his former employer. Despite their efforts and letting go of most of their employees, they couldn't keep the boat afloat and three years ago, they folded, and their unit was up for rental. This is where the mistake occurred.

Granted, by then, everyone was just about giving a saddened Steven plenty of room. Hard to say if the error proved unintentional or just committed to help him cope with his grief. Simply, perhaps, made out of fear of a potential murderer. What he ascertained for sure involved the new tenants, an accounting company. They ignored they were signing not for one, but for two shipping docks. They ended up covering the rent and taxes for both units. In fact, they even reimbursed his electrical bill, without their knowledge. Steven didn't even question his good fortune until a few months later, when they offered him a freelance contract as an IT superintendent, allowing him to steal their Wi-Fi connection!

Now, Steven wasn't an IT administrator, but he understood his way about computers. He discovered a USB stick that accommodated most software issues. He found a few books to help him with networking problems. With no full-time job, no wife, no kids and no friends to take slices from his life away from him, he managed to focus on the fundamentals: handling their basic IT needs.

Most of the tasks implicated their printer jams. That's well within his main line of work! Steven had been sleeping on an inflatable mattress in a corner of his shop for over two years by then. He had built himself a makeshift shower. Thanks to the accounting office, he now had access to several bathrooms, and even a cafeteria with a properly functional oven!

Back with the CD company, two deadbolts had been installed on the door: one on his side to prevent his employer from getting into the workshop without his key. On the other of the door, another one stopped him from going into their section from his garage. Granted, it's not as if he could prepare lunches in the day, with the department occupied. At least, over the weekends, he could cook a few meals. He had taken his refrigerator out of storage, so that helped him a lot. Now that he managed the payroll company' IT, they let him keep the key for their dead bolt. They even had cable TV in the cafeteria!

28

It's only a few months later that he acknowledged that he could exploit the difference in ceiling heights. The office had a normal nine foot-high top, while his workshop had its own at twenty-three above the floor! After buying a ladder, he climbed above the payroll department's half only to realize that aside from a wall dividing the loading dock from the front, it seemed like an unused empty space. Partially because ventilation systems blocked some of the way, but they mostly rested on top of their ceilings.

He laboured 14 months, over long complicated weekends and cost him most of the little money he made by selling his house, but once completed, the results blew him away! The worst part was adding the plumbing, but he had some water pipes in his dock, so he just extended them upstairs and covered them with drywall he painted to hide what he was doing. The pipe to eliminate the waste liquids proved more problematic, so he made sure to put his toilet as close as possible to his place's edge.

With plenty of sound insulation, he had constructed himself an operational apartment above the front area of the building. Granted, the only windows were on the rampart toward his workshop, but he finally had a closed bedroom, for the first time since he had to flee his house to avoid the reporters. He even had a fully functional kitchen and an actual toilet he could use twenty-four seven. The spiral staircase wasn't practical to move furniture in, but he simply borrowed a nearby client's forklift (he had the keys anyway) over a weekend to finish the job. Steven now had a home, rent and tax-free. It remained unlisted and unknown.

It ended up his secret cave, finally allowing him some peace and quiet, away from the news and the normal complications of life.After a few months, he even added a sort of wooden base, and found a way to hide the door to his residence. The platform provided an alibi as to why the staircase was there. It probably wouldn't resist a police search warrant. It might remain concealed just enough so that when rare customers visited his workshop, they wouldn't see it. Looking at his apartment, he realized something. The fundamental guideline for financial stability is to reduce your expenses and maximize your incomes.

If it's so simple, why doesn't everyone do it? Because while most can easily grow their standard of living, going in the opposite direction proves itself complicated and requires a lot of challenging to make decisions. Worse, plenty of choices you can do to decrease your actual budget end up counterproductive to the other half of the rule: increasing your revenues. Steven found himself stuck because his reputation prevented him from finding a stable job: who would hire an employee with a risk of arrest for murder at any point? And yet, it was also reducing his bargaining power when negotiating contracts.

His biggest break remained his lack of a rent and electrical bill to pay. That didn't help with the rest of his expenses, such as food, clothes or his truck, which he needed to go effectively see his patrons. And yet, most of his actual clients were near his workshop. Being the only electromechanical technician living in an industrial park allowed him to get much faster response times to problems.

Chapter 1.7—Line jam

Today, DryTek Fabrics had a massive jam in their production facility and required immediate attention. Steven understood DryTek's assembly line like the back of his hand, as he not only fixes it several times per week. He actually installed it a few years earlier, securing what he then prayed to constitute a lucrative maintenance contract. Walking toward their factory with his tools, Steven performed a mental calculation. Knowing he holds no leverage, they cheated him and lowballed his price. They cut his project margin to almost nothing.

The base agreement would pay him only one hundred and twenty-five dollars a month to be on retainer, and he would receive twenty-six dollars for each trip plus forty-five for the first hour of his visit. Subsequent time was at twenty bucks per block of fifteen minutes. That almost equated salaried wages and well below a subcontractor's rate. They knew it far too well. So, back to the work today, the fabric stuck to the machine. A fold in the fabric often results in this mess.

Once the jam occurred, he knew of three main actions he could take without cutting the output: dismantle the fourth roller to resolve the problem. Back the assembly line up to the point before the wrinkle, and move it forward again, or simply loosen the driving belt to let the ridge flatten by itself. He understood the third option remained the recommended one. He even determined the reason for the frequent congestion occurred due to the overtightened zone. Furthermore, he knew because when he had installed it, the manual explained it according to the fabric's thickness. Plain and simple.

They never paid for him to supervise these operations. They cut their cost too much to even think about negotiating a rate for this oversight. Therefore, when they began production, the fourth roller got hardly calibrated. Well, that roller remains the most finicky… to loosen a belt, you would lack traction. Waves would ruin the stitching.

In the manual's *Troubleshooting* section, a guide explains how to configure the strap's tightness. Steven consulted it. From cover to cover, and his client should have read it only, since they didn't hire him after the installation, he neglected to deliver them the actual book. This constituted the third jam since the month began earlier this week. If he disassembles the fourth roller, it should be sorted shortly. This translates into sixty-one dollars for a total of forty-five minutes from the moment he left his workshop to his return. This meant an effectiveness worth about eighty dollars. On average, he would make fourteen such trips. That guaranteed him nine hundred and seventy-nine dollars in income, approximately.

The second option consisted of rewinding the production. It would occupy him roughly for ten minutes to resolve the issue. This increased his hourly rate to almost one hundred and five dollars per hour, for the same monthly income, just made in less time. The risk, however, was that if the foreman ever saw this solution, he would be able to fix the problem himself and Steven's main source of income might vanish out of thin air.

The third option, adjusting the roller, would require about five minutes to implement and would force him to stay for another two or three hours to monitor the adjustment to make sure it proved adequate. He could probably stretch that up to four hours, which would yield him three hundred and one dollars, but would stop any future visits to remove the jam in the fabric since it would now be fully calibrated. This is why the manual recommended it.

So, Steven picked up the first option. It might end up the worst for his client. It might show as the most labour-intensive. It might even remain the one that jams the production line the longest, but no other guaranteed him a minimum level of income from a client who clearly undervalued his work. They consistently underpaid him, abusing his condition.

Steven didn't have to perform the mental calculations. He did those exact ones, numerous times. In fact, each time he walked over to their factory. He now knew the numbers by heart. And in a way, he always knew he was breaking his code of ethics, but as he rationalized, he had to find a way to eat. Plus, they were short-changing him anyway. If they paid a good retainer, he would treat them better. They reap what they sow.

In his mind, he considered himself a victim of the prejudice of people who didn't have any imagination. In their mind, only he remained a suspect. Yet, maybe a rival historian harboured jealousy of Lily's success. Perhaps she threatened an electronics giant with her ideas. Of course not. Even Steven couldn't imagine it. Everyone loved Lily, and no one knew of her electronic projects but him. Every day, he would walk in his mind the theories about why Lily disappeared. At least, he no longer considered an alien abduction!

Something new popped in his mind today. The calendar revealed his father's birthday today, so his mother would prepare a pot roast to celebrate. He knew he was technically invited even if he no longer bothered with social events, but something told him that for one rare time, he would have good food at his table. While disassembling the fourth roller, as he had expected, the imagery on the fabric made him think of his sister-in-law. He shuddered at the thought of probably eating at the same table as her.

Growing up, Steven thought he knew what a dysfunctional family was. Burned by old money, his self-entitled parents had always focused on performance and appearance above anything else, including emotional wellbeing. He knew most of his problems came from his upbringing, but what he never anticipated was that his brother would marry someone objectively worse than their own mother.

He grunted at one of the screws which was starting to strip due to too-frequent abuse caused by his improper fix to a simple solution. This reminded him of the angst he felt toward his own sister-in-law, Camille, one of the community leaders trying to get him arrested for the murder of a woman she hated. Someone she herself utterly and completely despised. Saying that Lily and Camille were like oil and water, didn't do justice to their relationship. Camille consistently showed anger, manipulation and sarcasm toward a Lily who simply accepted the abuse with a smile and still accepted the horrible lady with empathy and tenderness. This probably infuriated Camille even more than the facts that Lily possessed a good education and came from a modest family, neither of which applied to Camille.

Thinking about his sister-in-law, Steven finished a good minute faster and soon enough, the production line resumed, and he got a happy foreman to sign the worksheet for the end of the month billing. He put a note in his mind to order another one of the screws to replace the almost stripped one. He wouldn't charge DryTek, since he imagined a limit as to how he can abuse their money, but he would prevent requiring himself staying any longer at their factory than he needed to be.

"Is there anything we can do to avoid such folds, Steven?" asked the foreman, but Steven knew how to answer...

"They don't make machinery in the same quality as they used to be. Now, they build everything in China and we can never fully calibrate them. The old machines would last years before jamming, but we had to oil every day. These new ones require almost no maintenance, but they jam so often. You're not the only clients I have service so often... These pieces of crap are killing American factories!"

He knew how to rile up the soon to retire foreman! After working almost forty-five years for DryTek the foreman had seen the number of workers drop like flies, from over 50 when he started, back when DryTek occupied four units, down to the four he now supervised. And yet, the profit margin dwindled as competition drove the prices to the floor.

The foreman began reciting his usual tirade against China, Bangladesh, India and Canada. Yes, against Canada. Steven could understand why he showed anger at those three Asian countries but could never figure out why he put Canada in the list. Each time, he would repeat how much he hated Peerless with a passion, without Steven bothering to even look up what Peerless even is and what they could have done to the foreman. But he wasn't the only one complaining about other countries.

Precision Dynamos, an old name no longer appropriate for their business line, lost over ninety percent of the revenues to China. They used to make fly wheels, about a generation ago, and now they made weights.That's right, weights. If you create a plastic gadget that feels too cheap or rattles too much because it lacks mass, you can hire them to produce a bar that will perfectly fit in your gizmo. But now, they make those devices overseas and used local suppliers. As a result, they only survive by virtually always being under the protection of Chapter eleven and machined recycled metal found in scrapyards to provide for their few clients.

In a way, it's not that different from their origin. A flywheel consists of basically a round weight that you spin when power becomes available so that you can retrieve some or most of that energy when without other sources. Now, they used the resources from when they had revenues, to sustain their operations after clients moved overseas. Back in the thirties, forties and even fifties, flywheels were envisioned as the future. An inventor even tried to build a car somewhere, that would run on the power stored in two flywheels, running counter rotation from each other to eliminate the gyroscopic precession caused by the rotation.

Lily ended up excited when she heard he had them for a client. She explained to him that flywheel in the past would smooth out the power output of some steam engine machines. She also heard that they received a contract for early satellite production, creating gyroscopes to keep them oriented. She asked for a meeting with their product manager to discuss a gyroscope she had in mind and left frustrated. Despite their aging website still featuring precision gyroscopes, the product manager not only couldn't help her. He ignored his company once made them. She fumed that night.

"We need companies to keep a better track on their history. This sounds pathetic! I don't mind if they stopped making them, but that they forgot even making them, that's absurd!"

GTW, a machine part fabrication manufacture and one of Steven's clients, by comparison, had pictures on the wall retelling of their history, and often, parts on the wall. Lily, when she learned about it, even took one of her days off to come to the office and meet with the gang. That afternoon, no one worked. Everyone, including Steven, only focused on the conversation between Lily and the aging Henry Tuckerman Jr. still the CEO for a little while.

As they elaborated on the industrial history of the town, Lily explained with excitement that GTW had been at the core of it all. Present at every twist and turn in the industrial progression, and ironically, the geographical evolution. GTW had moved four times, but each time, they had been in the industrial heart of the city, or close enough to it.

"It's easy to see it coming, Elizabeth," the elder explained. It took him a lot of convincing to use her first name, but no amount of pleading would convince him to use her nickname.

In his old gently patriarchal ways, men had nicknames, he got "stinky" and even as CEO he didn't mind people calling the nickname he got before realizing his lactose intolerance. During the talk, they even went along the walls, looking at the pictures, and "stinky" was shocked how much one of their old clients, in the early 1900, looked like Lily. She laughed, explaining how grainy and blurry the picture was, but took the compliment as the lady in the picture looked, indeed, rather cute, despite her old style of clothing.

Chapter 1.8—Laser work

Once he managed to exit Drytek, he was still thinking about GTW, so Steven went next door to go see them. GTW was now also struggling financially. They used to fabricate replacement parts of old factory machines on demand, using CNC drills, sandblasters and more recently, a high-powered laser. The third generation of sons (and two daughters) now worked in the company and, as they often said, "We'd never be able to pay anyone's wages. Not even our own. We only survive thanks to the fact that we own the company."

They had explained how three of the children simply kept living in their parents' home, and one of the daughters now lives mainly thanks to her husband's salary. Steven mainly bartered with them. Most of their remaining clients needed someone to install their replacement parts. Steven would often do it for free for GTW in exchange for the opportunity to pitch his services to their clients and get free parts for his own clients. The lack of money exchanged helped both parties in reducing their taxes and made it much easier to navigate when contracts dried up. Often, Steven managed to sell an expensive replacement part built at cost by GTW so that he would generate more profit than the actual cost of the installation.

What drove GTW to the brinks of bankruptcy, however, consisted of the mandatory use of certified parts, which rendered the use of third-party pieces impossible and would void warranties. In the past, factory machines would last decades after their warranty expired, but nowadays, most factories prefer to buy extended warranties and replace the machines once even those run-out. And we aren't even talking about the numerous factories that closed in the area! Steven picked up his antenna enclosure, which GTW had built perfectly to his specification. He couldn't wait to install his electronics but remembered his father's birthday.

"Hey Gary," Steven asked, "Would you be able to quickly make a logo in metal for me? It's my father's birthday…"

Gary remained Steven's favourites. The only child to Stinky, Henry Tuckerman Jr., who was himself the son of Henry Tuckerman Sr, who gave the T for GTW. Both Henry's financial genius managed to turn their little shops into a financial powerhouse, each retiring as CEO... until the third generation took over and left Gary instead as a bona fide metal artist. The joke running around was that had Gary been Henry Tuckerman the third, the company would have gone global, but in reality, his father or grandfather could have done nothing to help the company. Steven's idea sounded simple: a round medallion with the family crest on it. Yes, the Clark had a crest. His family used to own land in England, plenty of generations ago, and received a crest after one of his ancestors was knighted.

He didn't care for it, but his father did. One of Gary's specialties was using various tools to give different textures to metal, allowing to use a single block to simulate different colours. Talking with Gary brought a breath of fresh air. Almost everyone had been on Steven's back, but not the people at GTW. It's not that they thought him innocent, it's more that they didn't care about the rumours. Maybe because Lily often enjoyed hanging out with Steven and them. Often, on Friday afternoons, when she didn't have classes to teach and Steven was still technically on standby for his clients, the two of them would just go to GTW to speak with the team.

They formed a family. Granted, not by blood, but after three generations of the three family trees united by a single company, they remained as thick as cousins or even brothers could be. In fact, he knew of marriages between some of the members of the second generation, giving some team members a dual heritage, and one young child, Jaclyn, could claim the three of the founders as her ancestors. She didn't want to join the company, but then again, she was eight so her dreams of studying to become a horse veterinarian might very well change over the years.

Jaclyn wasn't born yet when Lily disappeared, but her parents had seen the love between Steven and Lily, and so did almost everyone else. Steven was actually shocked at how well Lily and the GTW staff became close, talking about their sex life close. It put him ill at ease, but Lily kept telling him to relax. That she belonged with them, as part of the same class of people. Simple, honest and hardworking. Talking to them was like a charge of his social batteries before having to deal with his family.

Susan came to see them. Her paternal grandfather, David Granger, constituted the G in the GTW, and her maternal grandfather, John Watson, supplied the W. Unlike Henry Tuckerman, neither of them wished to impose their first name on their child. Lily often joked that just as the Tuckerman patriot seemed to act as the rigid backbone of the company, David and John formed the creative team who wished the company to become agile and adapt with the generations.

Their complicity and cooperation created the mood which allowed their own children to intermarry and produce Susan, who married Gary's brother, with whom she had Jaclyn. Susan's husband, like most Tuckerman men, works as a hardworking accountant for a large firm, which allows them to provide for their daughter despite the hard times for GTW.

"Hi boys, I just heard that Kellerman will go out of business."

"Seriously? I was there last week, and they seemed fine!" says Gary. Kellerman operated a printer cartridge ink factory. When you go to the mall, you can refill your old cartridges, well, Kellerman makes the ink in those bottles for those places.

"They did, and they were, but two of their big clients just got acquired and will use the supplier of their buyer," explained Susan.

"This town is going to shit. We won't survive another generation, Susan. Mark my words. They will raise this industrial zone and build a shopping mall instead. No, a supercentre. Or worse, condo units", sats Gary.

"In which world do you consider condo units worse?" asks Susan.

"They don't provide us with any work," says Steven, which prompts Gary to point to him with both indexes, while still looking at his sister-in-law.

"But if we close, what does it change?" says Susan.

"Oh, you actually offer a good point," says Gary.

"My husband's employer might hire me as office manager. They don't have one anymore, and they're keeping the position open for me."

"Wait, do you want to leave?" says Gary.

"I might, it doesn't look that we'll have a great future anyway."

"No, I think it's a great idea! We can finally get rid of you," he says, pulling his tongue out.

"Steven, do you see how my colleagues remain children!" she says, but she's laughing.

Gary grew up teasing Susan and Susan pushing his buttons. Apparently, everyone was convinced that they would end up married to each other. Three things ended up in the way of a possible relationship. Perhaps, she jokes, without these three things, she could have married Gary. First, Susan fell in love with Paul, Gary's younger brother. Paul's the one with whom she always possessed chemistry, while Gary was more like a friend, one with whom to play.

Second, Susan couldn't date anyone working at GTW. When she accepted the mission, the responsibility of managing the daily operations, she knew the company was in trouble, and she didn't want to subject any children she would have to instability from both parents. The third one remained rather important, too! Just as Susan showed zero interest in Gary, he too felt no romantic or sexual interests in her at all for the simple reason that, Gary, is gay.

But apart from these three little details? Sure, a world might exist where they form a couple, both of them joked, with Paul usually rolling his eyes at the idea. And yet, Susan showed interest in Gary's work.

"Of course, your stuck-up family has a crest?" says Susan.

Gary gets along with everyone, and tried to act nicely to everyone, at least, that Steven sees. Susan remains a lot more selective about whom she likes and offer real pain to those she hates. Steven's relationship with Susan started rather indirectly. Gary, her brother-in-law and business partner, sees Steven as a friend, so she has a positive opinion of him by association. She also hates his family, not so much personally, but the type of people they are. Since they rejected him, it makes her have a good perception of him by simple opposition to them.

But Susan lived in a male world. Surrounded by men who worked in factories, both GTW and their clients, she always felt isolated from her gender. Even Catherine, her cousin, looks more masculine than feminine and mainly talks shop. That's where Lily came in, she became the only beacon of womanhood in Susan's mind. Only she brought some colour to Susan's world, but she also helped the GTW male employees (and Catherine) open up to the realities of the fairer sex.

Catherine even learned, for a while, to let her hair grow and instead to tie it in a bun, liking the look Lily presented with her pencils in her hair. Well, Catherine used screwdrivers, but still, it softened her otherwise harsh look. Susan found a best friend in Lily, and even took her as a maid of honour when she married Paul, which came as a shock to Steven, but not Lily.

"You know, Steven, not every relationship ends up symmetrical. Sometimes, we meet an acquaintance we enjoy the company of, but might not see as a friend, and from their point of view, we're their best friend. That's why I'm kind to everyone, I might know how much these people matter to me, but I can't imagine what I'm worth to them."

That, came too late to make Steven fall in love with Lily or want to marry her. Both of those remained firmly in the past, but now, speaking with Susan, Steven couldn't help thinking back to the days when he would arrive at GTW to find his wife already on location, laughing with Susan! She chose to spend a moment with Steven at his work, and stopped first to talk to a woman who considers Lily as her best friend, but who wasn't in Lily's top friends at all.

Lily thus didn't go out of a desire to see her, she focused on her because she knew of her importance in this woman's heart. How she would brighten her day by just giving her some of her time to listen to her concerns and validate her about them. Steven decided to remain honest with Susan. Lily served as her best friend, and she had always been there for his wife.

"Yeah, I never cared for the crest, I told you that, but my father does and even as horrible as my family is, they're my only family left."

"And I'm taking that personally, Steven. What is our relationship if not one of siblings?" she says, grabbing hold of his shoulders.

But the truth is that whatever Lily might have been to Susan, she did lighten the place, but Steven would only ever serve a business partner and the widow to Susan's BFF. Did Susan offer help when he had to run from his house? Did she offer him shelter, food or a job? No. And she knew it. She knew it consisted only of lip service honouring Lily. Because Lily would have done that, and Susan wants to respect her desires.

Steven, however, can't blame her. GTW as a whole lived with their own issues, and Susan was fighting to keep the lights on. Her daughter also took a lot of her attention away and before that, she was, too, mourning the loss of her best friend. The reality is that Lily meant a lot to the few people that Steven could have asked for help, as a widower, most usually remained deep in grief too. He called it the curse of having married such as wonderful woman, her loss deeply saddened everyone she touched, and that was everyone Steven knew.

Susan didn't stay long. She never stayed long in one place. Lily used to joke that there existed only two constants in Susan's life: Paul, and GTW, with Lily as a distant third. Now, Susan's adorable daughter got the affection previously given to Lily. Gary kept joking about, but soon enough, with a little sandblasting here, a fine mesh drilled with a CNC there, some laser polishing next to it, Steven held a pretty good replica of the crest. All completed in less than 25 minutes.

Even more impressive, Gary programmed his tools in only a few minutes. In reality, both men managed to talk while the machines worked. Susan's interruption hadn't even delayed the delivery. The machines just kept on working… machines which didn't break enough, Steven surprised himself thinking. Still, he knew GTW would never provide him a source of income. But it was nice to be with people who accepted he could have never hurt his wife, and who truly appreciated her. A little nostalgic, with the antenna enclosure parts and his crest in an old cardboard box, he thanked everyone and returned to his workshop. This left him wondering how, after paying for gas to drive to his parent's home, he would manage to get enough food to last until the end of the month.

Chapter 1.9—Linda Clark's Supper

Steven found a nice box in which to place the gift, but still stopped at the dollar store to pick up a gift bag and a card. He knew it would show on the back that he only spent $2, but that consisted of a huge percentage of his monthly budget, and he simply couldn't spring a fortune! It saddened him. Steven was stuck with the idea that his parents didn't really work a single hour in their entire adulthood. His father basically lived on a portion of the interests of the money he inherited from his own father, and also received the family mansion (which never even had a mortgage) when he became the patriarch.

Driving to his childhood home, he felt panic seeing himself in the rearview mirror. Unshaven for four days, unkempt hair deserved a haircut weeks ago and an old stained t-shirt which he should have known better than to wear. Resigned, he kept going. He wouldn't make any of them happy anyway. He had as much chance at warming up his family by his presence than an Inuit had to get a sun burn in the middle of winter. Fine, bad analogy, he acknowledged, as not every Inuit lived in their ancestral grounds, but he still smiled at the thought. Was Inuit even appropriate in his day and age, or did it become pejorative? Steven certainly admired their hard work and, thus, didn't wish them any harm. Plus, the little he knew of them, they appeared to care about their offsprings, unlike his parents.

His old, rusted truck clashed with the almost brand-new vehicles already in the driveway. He recognized his father's Porsche from the last time he had visited him to fix a plumbing problem—no use explaining that electromechanical technicians didn't repair pipes—but the remaining two showed how recently they were purchased. He guessed the BMW was his mother's: she usually put less than 1000 miles on the odometer. She still faithfully changes it every two years: not just purchasing a newer German car, she needed to switch the model to make sure the whole city knew she had bought another. Alternating colours weren't an option: her ride needed black paint.

The Lexus minivan, he realized, was obviously his brother's, and most likely paid by both of their parents. Steven felt disgusted at the thought that Michael probably got both their mother and father to pay in secret for it. He thus pocketed the full value of the car after paying cash for it by playing their parents against each other. It's no wonder he married Camille.

Steven rang the doorbell. Before Lily's disappearance, he would just walk in just as he always did, using his key should it be locked, which it seldom did was back then. The door mysteriously changed locks the day he became a suspect. Camille opened the door. Steven immediately thought that she looked presumptuous, but thought that he should instead to compliment her on her dress. It's simple, Camille wore dresses everywhere. Gucci, Versace and God knows which other high-end dresses, usually to show that she lost her baby fat after two pregnancies. In the end, he just looked at her.

"Oh, Hi Steven, good of you to show up," she said, with such a bored tone, she actually was missing her usual sarcasm. Steven had to restrain himself from laughing at one of the rare jabs that his mother, Linda, had made at her daughter-in-law: "She might have lost her baby belly fat, but have you seen her thighs? You could support a crane on them!"

But that was before the disappearance; now, the family unit had formed a thick coalition to distance themselves from the black sheep. Now, rumours and acid comments targeted him.
He also decided not to comment on the dress. Her bored tone came as a shock to him.

"Come in, we have hors d'oeuvres," Camille said, without realizing that Steven hadn't said a word yet. Instead, he was wincing at her horrible pronunciation of the French word for "appetizers…"

Camille walked toward the dining room, only via small steps in her impossibly high heels. Lily never understood how the woman could stand with these! Camille grew to only five feet four, so she wears five or six inch-tall heels to make her look an acceptable height next to her husband. Not that Michael grew tall… he remained the runt of the family at only five feet ten, while the men usually rose to a good six feet 2 or 3. Steven himself had peaked at six feet three and a half, but now that he was entering his forties, he had lost almost two inches without really paying attention to it. Noticing his smallness hardly scored high on his list of priorities.

Taken from his thoughts by his father, who greeted him with a firm handshake, he simply gave the present to his progenitor when he was asked if Steven held his gift. Opening the bag without even looking at the card, the great Richard Clark shook while holding the logo.

"Steven, I didn't know you even liked our crest. This is beautiful. It's a wonderful gift! Thank you."

Steven nodded, noting mentally how he didn't refer to him as his son, or by the nickname "Stevie" he used in the past. Steven tried to reply when Michael winced and Steven noticed that Camille had hit him in the ribs.

"Steven, did you lay your eyes on the fountain on the front lawn?" Steven just shook his head, as if he hadn't really cared about it. "Ah, well, Camille and I rebuilt it! Just like when we were young! Take a look when you leave, and you'll see, we paid attention to every detail…"

What bothered Steven the most wasn't that Michael probably fixed the fountain from the money he made scamming their parents. It wasn't that his gift proved bigger. It wasn't even that he was boasting at this exact moment. What fully annoyed Steven is that he noticed that he didn't even hear what occurred to the old one, and he missed the window to ask about it. He felt initially ashamed for not knowing what happened, but he also realized that it's his family members who kept pushing him away.

Linda, always trying to act like the iron matriarch of the clan, invited everyone to sit down at the table. This meant putting Steven apart from everyone, with a table place clearly put by his side for Lily, just to torture him in silence. It also meant that his niece and nephew, Sam and Sarah, would sit at the kid's table in the other room, even if they were teenagers now and the main table could sit the whole family. With the Clark, the special dining room always remained for adults only.

As always, Linda Clark wouldn't serve her guests and instead, a maid hired just for the occasion would do it. Manuela, their cleaning lady who usually prepared the meals, wouldn't do. She consisted of the normal help. What Linda needed today required a special maid, white, not Latina. It certainly never escaped Steven's thoughts that most of the family money came, before the civil war, from a huge plantation in rural Kentucky. While the Clark always maintained it operated as an honest plantation, anyone knew that with the money left, slaves most likely operated the plantation. His mother's disdain for the "coloured people" as she called the African American and Latino people, came from her own family, but Steven knew that both of his parents shared similar thoughts.

45

Steven ate the salad in silence as Camille rambled on what Sarah had achieved at school, while Michael, the first proper Clark to have held an actual job in generations, would brag about his most recent transactions. Michael became a real estate investor. In reality far from what most people would call a job, it consisted much more of a job than Richard or his father ever held. Steven felt actually impressed at how well Michael managed to become a somewhat productive member of society.

Granted, he mainly preyed on people who lost their jobs and couldn't afford their mortgages. Unlike banks, he would give them a chance to become actual tenants, often giving them a few free months before slowly ramping up the rent until it made him some of the money back. Camille, of course, talked about her boutique shop. You know the type of shop. It's in a strip mall and occupies the smallest rental unit. With a backdrop of pink walls, the schedule on the door shows official opening hours only from 10 AM until 2 PM, Monday to Friday, or roughly when Sam and Sarah study at school. It usually sells about one item per year outside the family.

Steven wondered why the store remained in business, but Kyle, from GTW explained it to him: It's something to keep Camille busy while Michael works, and it's a great source of expenses to reduce income tax. For Michael, it mainly avoided leaving his wife alone at home with a pool boy or a horny neighbour. It's not coincidental that most of these boutique shops have a networked camera that allows the husband to ensure his wife is present when she says she is. Of course, Steven mainly listened to his brother and sister-in-law because they remained only slightly more bearable to listen to than his own parents!

By the time the roast arrived, his mother had commented three times about how Steven was only wearing a t-shirt, twice on his beard and at least once on his hair. But that was for the salad and the soup, which Steven had eaten while lost in his thoughts about how superficial his family was.

For the main meal, his mother changed the subject and began talking about crime in the town with Camille. Steven's mother barely masked her contempt for her son, and both women constantly inferred that not enough men were in jail for crimes against women. Even Richard, the great Richard, put his foot down that the death penalty remains the only penalty appropriate enough for criminals. That some people just deserve to fry, or better yet, to get shot.

Steven worked hard on his roast, trying to concentrate on his food, but still feeling the eyes in the room staring down at him. He missed Lily, these horrible people never accepted her modest origins, and yet, they blamed him for her disappearance, strike that, for her death instead of standing up to their blood kin. Granted, they also poked fun at his choice of a profession. His father, who never worked even a single day of his life, insinuated that had he picked a better, more honourable job, he would have succeeded in life instead of fading away in a dirty loading bay.

Dessert didn't come fast enough, but once it did, the mood lightened up and finally, Steven managed to sneak away as the rest of his family opened Porto bottles to celebrate Richard's 64th birthday. Driving away with a heavy heart, Steven replayed in this mind, whether he wanted it or not, the conversations of the evening, only to realize, without much surprise, that he hadn't said a single word.

Chapter 1.10—Lily's past

Steven didn't drive back directly to his workshop and, instead, took a little detour to pass by the high school where he had met his wife. Parked in clear view of the old building, he thought back and still wondered how he had managed to get Lily to even pay attention to him. He still remembered how as a new student, in ninth grade, after his parents just decided to stop paying for private school. Oddly enough, he couldn't quite remember why, especially since they paid handsomely for his vocational education.

Anyway, Steven shrugged off the repressed memory and instead, remembered how Lily had volunteered from the beginning to become his introduction buddy. She showed him around school, always paying attention to his jokes and smiling the whole way. Michael proved cruel that night, he implied that, coming from a poor family, she only wanted him for their money, but Steven doubted it. How could she have even known they had money? Everyone, including him and her, wore stupid school uniforms which also included shoes for some reason. Even his private school gave some flexibility in footwear.

No, Steven was confused that unlike his family who seemed to just use people, Lily acted nice toward him because she liked him. Genuinely. As the days went by, their relationship grew, and he quickly discovered how smart and agreeable she was. She seemed to really care about him as much as he began to care about her. His private school showed a dog-eat-dog world where everyone was just fighting for a better position. Sure, the same occurred at the public school, but it felt optional. Parents, notably, didn't cheer from the sidelines. His family would select his friends and group partners depending on their own incomprehensible adult drama.

Plus, after being born and raised in a cold family, Lily's empathy and generous nature provided a striking contrast to the relationship skills he had learned growing up. In a matter of weeks, their relationship quickly grew as complicity settled in. Rapidly, Lily managed to spot Steven's weaknesses and help him with his learning, while never hesitating to ask for help on the few subjects where he outsmarted her. Not once did she laugh at him for his mistakes. She never even gave him the cold shoulder when his bad social skills insulted her accidentally. Instead, she would patiently tell him how inappropriate a comment or an expression was.

In truth, Lily wasn't like the other girls in high school. She was already thinking forward, thinking about adulthood, about how she wanted to live her life. She would reveal her rage today at the gossiping occurring around her disappearance, as she never paid attention to those wastes of time. Even back then, in her ninth grade, Lily knew she would become a historian, and already she had bought industrial era clothes she wore for Halloween or other costume parties.

Steven kept growing a little, but Lily's clothes from ninth grade still fit her as an adult. Did she give them room to grow the one or two inches she gained since her teenage years? He can vividly recall how he ended up seeing her as a potential partner. She would probably mention the agriculture fair. But that's when they both connected. His interest had already sparked. A few months earlier they worked together for the science fair. In previous years, it was possible to perform the experiments alone, but that year, working in teams became mandatory.

Lily desired to make a steam engine electrical generator, which would power an electric pump, which would fill the water tank of the steam engine, and she wanted Steven as a partner! What she neglected to mention to him is that not only would they manufacture the components of the experiment, including the generator and the electric pump! It consisted of a long project, often worked at her house, with Lily insisting that her parents not help with the main tasks, but her father nevertheless occasionally lent a hand with sheets of metal or using certain tools.

Steven was surprised at how much fun creating a makeshift engine gave him. It wouldn't look professional, but it functioned! But then, he had to wire two of them: one for the pump, and the other for the generator.

"Lily, wouldn't it prove more efficient if the water supply remained mechanical?" Steven proposed.

But the project, she decided, was about steam generated electricity. The motor was just to prove the system worked. And so, they began the process. Using recycled aluminum from sodas and soup cans, Lily toiled on the boiler. Her fuel source consisted of an array of candles, which would heat two important things. A container of water which produced steam by boiling, and a coil wrapped in the hot liquid to warm the newly supplied water without cooling the main recipient too much.

The pipe went from deep in the bowl and coiled up to drip at the surface of the scalding liquid instead of doing so at the bottom. This means that the slower the pump operated, the longer the water travelled in the tube, giving it more time to heat, helping the whole assembly to a warmer equilibrium. It also allowed a few turns at the start of the spiral to be in the path of the fire from the flames, providing a rapid rise in temperature, both in the piping and the water. Granted, the metal tube was bought, but they didn't have any way to fabricate it themselves, same with the magnets for the two motors.

Stubborn but positive, Lily tweaked her boiler bit by bit and by the time it she considered it perfect, Steven had finished wiring his first motor, which he quickly mounted on the rotating shaft. They were now making electricity! Not a ton of it, but enough. While Steven wired the second engine, Lily worked on the mechanical part of the pump itself. For this, she required help from her father as she decided to mould aluminum foil into the shapes she needed.

Steven observed, in the backyard, envious that Lily had such a present father. And her mother wasn't far, in fact, she was sitting next to him, looking in and wishing good luck to the two people she loved the most. Never had Steven seen such affection. Now, he would begin to imagine that having a wife and kids would feel. He visualized the passion between the parents and the devotion for their offsprings. This would be unlike the relationships in his family, who always bickered and didn't feel fully in love.

The pump, when activated manually, worked. George supplied them with a big bucket of water from Home Depot, and Steven mounted his part of the project on it. A flexible tube, also from Home Depot, connected from the motor to the coil. The initial run of the system, without the second motor, revealed a success! The boiler produced steam, which the generator converted to electricity with which his other engine pushed new liquid into the system without cooling it, provided the pump operated slowly enough. It only needed to replace the evaporated portion.

They spent two longer evenings waiting for Steven to wire the additional motor, which he completed faster than the other. He couldn't complain: Lily drafted the plans, created most of the parts, made the tests, his only requirement remained to build two electrical engines. Once in place, however, the first run left him sorely disappointed. Instead of moving at a slow pace, the capacitor they placed to start it would take a few seconds to charge from the generator, and then, the pump only made two or three leisurely rotations before stopping again.

Lily, far from sad, instead decided to calculate, in ounces, the water output from the tube, and then compared it to the evaporation of liquid to steam and came to the conclusion that they remained close enough! If the water container began at least 75% filled, the candles would burn out before the boiler would run dry. Granted, when the candles got shorter, the engine slowed down and eventually stopped from the loss of heat in the gap between the container and the remaining wax stubs. Lily noted that this entropy took long enough for their presentation to complete and for a long question and answer session.

In their mind, they produced a major success and the teachers agreed, giving them the winning place! The kicker, however, was Lily's authentic looking industrial era dress, which really helped set the mood. This consisted of their first project together, and soon after, they would meet at the agriculture fair, and their lives would begin even more connected as they discovered their greatest experiment: love.

Reflecting back about Lily still made him suffer. They had grown so close and their stories had become so intertwined that he truly felt like a piece of him was missing. Half thinking due to the pain, he drove back home and couldn't help himself, having a particular Meatloaf song stuck in his head. The lyrics "I'll probably never know where she disappeared" always struck especially hard each time he listened to it, but sometimes, just sometimes, it was what he needed. Even if objects in the rearview mirror may appear closer than they are.

Chapter 1.11—Lab Tests

He tried to change his train of thought as he began mounting the parts of his antenna into the enclosure that GTW built as per his specifications. As always, the part proved itself flawless and had almost no deviations from his plans. The cover over the antenna assembly fitted perfectly would provide excellent insulation for the system.

Yes, he thought back. This remained a completely crazy project...

A reception antenna usually consists of an exposed wire of a certain length, which you size proportionally to the wavelength of the frequency you tuned. For example, the local classic rock channel emits at 93.4 MHz, which produces a wavelength of a little over 10 feet. Having such a long antenna isn't practical, so instead we generally use an antenna that measures the quarter length of the wavelength or in his case, 30.06 inches.

The shape of the antennas doesn't matter. He worked with straight ones, coiled ones, and even directional dishes.

What they have in common is that they're exposed to the radio frequency wave you're trying to either receive or emit. It's common sense... to see something with your eyes, you need a direct line of sight. To catch something with your antenna, you need a direct connection.

Lily thought of other ideas...

Granted, she worked as a history professor, more specifically, an industrial era history professor. One of the youngest professors to get a full chair in well, any universities, thanks to her doctoral thesis which re-examined how the centrifugal governor evolved since its original creation by James Watt. She gathered parts Steven and her salvaged from antique shops scattered around the area, as well as pictures she requested from various museums. This allowed her to paint a much clearer image of how this ingenious piece enabled the Industrial Revolution.

Steven always found it odd that such a brilliant woman, who could have done anything with her life, focused her thesis on such a simple device.

"It's a feedback loop, Stevie…", she had explained to him numerous times. "It rotates at the same speed as the steam engine itself. As it turns out, the centrifugal force raises the two fly balls on either side, and it opens a valve which releases exceed steam, which in turn, slows down the machine and slightly closes the valve."

Feedback systems always fascinated Lily, and when Steven had shown in science class proficiency with mechanical things, she encouraged him to study in electromechanical maintenance, where he learned both electronics and mechanics. In fact, most devices work via feedback loops. The loom at DryTek uses the tension between the driving belt and roller #4 as a feedback system to preserve the appropriate friction on the fabric. The only reason the system introduces creases is that Steven, in order to keep his revenues, prevents the system from properly operating. A more advanced version could detect folds and tweak the tension itself. Such systems proved more expensive in theory and a good honest and competent technician could easily adjust the tension and forever stop the wrinkles. While Steven counted himself as competent… he just acted less than honest with them.

Shaking his guilt away, he instead thought back about how, on long road trips, they both felt excitement at finding odd, rusted parts of old machines. It would mean spending a few hours working together restoring them with rock music blasting out of their radio and laughs all-around. They would frequently stop at concerts for local independent bands (a few of which made it big in the meantime) and find local restaurants. Once again, Steven returned to his original thoughts, so, Lily imagined an idea about Quantum computing. "Focus Steven… Focus…", he thought. It remains one of her craziest ideas.

Her personal hero, Hedy Lamarr inspired it. In 1941, the Hollywood actress, officially renowned for her beauty, co-filed a patent for the invention of a method to transmit unbreakable radio transmissions by manipulating radio frequencies. Her invention directly allowed a series of spread spectrum technologies such as cellphones and fax machines. Just like Hedy thought of a crazy idea about how radio signals worked across frequencies, Lily had a crazy idea about how radio-frequencies worked at the quantum level.

Traditional computing uses electronics, just like radio-wave's kind of do. In short, electricity, whether in PCs or in radio communications is the transmission of electrons, hence the name, electronics. Quantum computing, however, occurs at that level, within the uncertainty of the position of electrons and such.

"What if both block each other? What if the actual flow of electrons blocks the data?"

She thought that to have a proper exchange of information, whether within a computer or via a radio-wave exchange, we had to isolate the electron flow and restrict the data only to the quantum level. Lily's goal was to create not a new quantum computer, but a new way to receive information remotely at that level. An antenna which offers a way to receive information instantly at huge distances, even across the Earth's crust itself.

This flew right over Steven's head, but she inspired the schematic and that, he did understand. It remained just an idea, strictly on paper. In fact, originally, not even on paper as Lily lacked the structure, the capacity to note down her proposals properly. That consisted of Steven's contribution. That and the reality check about how modern technology functioned. Because Lily worked with steam engines, not wires, and she was trying, as a hobby, to design the most advance electronic device ever built!

"But it's not, Steven." She would say, never getting his objection.

He would explain. "Lily, if electricity powers it, and if it sends a signal I can measure by an oscilloscope or a multimeter, it's electronics."

Yet, Lily dismissed him. And Steven would give up. When Lily wanted to do something, anything, it was better to follow along than to question her. If it ended up a bad idea, she would figure it out and stop. But often, she had frightening but astonishing ideas. It's only recently that he had found his old notebooks and began implementing her plans. He didn't know yet what he would do with the antenna. Lily frequently explained that, perhaps, it would be able to listen to distant stars.

However, Steven didn't want to just receive... he also ached to transmit. Lily initially saw her invention as a passive device. As a receptor, but in reality, they're bidirectional, in the same vein that any speaker can become a microphone (even if a poor one), and any electric motor can function as a generator. As such, any radio frequency decoding system can emit if you supply it data instead of reading from it. In fact, most wireless routers only need a single antenna to send but also receive and that's, in a way, what Steven had carefully built over the last year or so.

He felt it wasn't named properly. Anything considered "Antenna" would need a wire, a coil, something conducting, open. Anything conductive which isn't connected to the ground, and able to capture an electromagnetic signal. Lily, had weird components in the core, which she had already built with his help, and was planning to wrap her components in a Faraday cage. She would attempt to isolate her antenna!

"Of course, I want to get quantum signals, you know, like neutrinos, but they don't respect the speed of light. I could get data from the past, from the future, from far away! And from there, peek across the veil of time"

He would always look at her as if she had lost her mind, but she hadn't. Lily remains the sanest person he knew. He believed the project to remain futile and useless. He absolutely thought it would never work. But everything Lily touched, always worked. Everything. They said she couldn't make her thesis subject interesting, and they were captivated. They said she wouldn't find enough artifacts, and she did.

This time, however, what was blocking her wasn't even the antenna part. The problem lied in the amount of data. She could find her way to code and had already written the software to analyze the result. The problem centred on the bandwidth required to extract the data and the speed of computers to process it. Her antenna would have to supply close to 4 GB/s of raw data that her code would need to be calculated. Before she accepted it could send, Lily simply hoped to save the input but by then, she fully jumped onboard his crazy idea. She needed to crush the numbers.

Sure, they could check the raw frequencies with a spectrum analyzer to form an idea of the input. To get an accurate "picture," the outbound signal had to include some level of modulation, just as a radar had to turn. And to modulate properly, you had to do it as a feedback loop from the inbound signal. This is just like how cameras autofocus. For that, the raw data needed to be crunched in real time. In 2000–2002, with USB2.0, since each second of capture would produce 4 GB of data, it would need at least 8.3 seconds of transfer, and close to 400 seconds of analysis. But only if the computer possessed enough memory!

And that's every second. Lily thought it would require hours to tune properly and focus. It's why she didn't consider any transmission. As a passive device, she would lack control, but wouldn't need those complications. To work, she needed hours of data! It remained simply impossible... When she disappeared. USB 3 needing years to arrive. The project was thus shelved, she disappeared, and Steven had to move to get away from the attention the police and the press put on him. Time, then, got in the way. Weeks alone changed to months and years.

Twelve years after Lily's disappearance, in 2014, computers became so fast, and USB3 so superior that he found bandwidth to spare. He can hold a capture in memory and the several minutes of summarized information without needing to even write to the disk, a process magnitude slower. While receiving the next second, the program analyzes the previous one and once done, deletes the raw data to leave space by using a more memory efficient model. In just twelve years, Lily's project went from impossible on three fronts: USB, CPU speed and RAM capacity, to being within the specs of ordinary computers. Even his current laptop would be able to do, now that he upgraded it to thirty-two gigabytes.

So, alone, in 2014, he dug out the schematic and completed Lily's antenna. He would finally see what she was hoping to find. He remained with plenty of time to finish the build, and already had most of the parts. The rest, he ordered from AliExpress, something that didn't exist in 2002, or he got it made by a client. So, he booted up his emission program on his ancient laptop. She had guided its evolution and while neither of them knew how to really develop, they found the code simple enough to implement. Plus, they had the software construction kit for the interface they purchased.

Today, an Arduino would do the job better, but Steven hadn't kept up enough with the progress to allow him to replicate the old code on the new platform. In short, the module would send massive pulses on a stable carrier. It would emit on a fixed frequency, while keeping Steven's spectrum analyzer in the foreground to see if anything bounced back to him. Lily had conceived a frequency multiplier into the system itself. He had no idea how it worked, but if he gained a two-megahertz signal, it would actually mean he would have received a two-terahertz pulse.

It didn't seem possible to devise such a circuit, but once designed, he was able to build it, and for this, he could employ a normal cheap device he had bought second-hand when studying. A spectrum analyzer, even his low-cost one, would serve a very useful purpose. Most people use oscilloscopes for measuring amplitude over time. Usually, it measures in volts, so you can perceive the evolution of a repeating signal, synchronizing on a certain timing. But waves have a frequency, and they can overlap. When you tune your radio in the FM range, you select a specific channel, say 93.4 MHz, his local classic rock station, but that's the middle of their range.

The input of an FM station will move to transmit the music, something missed using an oscilloscope, which only displays the signal itself, not changes in its frequency. That's the job of the spectrum analyzer! It shows the amplitude of each peak, allowing us to clearly see the encoding of an FM radio, for example. With Lily's Quantum antenna design, however, she theorized that the signal would work marginally like the Doppler effect.

If a car is speeding away from you or from you, the sound it makes will rise or lower in pitch predictably in a measurable and predictable manner. This means that any drift in the frequency of replies could reveal their relative speed and movement when compared to his own fixed location. With the frequency multiplier in place, now used as a divisor when reading back, any close objects would stay invisible and only massive speed differences would show up. Perhaps Mars or Venus would show! Maybe even the Moon, but not a car down the street. Now that he completed his enclosure, he considers himself ready to make a test.

He had already planned what he wanted to do tonight. First, he would listen to try and gather the noise floor: every antenna can gather noise: random signals from its own system, from random waves and from the very fabric of space itself. Once he knew the noise floor of his antenna, he would see if he could pick up anything above it that sounded like a signal. Since the enclosure shields the antenna, it would only pick up quantum signals and as far as he knew, no one else had ever built a quantum antenna.

"Prepare to break your expectations, Stevie, the range of such an antenna might multiply light years," she had told him.

Nervous, Steven turned the system on.

After plugging it in, he took measurements. He did pick up spikes, which felt odd, and he wondered if, perhaps, the small Faraday cage he had built around it wasn't perfect. He grabbed some aluminum paper and wrapped it around with no reduction in spikes. In reality, he couldn't imagine how aluminum paper helped in such a case, he had grounded it, so in theory, it shouldn't help and yet, he had signals.

At the moment the countdown ended, once the waves found themselves propelled, new signals surfaced in the two almost two point two megahertz range, including a peak nearby. Lily had explained that in theory, thanks to neutrinos' ability to travel faster than light speed, the first echoes would possibly show up before the antenna radiated and once again. She seemed right!

At the moment the countdown ended, once the waves found themselves propelled, new signals surfaced in the two almost two point two megahertz range, including a peak nearby. He probably picked up his own wave. That one, being near, wouldn't appear before or after: the distance appeared just too close for any time distortion.

The stability of those signals fascinated Steven: it's as if the one he was emitting bounced back to him at new heights, with a few neutrinos arriving from the round trip, returning before they left.

Part 2

Chapter 2.1—Interrupted

A spike appeared on his spectrum analyzer, but it wasn't so much a new carrier, but almost like a dancing signal. Several new peaks appeared on the display and seemed to drift left and right, as if someone was scanning the antenna.

Almost like a fly buzzing around.

Worried, he turned it off and suddenly, a faint but clear smell of ozone filled the air. Thinking he had scorched his antenna, he swiftly turned it on again and witnessed that it remained functional: he could see the same signals he had previously gotten and no sign of the erratic one. He rose from his seat and hazarded quickly to touch the antenna to feel whether it became hot. He knew he should use a thermometer. He burned himself quite a few times checking client's machinery, but despite buying a quite effective infrared sensor specifically for that, he always relied on his fingers to experience the warmth of an object.

It seemed tepid, at best. Still, not even close to the heat it would have gotten if an arc had formed when he turned it on. In his experience, this remains the usual source of ozone when working with electricity. He touched other parts of the antenna and circled it, looking at every square inch of surface for darkened spots, when he saw something in the corner of his eye... it was, well, a box.

A metallic one. The size made him think of those photo booths from the mall from his youth. Perhaps barely bigger. Faint red lights came out from inside. It made him think more of it as a machine than just a simple container.

The dim ozone smell dissipated. As he gently approached the cubic object... a thought unsettled him. He didn't hear it at first: it felt like the universe tore open silently. The next moment, the strange container solidified its apparition in his workshop, placed as if it had always been there.The machine reminded him of a Faraday cage he had seen at one of his client's locations. It displayed a dull, grey metallic colour. What looked to be multiple panels invited him to open them. Various connectors seemed visible on the side, most of which he couldn't begin to guess at their purpose.

One of them, however, looked like a male power plug in a socket which made him think that perhaps that apparatus could be recharged in a simple one-hundred-and-ten-volt electrical outlet, but otherwise ran on batteries.

He circled it and noticed an actual door in the middle, to the left. The bar handle gently turned when he tried it and allowed the small entrance to swing open, revealing inside the machine what Steven thought of as a cockpit. What surprised him the most wasn't that he found a gorgeous maiden sitting in the dark, wounded, in the pilot's seat. He found himself shocked to find Lily, his wife, as beautiful and as young as at the last time he had laid eyes on her. Not Lily 12 years older. Not Lily from 2014. No, Lily from 2002.

Lily didn't vanish. She had travelled to the future in a time machine and failed to come back. She was holding her chest and blood was oozing out, in fact, the floor felt wet with the sticky liquid pouring out of his wife.

"Wait what? Stevie?" she uttered out of breath, almost inaudible.

"Lily? What's happening, where have you been? You disappeared over 12 years ago!"

"What? This isn't 2002. Shit, I'm seriously hurt. The bitch really got me."

Steven runs closer to her and sees that she isn't grasping her chest but rather her actual heart. Hearing her speak filled his head with memories of his life with her. He had so much to tell her, so much to ask her and yet, nothing could come out. He wanted to say that he was there for her. That he never forgot her. That he will do whatever he can, that he would forgive any shame, indiscretion or secret she kept from him. That nothing mattered but her. But he couldn't. His emotional range didn't allow it. He could express himself but had to reheat the room first. It wasn't natural for him. Hiding emotions in the deepest recess of his heart was what felt natural, so the only thing he could say, the only action he could take, is to speak from his head, not his heart.

"This is 2014 Lily… Let's get you to a hospital."

"It's too late, Stevie, the ambulance or your truck won't be fast enough. Let me get there."

With her left hand, looks at the console.

"A beacon? Oh no, why is there a beacon here? I'm locked out. Find the beacon, save me then, in…"

But Lily had lost too much blood and couldn't remain conscious or finish her last words. His wife had been there. The words he had wanted to say. The speeches he had saved up. So much remained left unsaid. They remained reduced to a few confused questions and a reply. Those remained the last words she heard from his mouth.

Completely factual. Absolutely emotionless. He grew up a robot before he met her and returned to a robot as she died. He cursed in his breath. He just reacted. Simply took the pushes. Hadn't taken charge of himself, of the situation. She entered his life after he grew up utterly broken and left it without realizing how good of an influence she exerted on him. For over 12 years, he begged heaven and hell to get a last chance to say goodbye to her, and now that he had, he had blown it.

"Stop only reacting, Stevie. You aren't a machine. When you just react, you let others push your buttons and operate you."

"But how? When my brother makes a jab at me, he makes me furious."

"Yes, and don't think I tell you to avoid your feeling. Accept your emotions, but don't let them control you. He knows what triggers you, you grew up together, but how you react to his comments remains your own prerogative."

"But my anger needs to express itself!"

"No, Stevie. Your anger desires to express itself. But feelings remain just messages. They inform you that something is happening. And if you don't do anything, they will want to do it for you. When your brother tells you a comment which makes your anger show up, it comes with a message. You can tell your anger that you heard it, and even thank her for showing up and reminding you to do something. But then, you decide what to do."

It initially felt weird to elaborate on his emotions, but Lily showed him otherwise. Often, just communicating with them enabled him to calm down quickly. This is how he managed to survive those years without her. This is how he successfully didn't lose patience with police officers harassing him. This is what helped him grow. And today, with Lily dead in front of him, so many moods assaulted him that he couldn't identify them, let alone talk to each one.

Lily had vanished, and only came back to perish in front of him. Why did the universe torture him this way? Yet, he wasn't without an internal voice. If he found himself to address his individual emotions, he could yell to the whole lot to just be quiet and that he would contact them later. That wasn't as healthy, but repressing them, he learned on his own, growing up. It's tackling them that she needed to teach him.

And that's the neat thing... the present isn't yet ready for that. Action now, wellbeing next. Steven lifted her and laid her on the floor of his workshop. He checked her wound and noticed that it was a lot nastier than he initially thought. Gently checking, he could spot that the bullet had torn her heart. He picked up his cellphone to try and call 911 but realized that she possessed the right instinct. With such a gaping wound, he failed to see a possible treatment, not outside of a trauma emergency room. She had lost about five pints of blood and her body turned white from lack of it. Most of the fluid fell around her, and on her clothes. She would have needed to be in a chirurgical ward to keep a chance of survival, and the nearest hospital remained just too far away.

What should he do? Could he call the police to try and prove he didn't kill her? But since he was in his workshop, it would be really difficult to convince them. If he didn't, who did? And why was she as young as when she initially disappeared? Where does this machine comes from and what purpose does it serve? Almost the entire town believed he murderer her, how the hell could he produce her body without finding himself in jail?

"Shit, where were you, Lily? What did you get yourself into!"

He recalled the despair he had dismissed. The emergency ended, feelings could assert themselves. To vent the pressure building up. To have a partner to help him pass through this and grief provided a better guide than rage, in experience. He did perceive fury in his heart, but kept speaking to it, "Thank you, I hear you, I will deal with you later, for now, I believe the moment I should cry, reflect, stop."And that's good. Because sadness slows your life down. Gives you a pause to think. Anger accelerates everything. It prompts you to action. Steven, figured it out on his own, after his wife disappeared.

With tears flowing, Steven shut her eyes with a droplet sliding down his cheek. He at last could see Lily again. He finally could stroke her hair. He might be able to get closure. It remained one-sided. He couldn't tell her how much he kept strengthening despite her absence and his grief. He needed to inform her that with her, he felt like on the highway of healing. That without her, he could only hike in the hills of self-improvement because of his loneliness, that only left him to work on himself. He now could say whatever he wanted to her, to her face, but she wouldn't hear it. Not anymore. She would never know that even after these years, his passion forever burns for her.

This lifeless body couldn't understand how much he hoped to tell her how she remained the most important person to him. That he wouldn't just cherish her for her whole life... because now, it got terminated and he still loved her. Indeed, he would do so until his dying breath, even if she had already given hers. For years, to see her, he had to close his eyes, and now she was there, in front of him, on his lap, under his nose, wet with tears. She was there, but she wasn't. This wasn't his wife, this constituted her remains.

Lily always showed vitality. She radiated in whichever room she was. But this cooling corpse no longer contained Lily. Sure, it had her skin, her hair, but not her life, her energy, or her soul. She was less than a drained battery. She died. Left. Her body was there, but she wasn't. And sadly, he realized, he now had to get rid of her corpse. But how do you do that? You can't just dump it on the curb with the trash.

He knew he couldn't leave his workshop with her, since the police still frequently monitored his movement. The frequency lowered, but often they would just write their reports in the car outside his place. And so, Steven did the only action he could imagine himself carrying. He lifted and brought her to his secret apartment and put his wife's body in his large freezer he normally used to store meat bought on sale. He did have to shift the usual content around, but he managed to close the lid. It made him ill at ease.

He knew it remained a cliché. He knew it he could do better. Of course, he knew it showed a complete lack of respect. But he possessed no other ideas at the moment. He couldn't just let her decompose in his workshop, and he saw nowhere to dispose of her body for now. He quickly returned to the workshop floor, he grabbed his mop and his bucket and began scrubbing the floor to remove the blood when it remained still somewhat fresh. Crying, he mopped the floor reeling from the pain of having really lost his wife, but as the effort progressed, his tears turned happier at the thought that he would eventually start to find closure.

It's as if his anger saw that he was seizing control, and he was able to get back to sleep enough to let calm come back. He wouldn't be looking for her anymore. He wouldn't fear that some nefarious person kept her captive somewhere against her will. It definitely wasn't the ending he wanted, but it still remained an ending. A violent and abrupt one, yet even such an ending can lead to a new beginning. One where he was widowed and stopped obsessing over what happened. Once the floor was cleaned enough, Steven launched a scrubbing of the inside of the device, which proved to offer more challenges. Not only was there a lot more blood, but the cramped space made it hard to maneuver in. As he concluded, he remained left to ponder the purpose of the apparatus. How did it appear in his workshop? What did he do?

Chapter 2.2—Inspection

He could see the presence of a monitor and dials on what he could only call the dashboard. He can see dials, with one group digits set to November 3, 2002, which constituted the exact date Lily had disappeared. He located next to that group a single dial, set to "2", which he couldn't figure out the meaning or purpose. He saw what he evaluated as a power-level meter, showing a charge of 7% left. The monitor seemed to be off, but blood had drifted on it and on the keyboard, and both looked defective from short circuits.

Still cleaning up, he could see two seats in the cockpit, and a little storage room behind them. It contained snacks, some familiar, yet most remained new to him, with various expiry dates. Some seriously in the past, such as a chocolate bar best before 1997. Other far into the future such as a granola bar due in 2028. He knew most sold in stores lasted months, perhaps a year or two, but not decades. Setting them aside, he saw an old metallic bracket, the same kind Lily and him had found in antique shops when searching for steam governor parts.

He grabbed a notebook and smiled when he realized he had already seen it in the past: it served as Lily's diary. It's a book in which she used to record her important events in life, and which she had made him swear not to read. He put it on his desk, next to his spectrum analyzer, which was still showing the various carriers from his antenna. Returning to the machine, he began opening panels. One, at the front, revealing electronic contraptions. Nothing seemed really complex in itself, but the assembly appeared intricate, and he noticed that how sealed shut inside metal boxes several of the modules were.

He decided to leave this for a future review and instead, opened one of the side panels. It uncovered another storage compartment, this one filled with water bottles, soda cans and an old metallic box. Opening the box, he discovered a lot of old paper money from the 1800s, but in almost perfect shape. In the zone under it, he could find a few dresses, including antique-looking ones, carefully folded, as well as old leather shoes made manually by a cobbler. Odd, he thought.

At the back of the machine was a large, mostly empty area. It wasn't really deep, but he occupied the full height and width of the unit, apart from several plugged in rectangular boxes which Steven quickly recognized as batteries. They looked different than any he saw before, yet is still appeared obvious to him what they were: two pins sticking out from the top with a rubber cap on them, wires chaining them in a circuit.

He grabbed his multimeter, and touched two leads on one of them expecting them to be 12 volts, but instead, he discovered they supplied around 250 volts each. With 8 such small modules in series, this meant the system ran at 2000 volts! Returning to the front of the machine, he measured the voltage coming in the "engine" to only show 20 volts... why did anyone put a 2000-volt source when you only need 20 volts?

Walking around the box, it suddenly dawned on him: for power. Most batteries are limited at the current they can pump out since their reaction occurs chemically. So, a 250-volt battery, giving 10 amps, generates 2500 Watt of electricity. Chaining eight of them still produces only the same current since in a serial circuit, but the voltage in 2000 volt would provide 20,000 watts of power. If you converted 20,000 watts to back 20 volts, you could extract 1000 amps from batteries only capable of making 10.

Holy crap he thought... 1000 amps!

He returned to the front of the machine and began understanding the structure vaguely more. Many of the metallic boxes had multiple really, really thick wires going inside them, and they seemed to be connected in parallel. If in a serial circuit, the current is fixed, in a parallel one, you could add the current of the cables.He counted 10 such boxes, and each of them had 5 taps. If they configured in parallel, a unit could receive 100 amps, so with the multiplexing of 5 connections, they would individually receive 20 amps. That's reasonable.

He thought back to his classes, over two decades ago... the wire current travels into itself sets the limits: the bigger the size, the more amps you can carry through. It does cause heat, and electricity prefers to travel on the surface of the metal, restricting how big of a wire you can use. Amps is what can burn wires. You have breakers in your house not to prevent electrocution, but to prevent the cables in the walls from overheating and burning down, possibly starting a fire.

In North America homes most breakers limit to 15 amps, with some 20 and 30 also common. But not 1000 amps! What determines the voltage limits again? Was it distance and isolation? It escaped his recollections, but with 20 volts, it wasn't a problem. Even 300 to 400 volts would pass easily. He pulled the male socket he saw and indeed, it was connected to a spring-loaded coil. You could pull it out to recharge the batteries and if you let it go, it would slowly wind itself back. Quite ingenious.

After plugging it in and making sure the batteries weren't overheating, he looked at the craftsmanship, and the creator expertly made it using their own hands. This looked beautiful if one appreciated beauty in such installations. Inspecting the panels, he suddenly realized that this hadn't consisted of the first time he had seen them! Back in the '90s, when he was studying, Lily had asked him to help her with a project. She had wanted to build a metallic box to house the various pieces of antique she had found. As was often the case, Lily had the exact dimensions she wanted for the panels, and only needed him to cut them properly. He had helped her, but he now realized, he had never actually seen the finished assembly.

Once again going back to the engine part, he remembered buying with Lily metallic containers just like those he found for a design she hoped to do, but failed to complete. He thought back and realized that when they both studied in college, Lily had attempted a lot of weird electronic projects with him, without any of them panning out. Was she already working on this machine? Because the parts for these projects seem now to lay in front of him. Steven returned to his desk, and for the first time in his life, opened Lily's diary.

It wasn't what he expected at all. In the beginning, plenty of dates, and events narrated her life, including a description of him and a recollection of their first exchanges, a description of his family and how to deal with them. He also saw, almost written as if this functioned as a scrapbook, some of her more favourite quotes. Often detailed with hearts or flowers drawn around the quotes.

"There exists a place where you can touch a woman that will drive her crazy. Her Heart"

Or

"If you don't spend time getting to know yourself, you'll help up believing someone else's version of you."

A few weren't taking a whole page, but rather, many were just filling up random blank space around something else.One page, for example, is about Camille. It basically highlighted how it was useless to try to get along with her, and explained that she could be diagnosed as histrionic, whatever that meant. But then, at the bottom of it, was the quote "God save me from my friends because from enemies, I will protect myself," and then "Romanian saying." Lily often liked to say it to Steven, but she never clarified about whom he should see as his friends and whom as his enemies.

Hurting mildly and still very curious, he flipped quickly through those weird personal details, but once he changed section, he found detailed schematic on how to build the machine. Clear drawn or printed and glued over the diary pages plans of each of the components, with dates and locations when Lily obtained or built the various parts. Many did date from their college years, but the different inks used struck him. It clearly consisted of her own writing, she always showed excellent penmanship, but it's as if she revisited and updated the diary with either slightly different pens, or just with different ink levels. He also spotted at the end of the diary a series of dates set in the 1800s, along with longitude and latitude coordinates.

Lost and confused, Steven closed the book and inspected the floor and the machine to make sure no blood lingered anywhere. That night, Steven didn't sleep in his bed; instead, he grabbed his old inflatable mattress and slept next to the freezer, mainly crying

Chapter 2.3—Introspection

Steven woke up the next morning disoriented. At first, he couldn't remember why he slept next to his freezer. After opening it and finding Lily in it, he realized he hadn't dreamed about the previous night's events. Looking at her, he surprised himself speaking to her, as if she was there.

"I kept going, Lily, as you told me to do. You said that we have to work hard because we have no one else to fall on. That we constituted each other's only backup. I never believed you because, at least, your parents were nice and always there for us. But since you vanished, I lost my only backup. So I make sure to last. I made myself a home, one that no one could take away from me. You wouldn't like it. It's not pleasant to the eyes. I never did the joints on the drywall. I didn't paint any walls. But I'm safe."

He took a pause, grabbing the time to cry.

"You always told me, physical safety first, emotional safety second, comfort third and presentation fifth. Only, you never told me what you considered fourth."

He grabs a tissue and wipes away a tear.

"I miss you so much. I still think about you every day. Every single day, and now that I found you, you still elude me. And not like on evenings when I ended up distant."

Steven thinks back to evenings when Lily would tell him. "Where are you, Stevie?"

"Right here"

"Yeah, your body is, but your mind isn't. Where is it?"

Usually, however, it was nowhere. It's not that his mind floated elsewhere. It was that his mind went nowhere at all. He could describe it as feeling empty, inactive, lost. He was never able to put a word on it.

What he knows is that after years of Lily taking him out of his fugue state, he began visiting it less often and by the time of her disappearance, he had lost the habit. It's as if he has been drifting into an attention coma and Lily had taught him how to first climb out of it, and then, how to avoid it. Even after she was lost, despite the hard grief taking over, he managed to avoid this passive state which characterized his younger years.

"I love you, Lily," he said, caressing her hair, he closed the freezer and took a shower, leaving his still blood-soaked clothes on his bathroom floor.

Steven thought that showers felt nice, since it wasn't clear if you let tears flow due to the pain, or the water dripping from your hair. But today, he realized the source of his despair. He couldn't hide it.

"Men can and should cry when they need to," repeated Lily. "Sadness when necessary isn't a sign of weakness, it's a proof of emotional maturity."

"But even babies and children know how to cry."

"Yes, except, keep in mind that the reason changes. A baby doesn't know how to communicate its problems in other ways, and a child lacks the skills to form into sentence their complexities. But even as adults, we often lack the words to express our emotions. That's when we need to cry. To express what we can't say otherwise."

Steven didn't understand fully then. He sure believed he did, but he didn't. Today, in the shower, his eyes dripped from his sadness because he couldn't translate into thoughts what he felt, much less express it or even find someone with whom to express it. So he reflected back to another one of her talks. "Sometimes, with some emotions, crying itself remains the only valid reaction." Maybe the proper mourning to a reunion with your wife after a decade of fearing she died, only to have her die in your arms... is to break down in tears.

He remained too long in the shower, enough to drain his hot water tank, and still stayed a few minutes later, until he was shivering from the cold that was seeping to his bones. He absentmindedly dried himself, and without bothering to dress back up, he walked to his kitchen where Lily's diary now rested. Flipping through it, he noticed things he hadn't noticed the previous day. He now looked at the way Lily entered entries at the beginning of the book.

Steven felt like these were more like task lists than recollections. For example, instead of "Today I found an old governor part at an antique shop in Forestburg," it would say: "Governor part, third shelve on the 2nd bookcase at the back of Earl's Chest, in Forestburg, 234 Main Road, open 10 AM-7 PM."

She had dated the entries, like in a diary, but they weren't in chronological order! Not only earlier lines found themselves after later ones, even the years jumped around. The initial section was mostly that, a list of places where to discover artifacts.

At first, Steven thought that maybe she called in ahead to reserve the pieces, but for other notes, it didn't make much sense, like "Steven at the agriculture fair, 7:34 p.m., near the Ferris wheel. Green dress." Steven had remembered that event. He was at the fair, months after meeting Lily in school, and had bumped into her accidentally. He kind of visualized the green dress she wore. He found her particularly attractive.

Previously, she only played the role of a school colleague, that evening, he saw her as a woman. He felt interest before that date, but that night, it solidified. Anyway, the two connected, and spent the rest of the evening together and it's from that moment that he fully saw her as a potential love interest. Something in the way she seemed to just be in sync with him really made them connect.They had already spoken, back in school, about their families. The steam generator project gave them a lot of time together. Somehow, he managed to remain honest about how horrible they were. Lily prompted him to spill his secrets just like that. Something in her soul just made you want to open up.

It's only later, after their marriage, that she explained her tricks. The first consisted of active listening. That was asking open-ended questions to cultivate the conversation without guiding it, just as you water a plant. You don't tell the plant how to grow, you just give it what it needs to do so. When she explained, he could immediately see it. Often, she would rephrase what he was saying into a question.

"The key to active listening is threefold. Listen for the full meaning, like, what your interlocutor is really saying, but also the non-verbal parts of the message. Then, respond to the feeling of the message, not just the message. Finally, handle the cues because often, a deeper message lurks behind."

At first, he didn't get it, but then, it clicked when he saw it clearly. He doesn't recall today what he had said, but he felt angry, and she said something like "I can feel that you're angry, do you want to tell me what makes you that mad about the situation?" Often, her questions seemed completely out of context, but after a talk, Steven would realize that he was almost telegraphing emotionally what he couldn't express verbally. Shame, anger, sadness. It's not easy for him to identify those emotions.

The second trick consisted of energy. That took him a lot longer to understand. She explained that every conversation, every interaction and every room where such interpersonal interactions occur, possesses a certain energy. Her goal wasn't to adapt to the energy in place, but rather, to shift that energy to a more positive, open and creative one. Perhaps it's why she acted so nicely with Camille, despite how his sister-in-law treated his wife? Perhaps it's why his wife had weird subject matters at the family dinner, to divert from the clashing of egos which only existed to demean others.

After such that supper, Lily told him. "Don't look at yourself through their eyes. They don't mean you well." That remains the most helpful deed anyone had ever done for him. How else could he have figured it out? He grew up with them. They raised him. He had built his entire internal belief system in part by the lessons learned maturing with them. Lily acted as an external observer, able to see things clearly.

Speaking of which, near the middle of the book, he noticed a series of remarks about him, his family, common friends, colleagues of his wife and people he had never even heard of before. He also read notes on Lily herself, such as every time she fell sick, or her periods, which he thought peculiar. Weirded out, Steven put somehow and picked up his phone. He had forgotten to plug it overnight, but he had no emails, missed calls or SMS. "Good," he thought.

Steven returned to his workshop, realizing he couldn't actually eat breakfast that morning, and checked the machine again. It was still there, but the battery level now said 23% or 16% in about 10 hours. That meant that it still requires a lot of time to charge, possibly almost 123 hours or 5 days! His amp clamp which allowed for measuring the current in a wire told him the amperage approached 12 amps, which meant that this machine was stocking up over 1,444 kW at a time! This looks massive!

He saw that the antenna was remaining stable, but didn't bother turning it off again. Instead, he launched a peek at the machine and discovered that the keyboard and monitors proved easy to swap. He owned a replacement keyboard, except that the monitor itself needed to be a CRT, and he no longer had any around…

Chapter 2.4—In Laws

A double idea dawned on him. He had things he wanted to check, and a monitor to pick up, and he knew just where to find both. He grabbed the steam governor piece he had found in the machine and put it in a bag. After making sure he remained presentable, he jumped in his truck and drove toward the suburb. He would visit the Connelly house. Steven had joked about the watt equivalency of families with Lily. It did make her laugh, even if both knew his analogy fell short of the truth and remained purely coincidental.

If you take a 120-volt line and transform it to a 12-volt power supply, it will divide by 10 the amps you draw via the transformer. If you draw 1 amp at 12 volts, you draw 12 watts of power, and on the other side of the transformer, you will have 120 volts with 0.1 amps of current, or still 12 watts of power. You could say that they balance each other out.

Steven's joke was that money and niceness also balanced each other out in clans. His own family rested at the deep end of the cold, grumpy and detestable range of human qualities but didn't understand what to do with their vast fortune. Lily's parents, while being in the lower-middle class, were some of the kindest people Steven had ever met. Lily often claimed that this sounded ridiculous, that she knew plenty of horrible poor jerks, but she still giggled. She always laughed at his jokes.

Somehow, reflecting about her past brought back a new memory of Lily, from the early days of their relationship. She talked of a place in a woman's body where if you stimulate it, it drives her crazy: her heart. It puzzled him, but then, about a year later, after one of his bad gags, he asked Lily if she really found it funny.

"Men always think that we see them as more attractive when they make us laugh. It's why most pickup lines are basically joking, right?" she said.

Steven was trying to remember. It was in her family's basement, before it got crowded with their things when he sold his house. Then, it sat unused by her parents, but that night, like many others, they were cuddling on the old couch from her grandparents' home. He had put two logs in the wood stove, and lit it, so they could relax on that cold evening in front of the fire. Her father wouldn't get a lot of timber, but once Steven came into Lily's life, he could help his father-in-law split them in the backyard.

"It's not that being funny makes you more attractive, it's what if we're attracted, we laugh more at your attempts, our desire makes you hilarious when you try to make us smile."

And that explains why even his most boring jokes made her laugh.

"It's not that only men can be funny, it's that boyfriends, prefer to be funnier than their girlfriend. So, we goof off with our besties, not with our partners."

And yes, he found Lily hilarious on her own most of the year, and in April fools, she constituted a force to be reckoned with! Steven smiles when he recalls Lily explaining how she made a huge discovery and would reveal it after her following Thursday lecture. It occurred in the last week of March 1999, and she would reveal a new material never seen before in a steam governor. A unique piece she just discovered.

She had shown grainy pictures the whole week, and the design intrigued every teacher in the history department.
Seriously, she had presented it inside a glass display not unlike a cake bell. Her colleagues would alternate looking at the weird dark-coloured governor and her explanation that it originally came, oddly enough, from their town!

"But the best part is, after a good day of hard work in the factory, if you're hungry, you can just grab a snack."

Lifting the bell, she snapped a piece of the governor, and the room filled by the scent of chocolate. Most of her colleagues found it funny, and those that didn't were bribed with pieces of her gag. Sadly, for the following 2 years, April 1st fell on weekends, and then, she vanished. Not that her parents or him received any immunity from her April 1st pranks. Steven used to have an excellent relationship with the Connelly until Lily's tragic disappearance. At first, he thought they resented him or thought he somewhat caused it, but after a few years, he realized that they, too, were missing their daughter and that he reminded them of her each time he saw them.

Still, when he had to sell his house, he decided to offer to let them take most of Lily's things since they still had their house, and he thought he offered a nice gesture to them. They received him for supper, but clearly, without Lily, not much connection remained. Since then, he would only see them twice a year, to help his former father-in-law install in his winter car port and in the spring, to remove it.

77

They would barely talk and apart from a single beer offered by Sandra, his former mother-in-law, he wouldn't really socialize with either of them. Having parked in the street in front of their house, it's with a heavy heart that he rang the doorbell of his now officially dead wife's childhood home. Sandra opened with a surprise, and as always, remained perceptive enough, quickly asked him. "Oh my, Steven, you look as if you saw a ghost. Is everything fine?"

"Yes, Mrs. Connelly, it's just that... well...". Steven took out the steam governor piece from the bag. "I found this in one of my old boxes..."

"Oh my," she replied. "That's one of Lily's pieces..."

"Yes, perhaps something she was working on, you know... well. You have her notes. I was wondering if I could review and see if it should be sent to a museum."

"Of course, Steven. Her things are in the basement. Take your time... George ran out right now, but I'm sure he would be delighted to assist you, as he's the one who stored everything."

Steven thanked her and proceeded to the basement. He had fond memories of evenings spent with Lily watching TV or just talking away from her parents. They first French kissed on the coach, which, 25 years later, had barely moved an inch. The carpet in the middle of the room had changed, and the TV used to serve as their old living room television, which made Steven wonder if they finally bought an LCD model.

Steven found the room where George stored the boxes. He had helped put them there, but they were in a different order and most of the boxes got replaced by plastic bins. Two of Lily's old monitors were in the corner, one of which seemed the perfect size, so he quickly put it by the door to avoid forgetting it. Steven then grabbed a chair and began opening bins. A lot of them just contained clothing or personal effects, many of which brought great memories, including the actual green dress which now rested flat in his arms.

He wondered if he shouldn't bury her in it, but then thought that he should just change the minimum her cadaver. He respected her too much to actually undress her and dress her back up now that she lost her life. No need to turn the knife in the wound. Near the bottom of one of the piles, he found Lily's notebooks and binders. He could understand why it was at the bottom: George didn't think this through when he filled her books into a single container, it must have weighed a ton! Sifting through them, he quickly found what he was looking for: Lily's guide to identifying Steam governor parts. It featured pictures, drawings (some of which had she drew on her own) and descriptions to help identify steam governor parts.

That notebook would find itself absolutely priceless for anyone interested in steam governor history because of its uniqueness. In part because no one spent the time mapping the progression of steam governors over the years. This is in part because, well, no one really cared to do so. Steven had to admit to himself: Steam governors weren't that interesting. Lily kept saying they were what allowed the Industrial Revolution, but in reality, it's their invention and not their evolution which drove the revolution.

Flipping through the pages, he managed to identify the model and generation using the same process he had used numerous times to help her during her thesis redaction. This model seemed rather irrelevant, according to her notes, but it remained one she never recorded as collected. He didn't remember her ever finding a duplicate of a piece. His wife was one lucky gal. Speaking of it, he saw a familiar book near the bottom of the bin. He pulled it out to look at it again. When she had received her doctorate, he had hired a company to professional print in a hard cover her thesis as a gift. Now, with sites like Lulu offering such print on-demand services, it became easy, but he paid a fortune for this singular copy about two decades earlier. After flipping through the pages, Steven peeked at the stack to put the report back in and froze in terror.

He found another book under the thesis. One seen multiple times, but never read until the previous day. There, at the bottom of the bin, sat Lily's diary. The very same currently resting on his kitchen table right now. He took it out and skimmed through it. In appearance, it seemed identical, the same diary. He stashed it in his bag, closed the containers in the order he had opened them, and grabbed the monitor.

He ran upstairs, and just yelled to Sandra, "I have to go, the piece proved worthless. I borrowed one of her old monitors for a project. Sorry, I have an emergency at work…" Sandra replied something from the kitchen, but Steven left. He furiously drove back to his workshop.

Chapter 2.5—Idea

Sitting at his kitchen table, Steven had both notebooks side by side. Each with the same coffee stain on the cover caused from his carelessness when coming in for a hug. She didn't complain or scold him. He knew that it remained her most precious physical possession, but she only reminded him that he stayed more important than a simple book. And now, and he had two identical copies. How could this occur?

Flipping through pages one by one, he could see their similarity, down to the pen strokes and small tears and ink droplets on the paper. The diary from the machine did have a few more notes in it and seemed slightly more damaged, but other than that, perfect duplicates, line by line. Many sections of the book, about Lily's life, appeared identical, to the point where some things didn't make sense. Lily disappeared in 2002, but he located diary entries on her life well past her departure in both editions.

For example, she indicated that in 2004 that she had a cold from February 22nd until the 26th. When he initially read it, it strokes him as a note on what she was doing while away from him. Yet, the copy from her parents' house, sat in the basement between her disappearance and the moment he moved Lily's things to where he had found it. In absolutely no way Lily could have written her sickness in the diary.

An idea started to germinate in Steven's head, so he flipped to the parts with the coordinates. With each of the paid consisting of two strings of numbers which he began to understand. They formed a duo of dates, one of which in either the 1990s or the early 2000s, and another one in the 1800s or even 1700s. Then, the writing continued on a single pair of longitudes and latitudes. For example, 02/23/2001—07/23/1823 29.966667,-90.080556—Steam boat dismantled.

The first date occurred on a Friday, while the second fell a Thursday, and the location is in New Orleans. Steven guessed that it was when and where a steam boat that was dismantled, but it's not a coordinate by the river. Which led him to his breakthrough. Slowly, his idea became more in focus, so he put the notebooks aside, and returned to his workshop. The battery in the machine showed 29%. He proceeded to remove the broken monitor carefully and gently began replacing it with the one he had borrowed from the Connoly. Well, technically it remained his own property, so he didn't feel guilty, but still.

The Bulky CRT screens were starting to get really scarce and if it wasn't for the fact that it constituted a small model, he would have properly switched it to a newer and easier to lift LCD one. Steven saw that both monitors were of the same model. He thought they were alike, but under scrutiny they proved to look identical, and to possess similar serial numbers.

Once he removed the old one, he considered it would allow to sneak a peek inside the machine without disassembling a panel. Sadly, the screen was in a sort of housing, with both a power outlet, and VGA port. Once plugged in, the new display stayed blank. Under the space for the monitor he located two USB connectors, one for the keyboard and the other for the mouse. In the shuffle, the pointing device fell from the little counter and began hanging in midair and, as such, didn't get any blood on it.

Despite a few attempts, neither input peripherals seemed to wake up whichever computer was installed within the machine, so Steven had to pay attention to the various buttons on the dashboard. With a faint mechanical click, the meter turned to 30%. Most people looking at the output for the battery level or the other numbers would wonder why anyone would care for such mechanical numbers. It's the same type of old flight displays that were in airports in Steven's youth. It's obsolete. But not for Lily. She didn't fancy the term "old," she would prefer "classic" or "retro," or "antique."

"Stevie, ancient tools once began as cutting edge. We need to respect what our elders built because they're the stepping stone for what's next."

In fact, Lily still had an old alarm clock made from such flip cards. They produced no sound, unlike these, but when she changed the clock twice per year for daylight saving time, the fast speed of switching did make a faint clicking noise she enjoyed. Even better, you couldn't go back in time with it, so leaving DST meant moving forward 23 hours, since the 24-hour cards revealed the little AM and PM label next to the number. Newer ones could go backward too, but Lily stuck with her old one. If Lily had designed this machine, as he suspected, it made perfect sense that she would use those displays. Even the battery display, of course. Two digits, and he guessed that like her alarm clock, the left most ones could also display a 10, to make 100%. That showed one of the nice things about these displays: they weren't restrictive on what you could put on them.

He observed the four other groups of flip cards, each with a rotation dial under it. On the left, in the first row, he located a single number. Next to it sat a date, with, from the left to the right, the year in four individual digits, the month spelled out, and the day, with a single flip card. The following five allowed setting or the 24 hours, tens of minutes, minutes and even tens of seconds and seconds. On the next row, the following two groups clearly showed longitudes and latitudes.

They each had plenty of flip cards! The first went from -9 to +9 and allowed setting the tens of units. The next was simply from 0 to 9, for a total of nine flip cards each! Searching in his phone, this meant 7 decimals and would provide the precision of 11 mm, almost nothing! A rotary dial had been installed under each of the four groups, and a few random coloured buttons sat next to them.

The first rotating control he touched allowed to modify the date, still set to the day of Lily's disappearance. The time hadn't altered by even one second, but he could change its value with the dials, composed of three concentric segments. It resembled those found on oscilloscopes he used! It looked like a single knob, but it had three different parts on a concentric axis. The outermost piece was wider and shorter. The middle one rotated inside it, sticking out, and from that control, the innermost poked out.

On an oscilloscope, it made a lot of sense, as it enabled fine-tuning adjustments. Usually with only two levels. The outlying dial might allow raising or lowering the y-axis by one volt in the same motion that the inside part would only alter by a tenth of a volt. He tried manipulating only the topmost dial under the centre display, and it would shift the hours (represented in a 24-hour clock), minutes and seconds with some precision. Going over midnight, increases the date. Turning only the middle dial would change the days and the months much faster, while not moving the hours and minutes. Finally, altering the outermost dial adjusted the year without touching the date or time.

It constituted a rather ingenious method to edit the date in a mechanical form, and he wondered who made this. He also considered why the computer couldn't link to this, but seeing it no longer functioned, and the rest still did, maybe it's better this way! He also realized that if this possessed the same ports as a normal computer, it might not have a simple way to interface with an external system. Even today, you need USB boards, and it's easier with an Arduino microcontroller which you can connect via USB.

The same system worked for the longitude and latitude set of coordinates, but the final one, at the top left, was for the solitary flip card which was only for a single number. He returned them to their last values. The problem is that none of them possessed a label. Next to the display he observed a few buttons, but they presented themselves untagged. He imagined their colour and placements meant something, but at this point, it was too early to understand their individual functions. He also noticed a USB connector he hadn't spotted the previous day.

He did realize that two buttons resided under the dashboard, and pressing the first one produced a small beep followed by the booting prompt on the monitor. Finally! Progress! He could guess that these served as the power and reset buttons of the embedded desktop. Looking around, he couldn't see other USB plugs or audio interfaces. The operating system revealed itself as Windows 7, which kind of surprised him. He expected with such a monitor to discover a computer running Windows 98, or perhaps even DOS. He also realized that this created further confusion in his mind: Windows 7 came out in 2009, or seven years after Lily's disappearance.

He could see colour photographs of functional steam engines, often in their original factory environment. He loaded from the drive videos of interviews with people dressed in old clothes, including one of a middle—age Scottish man captioned as James Watt about his new invention, the Steam governor. Steven now had the proof of what's this machine was. It allowed time travel, and Lily, his wife, worked as a time-travelling historian.

Steven had a hard moment concentrating following his realization. Lily, a fan of Doctor Who, possessed in effect her own Tardis Would that explain why she vanished without a trace? Did she simply travel to another era and instead of resurfacing in 2002, she popped out 15 years later? When you time travel, does it feel like regular expeditions in that you wait while you navigate the years just as hours pile up while to drive through towns and states?

Was she shot in the future and forced to abort her way back to 2002 because she was dying? Did she make a sort of emergency stop on the side of the road instead of returning to the point she had left? That was now making more and more sense... Steven searched through the snacks and could now comprehend that she seemingly didn't store expired or long duration ones. She simply had treats from various eras she had visited! He acknowledged he still hadn't eaten since he had woken up and grabbed a granola bar best before 2024 and a chocolate tablet due in 2003, blindly trusting them to be within their edible phase.

He sat at his desk in the workshop, and while thinking that the peanuts in his bar had probably not been planted yet. Puzzled, he realized that he didn't even know the original source of peanuts. Returning to the task at hand, he looked at this spectrum analyzer which displayed the same stable patterns.

"Quantum antenna...", he said to himself. She most likely had him create some of the components of her machine, after all, the sealed boxes in the front compartment reminded him strongly of her plans for what he just built.

Thinking about how time travel and quantum mechanics intersected, he raised his arm to turn off the antenna. Just as he initiated the action to flick the switch he spotted movement on his spectrum analyzer, but not fast enough to stop his operation.

Chapter 2.6—Intruder

As soon as the switch was closed, the air filled with an ozone smell, which made Steven jump up from his seat and searched around the workshop floor. A new photo booth sized box appeared nearby! Black in colour, it seemed industrially made: its corners were rounded, and a number "D-325" was painted on the sides in a cool silver metallic font. Steven kept absolutely no illusions. His workshop now housed two time machines, and he couldn't know the occupant or what constituted their business. He grabbed his sledgehammer that was resting next to the wall behind him.

The door gently opened and a man in his mid-sixties emerged. With a short stature, he possessed a faint Asian look and mostly grey hair with a seriously receding hairline. Confused, he sought around himself. "Where am I?" he asked. Steven slowly moved toward him, trying not to interrupt him. The stranger gazed at the antenna. "Is that another beacon? Oh shit, when did a beacon arrive so early?" Surveying around him, he suddenly saw Steven.

"Who are you?" He asked, just before raising a gun of some sort.

Steven leaped forward and hit the foreigner's arm as fast as he could, knocking the weapon on the floor on the far side end of the workshop. The visitor left a yell out as he held his hand.

"When and where did you come from?" Steven asked.

"Hey, I wasn't cheating! I swear… no lottery tickets, investments or pillaging. I swear… I followed the rules. I didn't even visit myself!" the man pleaded.

"I asked you a question…", Steven insisted, raising his sledgehammer.

"Hong Kong, 2029. I have a permit! Don't report me… I knew I wasn't supposed to go more than five years in the past, but I wanted to lay my eyes on my daughter one last time. She died as a child, you see?"

"You're in the United States, in 2014....", Steven replied, thinking hard about the implication.

"What... that's a quantum beacon? May God have mercy on our souls." The father grabbed something from his back pocket, and Steven realized he picked up a metal stick, the kind police officers carry to control crowds.

The man quickly lunged forward at Steven and attempted to knock him down, but remained too slow and Steven dodged the strike. Turned around, Steven pivoted and pushed the stranger on the floor, making him lose his balance and plummet near the antenna.The visitor raised his stick one last time to try to destroy the antenna. So Steven, who stood just a bit too far away, threw his sledgehammer at the guy and missed his arm, instead hitting him directly at the back of his head.

Steven heard a crack, and his opponent collapsed, not very far away from where Lily had died just a short day before Approaching the father, he almost vomits after inspecting the gaping hole he created when he threw his weapon. Feeling his pulse, he realized that he accidentally killed the stranger.

Great, he thought... he now had two bodies to eliminate!

He didn't know what a beacon was, but from context, he understood what his antenna did. It disrupted the time travel machine while they were trying to travel through time, therefore stopping them at the moment it first encountered it. If it approached from the future, it would appear when he powers it off. If it came from the past, it would arrive when he turns it on.

For an odd reason, only one machine seemed to be caught at once, but he needed additional information to understand why. But he also realized that he now had two time machines to study. And more importantly. He created a plan. He would prevent Lily from even getting shot. Not only that, but he now knew she landed from the future, and he had the way to travel there.

Chapter 2.7—Information

The first thing on Steven's mind was to find a way to get rid of the body of the time traveller, but he still hadn't figured out what to do with Lily's remains. Unlike Lily, however, Steven possessed two major advantages with this one. First, he didn't know him. Plus, he left no traces tying back to him anywhere on his cadaver. The second one made Steven smile even more. The man came from the future, so if the police discovered his corpse, the only possibility would be that they link him to his present identity, something that didn't worry Steven at all.

Unlike his wife's body, Steven thought of an idea. He drove to a dump site he knew for having passed in front regularly and grabbed one of the old barrels, making sure to use gloves to prevent leaving any prints. Thanks to his closed truck, Steven managed to carry the barrel discreetly back to his workshop, but would wait until the cover of night to unload it. Back at his desk, Steven understood he caught not one, but two different time travellers in his antenna or rather quantum beacon, as he was trying to remind himself. He also recognized that Lily had appeared with an almost depleted energy reserves her machine and that it would take days to refill completely. Steven also grasped that to save Lily, he had to jump to another period and would thus potentially arrive in a place without electricity to charge and return. Finally, he understood that unlike a crashed truck, an out-of-service time machine isn't something you can walk home from when it breaks or runs out of power.

He needed additional information, and a lot more of it. He entered the new time travel machine, and peeked inside. This one appeared more modern: this dashboard was mass-produced and instead of dials and a CRT monitor, it had a touchscreen interface with an unknown operating system. The battery gauge on this time machine lower to 82 percent, so he ran outside and searched for the plug, but couldn't find it. Odd… he did discover that the front panel could open, and in it, he identified a very different look than in Lily's version. It still had the similar boxes with apparently the same sort of connector, but instead of just scattering randomly in the area, racks allowed to store them and to hold by metal straps. The wires were also well organized.

At the bottom of the compartment, he could see the batteries which looked identical to those in the other machine. He wondered if in the future, these batteries didn't simply become as widespread as those installed in vehicles of the last decades. In fact, he considered if these weren't mass-produced electric car ones. Following the cables, he understood now that the unfamiliar plug most likely came from an electrical car socket of some sort, possibly converted for this usage.

Steven's first reaction was to find this ridiculous: Lily's box allowed charging in pretty much any socket up to maybe 80 years ago, while this one required a dedicated specialized plug which didn't even exist in 2014 yet. Thinking, he realized that the man had actually defended himself that he knew he wasn't supposed to go back so far, so perhaps the connector became ubiquitous in his era. But does this mean that his wife had a prototype? Did she invent it or steal it? He had far too many questions to ask and no one to answer them.

Returning to the cockpit, he began exploring the user interface. He quickly discovered that the system was locked out and that the computer offered mainly preset destinations. This made Steven realize that this poor guy might not even own his ride, but probably instead rented it just as people hailed taxis to travel in a city or perhaps a bus shuttle from the airport.The controls possessed some sort of software restriction. It prevented the use of other locations and times. This grieving father found a hack to try and see his daughter, but Steven imagined no idea how the man did so. He also figured that if the system only offered few presets where, most likely, guards or "customs" agents checked the identity of passengers when arriving at the destination.

In that regard, it meant that this box, which he couldn't even charge securely, remained inoperable to him. It did provide one advantage over Lily's: small wheels were under the device, so he managed to push it against the back wall and cover it with a tarp.

Using his gloves and putting on a hat to prevent losing any hair on the body, he searched the poor guy's pocket to find a wallet. It contained a conventional driver's licence from Hong Kong (expiring in 2030) on the name of "Victor Kingsey". Next to it rested a temporary time machine operator permit granting him the rights to utilize the unit numbered D-329. The card was issued in a cheaper plastic, perhaps printed upon rental. In his pocket were Hong Kong dollars from the past, which he had probably picked up to use on location. He also spotted a connectable device, which he presumed served like a USB stick of some sort he installed for the hack.

Victor was wearing clothes which Steven found contemporary. Most likely because he knew he was going to see his daughter, so he decided not to undress him after checking each part, every inch, for any hint as to his identify or era. Outside, the sun had set, so he parked his truck closer to the loading ramp and carried the barrel inside. Carefully, Steven put Victor in the barrel, pushing to make sure he would fit, and closed the lid that best that he could. The seal wasn't perfect. In reality, nobody discards an intact barrel, but they held together well enough.

With the help of his trolley, he brought the barrel into his truck and after locking his place, he drove to the next town over and on the other end of it, found a secluded trail by the forest. Steven parked on the asphalt after making sure to slow down and not leave any tire marks, and rolled the barrel a few hundred feet into the trees. Using a fallen branch, he erased both his footprints and the barrel traces in the ground as he walked backward toward his car.

Once he gained enough confidence after failing to spot signs of his actions, he threw the branch into the forest, still wearing gloves, on the other side of the road. He promptly returned home after making a huge detour to avoid going back the same way. Steven couldn't imagine if this constituted a perfect crime or if the police will eventually catch him. Since he was planning to visit the future soon anyway, he would know in advance of any mistake he might have made and thus, might be able to return to the present to fix them.

He drove home while filled with doubts and regrets. He realized that had he not built his antenna, Lily would have arrived at the time she left and would have either been able to call 911 to get an ambulance. He would at least have avoided becoming the number one suspect of a murder, again. Speaking of murder, had he not turned back on his antenna, Victor would have come back from seeing his daughter and would have mostly likely returned home safely.

What he had wanted to do with his project was to see if Lily toiled on the right track with her quantum antenna. Now, he began the conviction that more and more, her project constituted a component of her time machine.

Chapter 2.8—Intermission

Once he was uneventfully back at home, he grabbed one of Lily's diary and looked at the included plans for various parts of the time machines. He also saw directives on how to build them, where to find them and what to do with them. He notably saw that in the diary, it mentions various purchases of car batteries on sale. Perhaps in the first version of the machine, those supplied the source of the power, and they were only replaced once she could buy more advanced parts in the future.

Steven also noticed something else he had missed: at the middle of the outside edge of almost every page stood a single letter or number. When he assembled them on a notepad, he realized he had found an address, along with two pairs of numbers: 245, and 165,628. Searching on his phone, he discovered it actually pointed to a self-storage space! His cellphone told him it wasn't 24 hours a day, but he promised himself he would look at it the next day.

Once again, Steven mopped the floor before going to bed, but this time, he elected to sleep in his actual bed. It's only while trying to fall asleep that he realized that he had only eaten a granola bar and a chocolate bar that day. It was too late to get out of bed, and he became afraid he would be too tempted to look into his freezer.

The night introduced a sort of restlessness, with Steven's dreams filled with visions of his wife, complaining about the heating and how freezing she felt, mixed with visions of a dying young Asian girl asking to see her father. Everything ended mixed up, with vivid images of police officers raiding his workshop in the middle of the night for both murders. He actually woke up sweating on those thoughts twice, but each time he remained alone in his apartment, and everything left no sound.

It's in his stomach, which eventually got him out of bed the next morning.

Part 3

Chapter 3.1—Visiting himself

After a good breakfast, Steven resisted strongly at his urge to go see Lily in the freezer. He now had a clear picture of his beautiful wife in his mind, even if the fact she died in his arms almost ruined it. He didn't want to add a vivid image of her frozen body next to it in his mind. He knew he would have to take her out of there someday, but not today, Steven read more in the diary and noticed that the last date in the diary of purchases was in 2019 on July 7th, so he set his mind to travel then.

He stashed one of the diaries in one of his bookcases, behind his reference manuals for his job. He carried the other one in Lily's time machine, which was now showing a charge of 42%. He really hoped it could last, but at least, he would be travelling to only a few months into the future, therefore reducing the risks of being stuck. He tucked Victor's gun in his belt and packed some food in a bag to add to Lily's stash. With a sigh, he sat at the console, closing the door behind him. He felt a knot in his stomach as he turned with the dial to the proper date, but didn't touch any of the other controls. He pressed the various buttons on the control until he heard a beep, and the battery indicator dropped to 31%.

Was he really in the future? He peeked outside the door, and found himself in the basement of his former home, in the storage room they never used. He definitely had moved places, but that meant he was now in someone else's house since after all, he sold it! He grabbed the extension cord and plugged it in the socket in the small room. It wouldn't do much, but even if he rose by two or three percent it might remain enough for now. As soon as he exited the room silently, he saw that the cellar looked much different than he remembered: new furniture surrounded him, new boxes and some posters on the wall he had never seen. Nothing from his former life was still in place.

Back when he lived in this house with Lily, they barely used the basement and from the surrounding look, the new owners did the same.He listened but couldn't hear anything at all. He tiptoed upstairs and saw that no one appeared to be home. The picture had the people to whom he sold his house, so he guessed they liked it and kept it. Searching around, he found a keychain and after making sure the street lacked witnesses, he opened the door to test the lock: he now once again had a key to the house he had shared with his wife.

Checking the street, he saw it deserted, so he carelessly walked toward the nearest bus stop. He had travelled through time and now had to walk to the proper destination! Grabbing his phone while waiting for the bus to get the schedule, he realized he didn't have any connection: perhaps he changed carrier in the present. Perhaps his Sim card no longer worked. That's something he hadn't anticipated. After a good twenty minutes, the bus finally came, but the fare rose even higher than he remembered. "Ah… sweet inflation," he thought.

He managed to get close enough to his workshop to walk there instead of taking a second bus. His now rusting truck was parked in the usual place and his key worked both on the truck and on the door itself. The workshop looked identical to the way it had been in the past, but without the antenna and without the second time machine. In fact, it looked as if the events of the past few days hadn't occurred at all. He called for his future self, but didn't get any reply.

After running upstairs, he searched and couldn't find either the diary or Lily's body in the freezer. In fact, in one of the boxes, he found the circuit boards for the unfinished quantum antenna and couldn't understand why. A noise came from downstairs, and when he looked up, he could see himself closing the door behind him. Steven waited until his future self climbed into the apartment before announcing himself.

"Steven, I don't want to cause you any harm… I just want to talk…", he said, from the storage room with the freezer.

"Who is there?" older Steven replied, with a scared tone in his voice.

"Listen, I'm coming out, please don't hurt me…", said the younger version, as he entered his kitchen.

"You are... me?" Asked the Older Steven, with a trembling voice.

"Yeah, listen, long story short. I came from 2014. I jump here to find Lily, but things seem very different from the year I left with Lily's time machine."

"Jump from... What?" he replied, confused...

"Yeah, our wife, Lily, is a time traveller. She skipped from 2002 to now, except on the trip back, the Quantum antenna I had completed stopped her from returning, and she ended up stuck in 2014 after getting shot."

"Let me properly understand. The reason Lily disappeared is that she died while playing Doctor Who?"

"Exactly. Now, I have to find her in this period to prevent her murder, so we can live with her. I just need to borrow my truck, well, yours..."

"And if you save her?"

"My guess is that we will both settle up in 2014, happily married, but with her 12 years younger than we are."

"So, we could start over... maybe even have kids!"

"Yeah, but sadly, I suppose that by returning to the past, I will erase you or something...", he said with some empathy for the visiting Steven.

"Hey, I'm you, and it's not like the last few years have been great. More of our clients are closed. I'm basically starving... So yeah, take the truck, save Lily!"

"Please, don't spoil me anything... Listen, once complete the errant, you'll find your truck near our former house, possibly only tomorrow."

"Sure... Good luck!" said the older Steven, with some sadness in his tone. He stood up and went to shake his younger self's hand.

"Maybe we shouldn't touch... in some movies, it caused an explosion or something..."

"Prudent call..."

The younger Steven left, not without some regret. This showed him his future if he didn't build the antenna.

Chapter 3.2—Victoria's treasures

He left his workshop and drove his slightly older truck, and as such more damaged, and rode almost 45 minutes to the antique shop "Victoria's treasures" mentioned in the diary. The door opened, but the only person in the store presented himself as the owner, named Bob. Rather nice, he didn't hesitate to strike up a conversation with Steven. Of course, Steven spotted the obvious sales technique to humanize him and make his assertions about his merchandise more valuable. And yet... despite knowing the conversation sounded as genuine as when a politician seeks your vote on the street, he found himself captivated.

After over a decade of being a social pariah, talking with someone treating him as a respectable human provided a nice change of pace.

"A steam governor? It's not every day someone wants such an antique. I mostly get asked about plates, commemorative spoons and old furniture. Anything but obsolete old machinery and coins"

"You don't get asked for coins?" Steven asked, surprised.

"I leave them to the specialty shops. Oh, and stamps. I don't deal with that either," explained Bob.

What Steven learned was that Victoria's name came from Bob's late mother. After retiring, she decided to open this antiquity store to help pass the time and distribute the old things her hoarding parents had left her in storage. Bob had taken over, buying old pieces from estate sales or from people retiring. He used to work as a carpet installer, and when his mother died, carpet installations had become less popular. Steven wondered if the pity act offered a way to sell more, or a way to heal, but then again, neither of his parents had worked a day in their lives, so perhaps this is how normal people feel.

Bob's mother began something, his business failed, he decided to continue her... her what, exactly. Her legacy? The only legacy his family would gift him consisted of traumas and issues. Everything else would go to his brother.

While talking, they walked down the aisles, with Bob pointing out interesting pieces. It was like an advertisement interrupting their conversation, but Steven kept the nagging suspicion that Bob's plan was simply to keep him engaged long enough to complete a sale. Or was it him again seeing the world with the filter left by his parents? The steam governor piece he had found in the time machine was still there, on the shelf, exactly where Lily's diary said it would be. This means she hadn't come yet.

He kept speaking with Bob, but the time of Lily's visit was fast approaching, so Steven decided to wait outside. After thanking the man, he returned to his truck and parked so that he would clearly see the entrance. Now, he had gotten this truck used after he had sold his house, so Lily remained devoid of hints he would be waiting. And he did wait, for hours, sometimes grabbing a snack from his bag, either from his workshop or some exotic candy bars from the past or the future. He didn't bother to check, eating without taking his eyes off the shop's entrance.

The shop was deserted.Twice he went to buy something to drink and relieve his bladder at the nearby convenience store, but each time, he checked, and the steam governor was still in place. He didn't miss Lily.

"If you really want the piece, I could give you a discount... I'm not going to sell it to anyone else anytime soon"' offered Bob. Steven just replied that he wasn't certain he wanted it.

So time flew by, and he decided to spend the last 15 minutes of the store hours in the store, talking to Bob further about his sales, his items, etc. He mainly wanted to know if he kept a record of his previous sales, including the date, and got confirmation he did He did notice that Bob offered the key duplication service, so he copied his former house key to keep it safe and secure... Steven wondered if it that consisted of the only sale made that day. Bob didn't seem to have received any other clients.

Soon enough, after Bob left, Steven was driving back toward the house he had shared with his wife. He could return the next day, and the day after, but it didn't feel right. She had picked up the governor today, so something went wrong with his plan that he just couldn't understand. He had a time machine, he could skip the need to wait in line for events to occur, and yet, Lily didn't show up. When he drove in front of his former house, he saw the new owners were home. Damn it, he thought.

He parked further down the street and waited again until 7:32 PM, when they both left in their car and left the house in the dark. Leaving the truck parked on a nearby street, he calmly walked to the house, unlocked the front door and left the keys back where he had picked them.

He found the time machine in the basement and checked the battery. It had gained a full 3% and was now at 34%. He sat in the cockpit and wondered what to do. Filled with hesitation, he set the destination to five years into the future, still early in the morning. He would repeat the same process: go pick up his truck, visit the antique place, and if the steam governor had been sold, he would ask the date to know when to return. He would need to find a way to sleep at some point…

Now seeing how lightly they furnished the basement, odds showed that he could sleep in the time machine and charge overnight even more. If discovered, however, the couple might remain on the lookout in the future, still he suspected that this room would stay his charging spot for a little while. Steven decided to risk it: not only did he need to charge from time to time, but he couldn't just travel to early in the morning, and return in the evening without resting for hours in a row…

He searched the basement and placed an old mop he found at the top of the staircase, lying on the door. If the owners opened it, the mop would fall and create some noise. Taking into account how silent Lily's machine had run so far, it might remain enough to let him escape. He also decided to improvise a way to jam the storage room from the inside, by wedging small pieces of wood into the frame. He tried to open the door but couldn't and considered it solved.

One of the things that Steven discovered that evening is that the USB socket in the dashboard is powered. That offered a nice surprise. Of course, it would be, but that means that by plugging a USB cable, he could connect his cell to top its batterie. And yet, Android asked between the file transfer and the recharge option. Hesitant, he selected the first option, and he mounted his phone to the computer in the cockpit.

Nice. Was this what she was doing to move her videos, or did she use a more common USB stick? When she left, cellphones remained primitive, but who knows if she bought a future model at some point in the future. The only reason Steven kept him, is that the technology after 2015 barely changed from year to year. He played a few more minutes with the computer. However, he got nothing done. He read some notes but found only a few more. It's almost a blank disk, apart from the videos.

Instead, he turned his attention to the diary. The forbidden book he hadn't been allowed to peek into, but of which he now had two copies.Under the light of the monitor, he managed to read a few more notes, notably the quotes that he has heard her speak to him.

He had noticed a few, but others filled the diary, including some he never heard Lily tell him.

"Leadership without vision is like authority without power."

And on the next page:

"Leadership without vision is like a boat without a rudder."

"Therefore, authority without power is like a boat without a rudder," with a smiley.

That's her kind of joke. He searched for one of her favourite ones in there, but couldn't see it. It looked like a series of algebraic substitution with "time is money," and another such saying, solving it so that it's making a funny new idiom. One that he didn't see previously, struck him.

"Sometimes, the black sheep is just the only sane person in an otherwise insane family."

But one of the pages struck him particularly. It listed a conversation Lily and him had early on.

"Do you know how therapy works, Steven?" she asked.

He can still picture her. He can still smell her. They were cuddling, in bed. In her childhood bed. Her parents left for the night, not that they disapproved of him sleeping over with Lily, especially since they both reached adulthood. She had her head on his shoulder, with her arms wrapped around him.

"You talk, and they help you get over your trauma?" said Steven.

"You aren't that far! You do talk, and they do help you get over the trauma. Do you know how?"

"No clue"

"Psychologists found multiple approaches but the best way to explain it's to help you isolate the trauma, see its effect, and find your way back to who you were before the trauma."

"That's nice"

"It wouldn't work on you. Do you know why?" she said. He could swear then as well as he could do so now that she tightened her grip on him. As if she felt sadness for him.

"Because I'm pig-headed?"

She laughed. "Stevie, you aren't pig-headed. You're dedicated. It's not the same."

"What's the difference?"

"A pig-headed person doesn't want to listen to the ideas of others, even if it would be good for them. A dedicated person still hears the ideas of others, but will act on their own self-interest, or for the interest of all."

"So why wouldn't it work?"

"That's simple! You can't go back to a pre-trauma Steven. He doesn't exist. No point in your life resides before your issues, since they reach back to your early childhood."

"So, I'm without hope?"

"Of course not, but it means that you need another way to find a trauma-free Steven."

"How?"

"Well, perhaps by having a Lily-filled Steven?" she said, laughing.

Which he did find funny, but today, seeing the bullet points of that conversion, with hints on how to have it, how to stroke his chest gently, how to reply to his pig-headed comment, it made him confused. He knew she somehow left notes about her future to her past self, but this felt spooky. It formed a crucial moment of their relationship, and she just followed a script. Written by her, but still…

Steven closed the book, and his eyes. This proved too much, and tears were forming in his eyes. He didn't go to sleep immediately and, instead, listened in until the couple returned. He could hear them talk very faintly, until they eventually appeared to have gone to sleep, so with a lot of relief, he turned and tossed until he found a good position to sleep on the chair.

Chapter 3.3—Vandals

The next morning remained uneventful. Steven waited for them to leave for work, noted the time, and used his former bathroom. Going by the kitchen, he stole some of their cereals and a little orange juice. Noting they would notice missing. He put the mop back in its place and didn't jam the door back. He unplugged the machine, now charged at 42%.

Setting the dial to five years into the future, he pushed the button and heard the same faint "ding" of a time travel. He noticed a drain down to 18%, which told Steven that the longer the jump, the higher the energy usage.Hesitantly, he found the house unoccupied and even if he saw new pictures of the same couple and new furniture upstairs, the basement had barely changed! The calendar on the wall confirmed he was now in July 2024. Amazing he thought.

His copied key still worked, so he left the house to explore the future. The bus station didn't move the place, but it listed a different bus route number and the cost of the trip doubled. By chance, it remained within his means, and they kept accepted old money: who doesn't have 10-year-old bills in his pockets?

He had to transfer to another bus to get to his workshop. Fortunately, tickets still paid the whole route, even if the trip required multiple buses just like in the past, and he ended avoiding a long walk on a rather hot July day. On location, however, everything had changed! The industrial sector had been razed to the ground and in its place stood city row houses, you know, the type where each house is connected to both its neighbours so that they created a sort of wall together.

Steven never understood the appeal but seeing the narrow land lots and the ridiculously small houses, he could guess it got reduced to a matter of cost. He spotted a convenience store around the corner, and he decided to approach it. Inside, a bored teenage boy was behind a bulletproof window. Steven used the microphone system fixed via a hole in the window to talk to him.

"Last time I was here, stood an industrial sector here… when did they build this?" Steven asked.

"I dunno, dude… I guess, maybe last year. I mean, they abandoned most of the buildings after the fire, so they tore the rest down and built these houses."

"Do you know when?" Steven asked.

"Shit if I know… check the Internet. It was in the news, you know…"

Steven thanked him and wondered if he could find any places where to access the Internet. He wondered if he should go back to his former house. Instead, he took another bus downtown, hoping the public library still offered computers and at worse, it would have hard copies of the paper. Waiting for the bus, he thought of an idea… He returned to the convenience store and found a prepaid Sim card he could activate with cash only. Bus fares might have risen, just like the cost of most of what was in the store, but prepaid Sims and data plans were priced now much cheaper than seven years ago.

Steven activated the Sim card (making sure not to lose his current card) in the air-conditioned store and, soon enough, was surfing the Internet for news about the fire and the destruction. The first news he got was from a chemical company on the other site of the DryTek office. He had never managed to get a contract from them, despite trying for years. So, they burned during the night, apparently the result of foul play. Was this the action of a competitor? A ploy to get insurance money? Vandals?

He kept searching for related news. DryTek also burned down, but it seems they had a good insurance policy and instead moved to the other side of town in a new industrial sector. He found no news of GTW anywhere, and their website was down. It didn't appear to have burned down, so perhaps the company simply closed. Maybe they each went their own way. It was already experiencing financial problems in 2014, so 8 years later they may have folded.

He found a note that officials determined the ground and the nearby building have excess levels of contamination and the whole sector (built in the 1940) was demolished for the decontamination. The investment company owning the rented buildings decided to deposit an offer to the few standalone owners and build the residential sector to recuperate their money.

The date of the expulsion was in the papers, October 3, 2022, seemed like a good bet. He created a mental note to check on October 2, 2022, to see his workshop one last time and judge on the progress of his future self.

Chapter 3.4—Visitor in his house

Taking the bus, he decided to go to his parents' house to try and find who would be residing there now.The ride ended up complicated, and it quickly reminded him that as a teenager, he found himself unable to commute by mass transit: the house was in a neighbourhood rich enough to never need buses. Instead, he had to stop nearby and walk the rest of the way, with the day running out on him. Looking at the houses, he notices that a lot of them had very different lawn decorations and that the cars, dating from the past few years most likely, looked odd and foreign to him. He did see plenty of cars with the Tesla logo, and the majority of them had an extension cord to the house. He saw cars with weird named like BYD or Polestar, whoever they are.

The few people he saw remained unknown to him, and he wondered if seven years proved long enough to change the owners. He then realized that he left this area over 25 years ago and that his few visits through the oak height development area occurred with his broken family in mind.The fountain was still in front of their home, and the landscaping appeared almost the same. Three cars were in the driveway, once again a Lexus minivan and a Tesla model he had seen parked at other houses, but not before that day. The other one was an older BMW perhaps his mother's.He walked to the entrance and grabbed his courage to ring the doorbell. After a few minutes, a young woman he didn't know and who was wearing a red dress, and high heels opened the door.

"Oh, excuse me, I think I have the wrong building…", said Steven, baffled…

"Uncle Steven?" the woman said, hesitantly.

Steven took a hard look at the lady and realized it had to be Sarah, his niece, now grown up.

"Sarah?" he said with surprise.

"Yeah, come in. Mom and Dad are in the kitchen," she motioned him to get inside, and yelled, "Mom, Dad, Uncle Steven is at the door!"

Just as Sarah was closing the front door, Michael and Camille arrived running. Michael was starting to lose his hair, while Camille still wore expensive clothes but was starting to show signs of aging.

"Wait, you're alive?" said Michael, surprised.

"Yeah, why wouldn't I be?"

"Well, you disappeared the day of the fire… I mean, the police went to look for you! When they couldn't find you, they even thought you might be a suspect."

Camille said with an accusatory tone…

"Yeah, where were you since then?"

Steven had to improve on the spot.

"DryTek remained my biggest client, and they burned down, so I began travelling around, finding great work with different companies."

Camille rolled her eyes.

"Stay for supper… I insist. Do you have a place to stay tonight? We have a guest bedroom… and Sam is at college, so the house feels pretty empty," replied Michael, visibly uncharacteristically happy to see his brother.

"Daaad…", Wind Sarah with a tone, he remembered from her youth.

"I know you too are here too, but I'm the only guy! Come, Steven, let's grab a beer…"

Michael grabbed Steven by the arm and pulled him toward the kitchen. In the Kitchen, Michael pulled out two beers from the refrigerator and gave one to his brother. Without saying a word, he motioned him to go on the patio outdoors where they sat on a new set of patio chairs.

"Did you at least hear about Dad…", said Michael, suddenly serious?

"No, I've been completely out of touch" he replied, in complete honesty. Time jumping had allowed him to fast-forward through his life, but it meant losing touch and a ton of information. He wondered how Lily had managed to navigate it, and he saw signs she went to the past too…

"Heart Attack. Sorry. He didn't make it."

Steven tried to show sadness and regret, but couldn't. Unlike Michael, he had never felt close to his parents.

"And mom?" he asked, out of curiosity, hoping she had met a similar fate.

"Still in Florida. You know about Florida, right?" Steven nodded in the negative and took another sip.

"Well, in the crash of 21, I made a fortune buying property and Camille and I decided to buy them a house in Florida while we moved in here. They became really, really happy until Dad had a stroke while playing golf. He made it to the hospital, but, you know, he wasn't the same, so he decided to sign a DNR order and a few months later he had another stroke and made it out peacefully. They buried him in town if you want to pay your respects. Same lot as Grandad and Granny."

Steven figured as much. His name had even already been carved in the stone, with his birthdate. He knew exactly where it was, but he possessed zero intentions of going.

"So how is your business?" Steven asked, more out of politeness than real interest.

"I got into a form of semi-retirement! My employees now manage my portfolio of buildings, now in 14 states, and I'm looking for partners to offer a partial buy out. Camille closed her shop, and we now spend a lot of time at home. I think it's been good for the kids."

Yes, the "kids" thought Steven. The children he had never really played with and which a nanny had basically raised for them. Well, for him. Camille did appear to take care of her daughter, not that she even did any homework, but she taught her about fashion style, looks and how to manipulate and complain against other people.

Sam looked like the sad one of the two, lacking a parent really showing interest in him, just as his father or uncle remained alone while growing up. Maybe he would find someone in college like Steven had. Or perhaps his parents had returned home soon enough to turn him into a perfect scheming socialite like his sister was destined to become. Steven had plenty of questions in his mind, but his nephew was the least of his worries. His wife died of a gunshot wound and the best person to get information from, his future self, vanished.

He had hoped his alter ego would have kept in touch with his family, but he honestly respected his choice not to make the effort. He knew he would have made the same decision… in fact, it appeared clear that he would have made the same decision. Michael talked more about his investments and grabbed two more beers when theirs ended up empty.

After what felt like an eternity, Camille invited the man to come inside for supper, and the four of them ate a delicious plate of pasta with a sauce Steven couldn't place. It wasn't tomato-based. It wasn't cream-based. Maybe pesto, or something like that? Lily never cared about cooking, and Steven felt the same way.

They apparently hired no servants, however. Potentially with both at home, they found a way to cope without hired help. Camille had shown disdain for servants in the past, so perhaps her hate of low-class people won over her own laziness. Camille served dessert, a Black Forest cake which she cut herself: two huge slices for the men, and two tiny pieces for the ladies.Once Sarah finished eating her slice, she asked her mother if she could go out with Jonathan that night. "Sure, but don't come back too late," she replied, half interested.

Sarah wished a good evening to her uncle but didn't even bother to address her father while leaving the room. Camille decided to explain the situation to her brother-in-law while both men were still eating their huge piece.

"Jonathan's father is a very successful investment banker. A very suitable match for our daughter, don't you think?"

Steven just raised his shoulders. He really didn't care. He had tried to connect with his brother's kids, but Camille had consistently blocked him since Lily had disappeared, as if his proximity to them would pollute them in any way. Of course, he did thank Camille for the meal and her hospitality and apologized to the bathroom.

Searching on his phone for nicer people, he discovered that George, Lily's father, passed away in a car accident six months ago. He felt sad for Sandra and promised himself he would visit her. He googled himself, but couldn't find anything other than a missing person article without an apparent follow-up. The article did mention he remained considered the primary suspect in the disappearance of his wife. Even after so many years, he couldn't escape it.

Steven realized that according to the public, the police named him a person of interest, but sadly, seeing the little blurb about him meant that it didn't make him an interesting person. He spent the rest of the evening nodding to his brother's stories but managed to slow down the delivery of beers. He smiled when he realized that the guest room replaced his actual former bedroom. They did redecorate it completely, but visibly didn't want their kids to sleep in the room where a potential murderer grew up.

Chapter 3.5—Vices

Sitting on the bed, Steven thought about his family and, more importantly, about the differences between his brother and himself. It appeared to Steven that his family, generations ago, had built a pattern in which the men were trapped. A kind of psychological construct built subconsciously (he hoped) to keep others at bay. He had thought in the past that it came from the shame of having built a fortune on the use of slaves. Today, he thought that just possessing more money than you or your descendants could spend on a luxurious lifestyle didn't encourage human contact.

Well, it wasn't just a lack of human contact. Each of the adults he knew from his family married someone and many, like his father and his brother, had managed to form friendships in high circles. Michael even managed to find partners and his employees apparently liked him. At least, according to his stories. It was more like a kind of preconceived notion of how the world works. A kind of self-importance or rigidity which reduced their capacity for imagination to a bare minimum.

To them, working remained only for poor people, and Steven's desire to perceive himself as productive with his life other than just investing money which they saw as something completely alien to them. Michael put all in real estate, his father preferred the stock market. In both cases, they remained pure capitalists in the sense that it wasn't them who worked, but their money. They made money because they had money to work with and a kind of flair of how to invest it.

Lily had thrown a doubt on their success and reminded him that he only really knew what they chose to tell him. It's like when you go to Vegas. You might brag of winning $15,000 but neglect to mention you came with $20,000 which you lost, apart from that singular win... Michael had also married in his social class, and from the evidence, Sarah would too. Camille's store had confused him because it initially gave the impression that she wanted to work, but perhaps it consisted of the same mentality: drop money in a pot and hope it would make more. Thinking, he remembered something that Michael had said. He laughed that the store kept Camille busy.

Was the store, in reality, a way to keep his wife entertained instead of letting her sleep with the pool boy? If so, it was even more pathetic than he thought. He always imagined that's why those store existed, but not that it applied to them. Camille wouldn't have laboured for a salary. She would have done so because her husband wanted to occupy her to keep her loyal while he traded investments. Steven, on the other hand, simply tried to have a good relationship with Lily, to make her desire only him, and yet, Michael still had Camille, and he didn't have Lily.

Returning to his thoughts, Steven thought that what he never understood, consisted of why he grew up so differently despite the same family raising both of them. Yes, Lily had helped him grow and had taught him work ethics, for the benefit of working with your own hands on your self-esteem and the, wait, he thought, how did she call it? The "Valour of hard work?" no, the "Honour of hard work" He couldn't remember her exact words, but it had resonated in him.

And yet, he felt unable to shake the feeling that he became different from them from an early age. He showed constant curiosity for the world while he just couldn't understand what's missing in them to make them perfectly happy to just live in a never-ending repetition of days which mostly looked the same. Ironically, he realized that this is precisely how he lived since Lily had disappeared, but he definitely didn't feel happy about it. He couldn't consider himself content. He instead stayed restless, felt trapped and isolated.

No, he wondered on the spark, the element in him that made him break that mould from a young age in which the Clark family members were stuck. Opening Lily's diary, he returned on a hunch at the section describing him. He realized now that this diary had a page on just that: that Steven needed encouragement to become a hard worker. That he simply didn't learn this as a child, but that he possessed the capacity for greatness. But nothing on why. Nothing on what made him an exception in his family.

Flipping through the diary, he took the time to re-read some of the key events of his life with his wife. He chuckled when he read about the Niagara Falls trip: the two of them didn't have much money at the point. His parents had just about cut them off already, and most of his salary went toward her remaining tuition. Lily had suggested that they rent a hotel room in Buffalo, to visit the falls for a low price. Back then, in a pre-9-11 world, a driver's licence was enough to cross into Canada and back, so their lack of a passport wasn't an issue.

They drove for hours, alternating between them, and reached their hotel around 11 that night. They were way off schedule because as always, Lily had insisted on stopping at various antique shops and buying off parts he now realized were listed elsewhere in the diary. Anyway, their place ended up small, and they smelled an odd chemical odour, but it didn't matter to them. What counted, however, was that after they went to bed, they both had a runny nose and a massive headache. After surveying the floor, they came to the conclusion that when they had cleaned it, some of the industrial disinfecting products they used spilled on the carpet and was making them nauseous.

The night manager didn't have any other rooms. After a quick scan at nearby hotels and motels, they couldn't find anything available at such a short notice. With their stay refunded, they turned back around and just drove until morning toward their city, without ever seeing the falls. This remained an element of shame in Steven's life until now, but on each occasion he proposed to return, Lily had dismissed it. He wondered: what if she knew? What if this excursion was only for the various antique shops?

Still, they had had a wonderful moment in the car, with deep conversations and a good amount of laughter. The trip itself, the travelling to and back from Buffalo that is, remained some of his fondest memories of non-sexual intimacy spent with Lily. It even overshadowed the long talks exchanged on the stairs toward the roof of their high school. That is where they had been able to discover a small corner devoid of foot traffic, finding the quietest section of their school where to eat lunch.

A few weeks later, Steven fell sick and needed to go to the hospital and ended up using the money from the hotel reservation to pay the medical bill. What if Lily already knew? After all, the visit to the doctor was listed in the diary, as well as the refund on the room, and even a summary of their finance. Steven fell asleep on the book that night and dreamed of good memories spent with Lily.

Chapter 3.6—Via Uber

Steven woke up late after having slept the previous night in a cramped time machine. And yet, he thought, could he think about it as the previous night? It occurred five years ago... but it was for him, from his point of view. He found his brother in the living room, using his laptop. Seeing no signs of his wife or daughter made Steven smile.

"Slept well?" asked Michael without taking his eyes off his monitor.

"Yeah," replied an equally uninterested Steven.

"Listen, help yourself to anything in the kitchen for breakfast." Said Michael as Steven was leaving the living room.

And Steven did, after living mostly on processed sugar and refined fat in small packets, cooking eggs and even bacon along with two orders of toast made for a very refreshing meal. The double toasters enabled him to prepare four slices at once. It wasn't the same one he last used in his parents' house. Steven thought that these bread grills didn't really seem to evolve. Most of his bread ended up browner on one side than the other, which always feels like a disappointment as Steven prefers the lighter side.

Once they popped out, on the lightly toasted side, he got margarine for the first two as he couldn't find butter in the large refrigerator, and the other pair got crunchy peanut butter topped by strawberry jam. He made certain not to put crusts in any of the three containers. He also ensured not to put any peanut butter in the jam. Michael might not care, but their parents did. Steven finds it difficult to just get rid of that conditioning, despite Lily voluntarily putting crumbs into the margarine just to make him relax about it.

It never worked. Especially not when she did it under his nose, grabbing crumbs from her plate and dropping them in the tub with a serious face. She tried to provoke him, but the reality is that he didn't care, his family did. After making sure the yolk cooked solid, something which always irritated his family, he left just the bacon to cook almost hard in the skillet as he served his plate. He realized they used the same plates as when he grew up in the house, making him wonder how in hell his family managed to keep them so long. He remembered that his mother had bought reserves and probably still had roughly 60 stored somewhere in the house.

This looked like the kind of behaviour that felt normal. Such as getting a new car every two years, but buying enough dinnerware sets to last four generations. The bacon finished cooking after he ate his first egg, and soon jumped on the thin strip of crunchy feast. How long since his last? And he laughed, as this didn't have a single answer, now that he was travelling through time.

Once finished eating his second egg, he wondered, was Michael really helping him out of brotherly love or simply out of social obligations? Still, Steven ate like a king for the second meal in a row after two days of questionable nourishment. He wondered if eating alone at the table didn't make him feel better than the awkward meal of the previous day.

He found a few snacks in the well-furnished cupboard, which he grabbed. He filled back a bag for the next visits: it's not as if they count anyway. After further consideration, he decided that he would wait a few days before returning to the time machine, to give it time to charge more. Seeing how little the new owners used their basements, he felt it consisted of a safe bet, he just hoped they wouldn't get the urge to clean the basement while it was charging.

Now the big question was about what to do in the meantime Sandra remained the only person he considered going to see, so after cleaning the kitchen and putting his dirty plate in the dishwasher, he saluted his brother.

"Wait, Steven, you don't have a car?" he asked.

"I'll take the bus…"

"Nonsense. Give me your phone, I'll log you into my Uber account."

So, Uber still operates, Steven wondered how it would have evolved. An idea suddenly jumped into his mind.

"Michael, how long have you had an Uber account?" he asked.

"Almost since the beginning. That way, no risk of being accused of drunk driving if you go out," he replied.

"Do you need to change your password often? Like every few months?"

"No, I think it's the same password as when I joined. Why?"

Steven smiled and thanked his brother. With any luck, he wouldn't need to take the bus after his next time travel trip. Using the app, he reserved a ride, and had to wait by the curb for a pickup in four minutes. When the vehicle arrived, it looked odd. It wasn't an actual traditional car, but instead, looked like a kind of minivan with four independent compartments. Only one of them unlocked, the one on the right side of the back seat, and found someone already sitting on the right side of the front seat, yet no one in the driver's place. The vehicle left after he sat at his assigned place, and he noticed that once inside the car, he couldn't see the three occupants: the dividers looked completely opaque and, apparently, pretty much soundproof.

"So, this consists of the future of Uber. Fully automated cars that let you ride alone, while sharing part of the road with unseen strangers?" thought Steven.

Still, despite the detour to pick up another passenger and drop the previous one, he made it to Lily's childhood home in a much faster time than if he had picked the bus. No wonder the mass transit system grew in pricing. Still, the Uber cost was over $40, money he lacked, so he felt surprisingly grateful for his brother's generosity. But then, he reminded himself, money wasn't a problem with his family: it's the rest that was.

Sandra opened the door when he rang the bell. At first, she didn't recognize him, but after saying hello, she hesitated and said a faint, "Steven, is that you?"

After confirming, they went up to her kitchen and reconnected. He offered her sympathy for the death of her husband, and she said that in a way, he remained the only person left in her family. She seemed surprised to see him, still looking so young, since she was under the impression he found death too. Steven repeated the same lies he told Michael about travelling but added that he didn't think that George and her wanted to stay in touch with him.

"Steven, you married our daughter... in a way, you're the son we never had. Would have felt happy to help you out, to let us stay at our place. I still have Lily's things in the basement. Neither Georges nor I could bear to go through them. It still hurts, you know..."

But Steven did know. He had been through 12 years of pain without her and only felt better now because he had managed to hold her in his arms one last time, and he now got a plan to save her. He made a mental note to stay closer to his in-laws if he did succeed. Spending some time with Sandra gave him some answers from the previous night. He couldn't figure what triggered the spark of his own empathy and desire to do something with his life. He realized what turned the embers of his difference into the bonfire of his adulthood: it came from Sandra's warm personality and George's hardworking habits, both of which had mixed and created Lily's extraordinary traits of character.

"Do you know if Lily showed interest in electronics at a young age?" Steven asked, trying to understand his wife in more depths, in detail he had never imagined questioning her with when he was still with her.

"Oh yes, she was building circuits at in elementary school. George was an electrician, you knew that, right? Yes, you did… So, yes, he was an electrician, and she often went with him on job sites. It was often in old buildings. I think that's why she wanted to become a historian."

Slowly, Steven was getting a new mental picture of his wife. He had known she performed well in school, but she always hid her interests in electronics and such, probably because of his own interests. He knew she had designed a few things, but she had always claimed he was inspiring her or that it came to her while reading an old book or something like that. That he inspired the work they did on electronics together, even when the idea clearly came from her, like the quantum antenna. What if she was both hiding her abilities to prevent him from growing suspicious and, at the same time, that she was trying to preserve his self-esteem? He had so much to ask her and couldn't get an idea on how to find her!

He thanked Sandra after a few hours spent with her and took a walk in the neighbourhood to try to clear his mind. Did he have anything to do while waiting for the time machine to charge? What else could he do to pass the time? He cursed the long recharge time, kept walking in the warm afternoon sun.

Chapter 3.7—Village Walk

Steven thought he had been walking aimlessly, but his feet were bringing him downtown, on a path he often took with Lily while in college. Back then, using your legs just represented a mode of transportation to him. Considering it an actual hobby remained something that never occurred to Steven as offering anything interesting. In his family, sport only mattered when points were awarded: football, golf, soccer, baseball or even tennis or volleyball. It's an activity you did for glory and if you weren't good at it, you just forgot about it. In short, no one in the family ever played any sports except occasional golf tournaments for charity.

But Lily's parents offered a different vision of sports. The three of them would ride with Lily in the neighbourhood on their bicycles, go cross-country skiing in the winter, and he had begun to enjoy taking long strolls in the city. Sandra even explained that as young adults, George and she earned the cute nickname of "the little couple who walked everywhere,"

Before meeting Lily, it had never occurred to Steven that you might decide to travel on your feet when you could use a car. But then again, his home was in a suburb where you couldn't navigate on foot at all. Lily's house was in a poorer neighbourhood in the inner city where you could stroll to the downtown hip area in about 60 minutes. When Lily first suggested it, he complained: "An hour?" Steven didn't even remember ever standing up that long, let alone walk all that duration, but he managed to do it, and to return afterward. His legs felt dead the next morning and less every few weeks until he looked forward to the following one.

A few years after, the two of them even went trekking in the hills and picnicked above a beautiful valley. That day, Steven had found the perfect place to propose and two years later, on another visit, it's precisely what he did. He tried to think back to that period, and he couldn't pull in him clear enough pictures of the landscape to see it in his mind's eye. Young couples all owned intelligent cellphones equipped with a camera to capture the magic occasion. His engagement would remain a private moment forever, a memory to cherish only in his mind, and hopefully, in theirs if he could just locate her and save her.

117

Wait, he wondered, what if he already did? He talked to his future self five years earlier, and now, this one vanished. What if he reunited with Lily since his departure? What if he too launched on a quest and discovered a clue, or something like that? Steven had found Lily dead seven calendar years before the current time. In those seven objective years, he actually explored less than a single subjective week, while his counterpart lived the whole duration, at least, until he evaporated.

What if he didn't disappear, and rather ended caught up with murder Lily and left with her forever to his era? Perhaps the answer wasn't to travel to the solution, and instead to take the long way to his wife. He couldn't wait, but this Steven already spent his patience for him. Steven needed way more information than he currently amassed and he started getting an idea in his mind. He approached the headquarters of the local newspaper still early in the afternoon. Much to his relief, it hadn't moved or closed. He had often gone to the office with Lily to place ads in the paper announcing her tutoring lessons. At worst, the public library could have helped, but the journal felt closer.

Fortunately, the building was still there and inside, after recalling on his cellphone the old article, he asked if Jake Minelly still worked there that he had information and questions about one of his articles. He only identified himself as Steven.

"Let me check if he's in, please sit back in the waiting area," said the young new receptionist. The old one that knew him probably retired in the last 20 years.

Steven was daydreaming about the odd fact that companies could remain almost the same for generations, while their individual employees changed as time went by. It reminded him of the paradox of the old Greek guy... He asked something like, if you change each piece of a boat one by one, until none of the original pieces was still there, could you consider it the same boat? He was trying to think of the name of the guy when a middle—age obese guy interrupted him.

"Steven? I'm Jake Minelly, you wanted to talk to me about an article?"

118

"Oh, yes… Sorry. Listen, it's about the industrial park that burned down. You wrote an article on its demolition, and I was wondering if you knew which firm took care of that."

Jake looked irritated. Steven had lied and said he had information and probably interrupted his writing. He thought the journalist would yell at him that he wasn't an information desk or something like that, but suddenly, his face lightened up.

"Aren't that man who disappeared that day?" he asked, piecing two and two together.

"Yes, Steven Clark, but I didn't disappear, I moved because my clients were moving apart from each other or closing down because of the demolition."

"If you give me an exclusive on your return, I can answer most of your questions!"

"I'd rather remain anonymous, if you don't mind…"

"Why?" he asked, puzzled.

"You don't know?" Steven replied, wondering if his infamous alleged crime had passed on or if this report had never put two and two together. "Listen, can you just tell me information on the demolition today? If my gut feeling pans out, I'll have a major exclusive for you in a few days. I think something really fishy occurred around it."

Jake looked around him as if someone were trying to steal his scoop, and got closer to Steven.

"Can you give me a hint?" he said, in a hush but rushed tone of voice.

"Listen, I promise, give me a week, and you will have your scoop… if it pans out."

The reporter gave him Steven his card and said, "Let's go to my office. I'll see what I can find." The two men walked the maze of corridors and cubicles but noticed that most remained empty. Perhaps the newspaper was struggling. Maybe most journalists worked from home.

Once at his desk, Jake began searching his old files as well as articles on the Internet, including databases of bids. After about 10 minutes of efficient work, Steven had plenty of information including the company name, the foreman name (Robert Thompson), the address of the office in town, phone number, etc. Thanking him, Steven took his leave and as soon as he was outside in the street, called the demolition company. The nice secretary explained that Mr. Thompson was on a job site, but after a lot of pleading (and pretending to be a family member from out of state), managed to get the address.

Being too far to walk there, Steven ubered away and soon enough, was in front of a massive construction project: they were demolishing the former Emerald Mall to make way for condo towers. Yet another city landmark that felt somehow unique due to the green tinted sunroof over the corridors would give way to boring architecture you could find in any other US city.

He asked to speak to Robert and, once again, tested his patience. He could still see part of the structure standing. Waiting, he remembered getting ice cream with Lily in the courtyard, or shopping for clothes there. Oh, he could picture it: the small boutique where she had purchased her prom dress. That one was now in a section completely destroyed, but the food court was in the still active destruction area.

Teenagers made that mall very popular in the '90s, but around 2010, it had declined in favour of the new super centre. You know, the type of outdoor mall where you park at each store and instead of an internal corridor, it remains wide open. Both Steven and Lily hated those, in part because when it was raining, you couldn't take a walk inside in the same way they could at the Emerald mall.

Strolling the whole halls lasted them about 35 minutes, so if they wanted a one-hour exercise sessions, they could just perform it twice. For a two-hour walk, four times. With AC, heating, protection from the rain and restrooms everywhere, it felt perfect for a walk on a rainy afternoon.

"But it was long ago, and it was far away, oh God, it seems so very far," he began humming to himself when the foreman finally arrived.

After an awkward introduction and some pleading, explaining and begging, the foreman began thinking back of the demolition of his workshop. He recalled the surprise of finding an apartment hidden above, on the second floor with some furniture and appliances, but in his memory, it appeared empty. He saw no books or clothes or even tools in the loading dock below. Only big, not easy to move, things remained. No computers, televisions, or anything like that. He only found a refrigerator, an oven, a couch, a bed, an empty freezer. Those consisted of the only things left in his secret home. Steven thanked him, but that didn't help him at all. That meant his future self had moved, but he conjured no idea when, where or why.

Chapter 3.8—Victor's Gun

He had a time machine at his disposition. He could travel to almost any day, but couldn't figure out which one! Thinking about it, he suddenly formed an idea... A way to simplify his expeditions. It was still early in the afternoon, so he Ubered back to close to his former house, and after making sure no one remained home or spotting him, used his duplicate key.

In the house, he called his new cellphone from the landline to save the phone number, and took the opportunity to check the charge: it was now at sixty-two percent. Great. After an Uber back to his childhood home and an equally weirdly silent supper with his brother's family, he sat down and composed a series of questions.

Taking an official tone, he called the landline of the new owners of his former house. He pretended to be from a travel agency making a survey on their past trips to win a five-hundred-dollar voucher for any future vacations. It took some arguments, but he finally managed to convince the lady to offer some insights on their past travels.

"We don't travel every year because we prefer to fly," she proceeded to recall their trips to Florida, including three cruises from Miami to California and to Las Vegas. With a lot of attention, he noted the dates, as this would give him windows to time travel without risk of interception. He even thought of the idea to ask if any were shortened, and wondered if they needed their house-sitting services.

"We don't have any plants or pets. My sister just picks up my mail after coming back from work," she explained.

He thanked her and told her she should get her voucher by mail in a week or so, knowing he would be in another era by then. Smiling, he managed to get a second good night's sleep in a row, in his childhood room. Inside him, Steven felt some resentment for Lily for neglecting to tell him that she could time travel. At the same time, now that he could, he has lied twice on the same day to people who didn't even care about him. He did so simply because he knew he wouldn't be there by the time they find out.

Lily once told him a quote. It was from someone else, but he couldn't for the life of God remember who wrote it. "The best motivation to always tell the truth is that when you do have to lie, people tend to believe you." He had never caught her lying, but that the focus on that affirmation changed, right? It now centred on "caught her". Now, her lies would appear on the surface and still, could he blame her?

Presently, he focused on only one mission in mind, to save Lily, prevent her from dying, but once he saves her, how will he resist the temptation to change elements of his past to improve his future? This worried him, so he decided to use a technique Lily taught him in the past. He noted on a piece of paper his "worries" and next to it, how he felt about them, and then, what to do with them.

The first thing he noted was to prevent Lily's death, but that was precisely what he was trying to do, and if he did get her back alive, it would become a moot point. The second thing he noted, since he remained destitute and with little money, he couldn't afford to alienate his father, his main source of income. His fear of his father cutting him from the family money kept him in line. He didn't know how he felt about it. He definitely knew that nothing, even time travel, could have avoided disappointing Richard Clark. They believed in irreconcilable differences in values. To his father, either you enjoy the family fortune or you work. If you work, you don't need the money. If you take the money, you don't get to work. His brother's investments felt borderline and not enough for Steven. You lived as a leader or a worker. His father saw no in between. Not that either Steven's parents led anyone, anywhere, anytime.

The third thing he noted was to avoid losing their house, but if he didn't lose Lily, they would still have it. As he began thinking back, the reality that sinks in: he didn't need a time machine in the long term. He needed to find Lily and would feel happy if both forever stopped their time travel. Steven once again returned to his former house during the day while the owners were away at work. The time machine had risen to 62% or more than he had even seen it.

He now had two periods to visit and wasn't sure with which one to start. The day before the demolition, which most likely coincided with the date his future copy disappeared. The other occurred several months earlier, in which the new owners of his former home took a vacation for two weeks. This would allow him to charge his time machine fully. In the end, he decided he would visit them in order. He was in the future, so he would first stop near the demolition, and after a stop to get additional information, would lay over during the new owner's vacation and whatever came next.

The third trip drained the batteries to 45%, but he wasn't worried since he would charge them for a few hours and the next jump would occur over a much shorter distance. The lack of cell signals initially worried him, but he now realized his mistake: at each time jump, he would need to purchase a prepaid Sim card.

123

Without the capacity to call an Uber (or even test if the app worked), he had to walk to the nearest store, which needed a good 25-minute trek in the rain (of course, it was raining). Soaking wet, he bought in the grocery store an umbrella and a prepaid Sim card, as well as a meal replacement bar box. He cursed himself for not having thought of that earlier!

He put his 2024 Sim card in his wallet and installed the new one in its place. If this continued, he would need to find a better way to organize his Sim cards. He wondered what Lily had done when travelling. He had failed to find a cellphone on her when she had died in his arms. Perhaps she lacked the necessity for one: after all, a lot of her trips were in the steam engine age, with no cellphone reception or even electricity. Still, the Uber app recognized him, which felt like a miracle in itself, but only after installing the current version from the store. When he reserved a car, however, the name of the driver appeared and soon enough, an actual person picked him up in a normal car.

The driver offered him snacks and a bottle of water and tried to make small talk, but Steven was lost in his thoughts. He was bouncing from trying to guess when he would find Lily, to attempting to figure out what his future self was up to, passing through how Lily even managed to navigate the various time frames. Soon enough, he was back at the industrial block. The traces of the fire were still there, and a construction crew worked on demolishing most of the buildings. His own building was still standing but the human resource company that leased the front of his workshop unit was closed and apparently long gone. Behind his loading dock, he couldn't find his truck. Perhaps his future self already left?

He used his key and came into the workshop. Sadly, someone, presumably himself, has emptied it, or rather almost emptied it. He saw a few boxes and Rubbermaid bins by the loading bay door, but most of the place appeared empty.Steven opened one, and saw it contained just some of his books. Perhaps his future self no longer wanted them. Perhaps he hadn't finished packing. He heard soft footsteps behind him and turned around to see the older Steven holding a shovel and swing to smack him in the shoulder. Steven collapsed on the boxes, hurting his back and making Victor's gun that he had strapped to his belt fall further away on the floor.

"What the hell? I'm you, from the past!" said the younger Steven.

The older Steven raised the shovel high in the air in the hope to hurt his younger self again. Young Steven rolled away, and the shovel bumped the top of one of the boxes, making the assailant drop it. Both Steven's hurried to their weapons, but the older one managed to grab his and strike the time traveller as he was picking up his firearm. It made him fall on the floor, yet he successfully held on to his pistol.

"Will you stop that? Why do you want to hit me?" asked the younger Steven.

"I'm not aiming to wound you, I'm aiming to kill you...", the angry shovel wielder Steven yelled while trying to pummel his doppelgänger again, but his more agile counterpart barely dodged it.

Running toward the end of the docking bay, he managed to get enough distance to raise his gun and point it at his older self.

"Dude, stop, I'm you from the past. I mean you no harm! We even talked once, remember?"

The shovel holding copy stood in place for a moment.

"We met twice, and I still have no memories of me time travelling, but I recollect full well what you did when we last crossed paths, and I know where this is going. I have to terminate you."

The older Steven raised the improved weapon while running toward his younger version, but stopped right in his tract when the gun fired a single bullet, which hit him straight in the head. Steven, now the only one alive, didn't really decide to shoot but rather, reacted instantly. Still, for the second occasion in less than a week of personal progress, he had killed someone in self-defence.

This time, it wasn't just a stranger. It consisted of him, from the future. His other self hadn't disappeared. Instead, it's Steven who killed his older copy. It remained entirely his fault. Traumatized, he grabbed a sheet of plastic he found near the book and placed it under the head of his victim. He observed surprisingly little blood, after seeing three people die, it looked like the only instance that not a single drop of blood had tainted his cement floor.

Discouraged, he went upstairs only to see it almost empty already. His freezer was still there, so were his other appliances, but older Steven removed everything small enough to carry in his truck.Completely demoralized, Steven took the biggest unused plastic storage box and placed the cadaver in it. Without a vehicle, he wouldn't be able to get easily rid of this corpse. He swore in his mind.

Why did he have so many bodies to hide? How did his life become so complicated? Why wouldn't this body fit in the bin? Still in shock, he undressed and began manipulating the shovel to try and cut the remains into smaller parts, and generally just filled the stupid Rubbermaid container with a disgusting soup, vomiting once in it. This, exceeded his limits.

"Shit, Shit, Shit."

In complete panic, he just doubled the efforts and with enough adrenaline and time, managed to split the corpse into three receptacles without making a mess on the floor, which Steven considered to remain a miracle of biblical proportion. He was now able to lift them but the sloshing blood at the bottom sounded rather horrid.

Tearing pages apart from some of the books, he placed them to try and absorb the slurry so it wouldn't remain as liquid. Once the covers were locked and the exterior of the sides wiped clean, it wasn't too weird, so he found a driver using the Uber app with a minivan and reserved it. It would feel tight for the trip back to the time machine, but he would arrive perhaps an hour before the new owners. He insisted on loading the suspicious cargo himself into the minivan. He didn't want to take any risks, and he almost hurt his back doing so, but soon, they were on their way back to his old home.

126

Traffic delayed them, and Steven's nervousness made the Uber driver uneasy too, but soon enough they were back at his former home where he unpacked the three containers beside the street. He only had 20 minutes left, so he unlocked the door, rushed to place the three bins in the entrance hall and extended the deadbolt behind him. At least, he made it inside now.

Winded, he almost flew downstairs with the first, and quickly returned to grab the second one. On his walk back up, he saw a car pull up in front of the garage and ran to the basement with the third tub just as he could perceive the opening of the front door. Panicked, he put the one he was still holding at the back of the time machine, over the batteries. He then slowly grabbed one of the other bins and deposited it on top. Three proved to occupy too much space, so he placed the last one on the passenger seat. He closed the door to the storage room just as he heard noises from the stairs.

"Is there anyone here?" said the female voice. "I have a knife…"

Steven knew the time machine would remain silent from her point of view, so he unplugged it without letting it roll in the cable. In the cockpit, he hurried programming the other date he had selected and pressed the go button. The machine left just as the question was repeated… He felt confident he acted quick enough to avoid detection, but only caught his breath when he arrived a few months earlier.

Chapter 3.9—Violence

Steven arrived to his fourth Time travel period, but this time, he would have several days in his former house with the new owners on a cruise. He knows he should learn their names, the lady even told him when he called her for the voucher, but he refused to learn it due to how he abused their hospitality. Well, not that they even knew. He would still need to pay attention to avoid neighbours mowing their lawn or watering plants, but he felt no intentions of sticking around. The end of the day would add risk as the owner's sister would come by to pick up the mail. His first order of business was to get rid of the body of his future self.

He had so far only seen future Steven once, so he knew that he would meet again from the comment he made, and that it wouldn't end well. With zero intentions of even meeting, Steven decided to plug his machine and wait for darkness. Coming out of his hiding place only to use the bathroom, he ate his meal replacement bars. The smell from the bins began to rise in the little storage area.

While checking his notes, he realized an off coincidence: the chemical fire would break out at 3:23 AM tonight. That gave him a perfect place where to ditch the body. The article had mentioned various strong acids and solvents and how much they had almost melted everything on the factory floor... it would provide the perfect way to eliminate this body. He did open the door to ventilate, but he was delighted when finally, 10 PM came, and he could leave the house, leaving the bins behind him.

Once again, without an Uber, he called a taxi from the landline and caught a ride from two blocks away up to a few blocks from his workshop. He had a body to hide, he couldn't take shortcuts. Gently walking toward his loading bay, he realized a flaw in his plan. He would borrow his truck, which he saw as perfect, but it required him to leave it parked for a few minutes in his former driveway with the new owners presumed to be away. Damn, he thought of his plan most of the day and didn't think of this until now. He would have to gamble it... At least, he knew from newspapers that his copy wasn't in jail, and, if you kill your future self, does it constitute a murder, or suicide? Can you even go to jail for killing yourself?

Without going inside, Steven entered his truck and gently drove toward his former home, a route he knew by heart. Instead of parking right away, he drove slowly and checked: the exterior showed an absence of occupancy and the lack of lights revealed that no resident was peaking through their windows. Chancing it, he parked in reverse and quickly loaded the three bins into the truck. He also grabbed a hammer from the house. He sneaked away from the house as if he had never been there and returned to the industrial block.

128

Avoiding his own unit, he parked behind the chemical factory, and using the borrowed tool, he smashed hard on the window above the rear door and managed, with some force, to open it. The interior of the room smelled strongly like acetone, and he wondered what they were doing in this factory. With such a high concentration of acetone in the air, it's no wonder the place would burn down tonight. He parked closer to the door, and unloaded the three bins from the truck, placing them just inside the building.

He looked inside. Plainly visible he noticed four vats of chemicals, as he had imagined, with one labelled sulphuric acid. He flushed the content of the first bin in the vat, trying to avoid any splashing toward him, but some did drip on the floor, which fizzled in the reaction. After some hesitation, he also dropped the mostly empty bin into the vat itself, and it managed to begin breaking apart, but the acid was slowly changing colour, as matter was dissolving into it. He grabbed the second and was repeating the process when he heard a noise behind him. Looking over the third, with the lid in his hand, he noticed current day Steven.

"What did you do?" he yelled, when it became clear to the time traveller that contemporary Steven was starting at his counterpart's dead head.

"It was an accident, I swear...", the younger Steven replied. You

"I'm calling the police!" the older Steven said as he picked up his cellphone.

"He's you from the future... and I'm from the past. If you contact 911, how will you explain this?"

The other Steven put his cell down.

"I have to stop you... you're ruining my life, and now I discover you killed me?" he said.

"Listen, even if you murder me at this moment, I only killed the other you in self-defence, but in my past. I'd do anything to prevent that, now it's too late... It has already happened."

129

"As if I believe you…."

The resident Steven picked up his hammer and charged forward. This made Steven drop the bin into the vat, which splashed hard against the floor. Steven, who was up on the rail, ran in the opposite direction, toward the back of the factory. Older Steven climbed a ladder and followed him, running toward him with the tool raised. This prompted a strong questioning in Steven. What in his emotional or psychological makeup made him want to charge at himself with a blunt object, first a shovel, and now a hammer? Or rather, the reverse? The other Steven reached a control room with a door and locked it behind him.

"Don't attack me, I'm trying to improve our life! I'm trying to save Lily! I can later go to a previous moment and erase our problems," he pleaded.

"You're one big liar!" the older Steven replied, while bashing the door with the hammer. Unlike the younger counterpart, however, he saw no logic to his actions: he seemed to just be letting his anger out.

The time traveller noticed a ladder dropping to the factory floor from a floor trap, which his copy hadn't located yet. Even better, it was on the opposite side of the room, out of view from the position of his other self. He could hear the contemporary Steven yelling at him, insulting him and swearing big words he had himself rarely used. He could understand why: he had (or would?) kill(ed) him and prevent his future. Verb tenses remain complicated when it comes to time travel.

Steven was carefully weighing his options. Would he rush and dash for the door? Could he find the time to start the truck and leave? Would the older Steven cause problems and call the police? He needed to dump the rest of the body in the vat and time was running out… Time… Running out… Steven looked at his phone and realized that the fire would be started in only a few minutes. He knew it began as a criminal electrical fire from the newspapers, but he still held no idea who lid it. Rumours were that it was for the insurance money, or that it came from a competitor. The cause escaped his recollection and the article lacked from his phone's cache.

130

The arsonist would show up any moment now and either ruin everything or allow him to flee. After all, they discovered no corpses in the wreckage and despite the blaze burning for hours. It remained hard to believe that if he died in the fire, they wouldn't discover him. A horrible thought crossed his mind, however: what if the arsonist carried his body outside the building and found a way to dispose of it, doing the same he had done for Victor's? Looking around, Steven found a heavy wrench which could very well serve as a weapon if the arsonist came close.

He knew roughly where the fire had started and if he thought right, it was precisely where he was, so the arsonist would have to come into the control room to start the flames. The older Steven managed to punch a hole in the safety glass, and suddenly, his voice became easier to hear: "You're just using me. You're just a killer…" and so on. He needed to survey the room better.

He spotted an emergency locker he hadn't opened yet with an extinguisher, an axe and a pair of gas masks. Steven dropped his wrench and equipped the mask and the axe. He found the courage to face both the arsonist and the older Steven now, even if smoke filled the room. A thought came into his mind. What if the older Steven, with his actions, had triggered the fire? He checked the time and realized that the door would hold longer. It wasn't possible. Older Steven couldn't start it…

Then whom? He wondered. The only humans present remained the two of them. A thought formed in his mind. The only way this made sense is for him to become the arsonist. He could imagine no other options. He needed to jump-start a combustion to solve all his problems. Searching around him, the only things he could see consisted of the controls, nothing he could use to really start a fire…. Unless… Steven jumped to action. He first swung the axe to break the window overlooking the vats. He didn't need a big gap, just enough to pass his arm.

After reviewing that the handle of the axe was in wood, he cut the power line connected to one of the switches and pulled the wires through the hole he had made. It didn't take much: on the next accidental spark, the room erupted in flame. It wasn't so much an explosion, as a rapid combustion of the acetone content in the air. The older Steven stopped banging on the door.

Checking around, younger Steven saw that the top of three of the vats were on fire, and for one of them, it became a blazing inferno.

Opening the floor trap, he ran toward the bin he had left, trying to exploit the confusion. He grabbed as fast as possible the remaining vat and climbed the stairs to drop its content in the same acid bath which had a more and more guilty looking colour. Without the fire, the police would have found something. He realized he was now on a walkway close to the control room, so he looked around and saw his doppelgänger lying on the floor. He ran toward him: he seemed correct but knocked out. The vats that boiled from the fire began dropping some of their liquid on the floor, making the whole factory more dangerous by the minute.

Without thinking, he pulled his adversary and dragged him by the arms on the rail until he needed to carry him down the stairs. By the time Steven finally reached the door, the room began filling up with odd-looking smoke and the smell was seriously worrying. One of the vats glowed red from the heat. He began fearing for his life enough to stick close to his older copy: while he knew this one would survive, he possessed no guarantees for himself. He put him in the back of his truck, which remained open, and quickly drove toward his workshop, only a few seconds of driving away.

On location, he dragged his future self into the workshop, locked the door behind him and fled the scene with the truck, abandoning it a few blocks away from his former home. Breathless, he climbed onboard the time machine, and quickly punched the previous vacation of the new owners. He was still shaking when he arrived at the new period, a year earlier, and ended up collapsing on their bed after showering quickly.

Chapter 3.10—Valiant

After a good sleep throughout the day, Steven plugged his time machine and began reviewing his options. He now knew a lot more about what had been occurring in the few years after his departure, but still drew a blank on where he could find Lily.

The elusive Lily. He realized she spent most of her travelling in the past, except he made it unreachable because of his quantum antenna, or beacon, like Victor had called it. She had purchased an item from a specific store in the future, but he stalked it, she didn't come, and yet, she possessed the piece with her when she died. He could count on her love for her parents, but Sandra failed to see Lily again, so she neglected to establish contact.

This remained something that troubled him at the beginning of his relationship with her. He just couldn't understand how a person above the age of 10 could even think to remain close to his or her family. To him, except when too young to know otherwise, they just were the adults that made the decision (or not) to bring you into this world. He loved telling them "I didn't ask to be born" during his teenage years until he recognized that it failed to shock them. I only pained him. Worse, it made him realize that he simply didn't matter in their lives. That he wouldn't wound them, due to their indifference.

Sandra and George, on the other hand, did things with Lily. They cared for her, and later for him too. They did so in a way he never thought possible: in a respectful, equal way. Lily explained to him the theory of Ericsson on connections. That there existed essentially three roles a person could take in an interpersonal relationship: Parent, Adult or Child. This occurred independently of the age or role of the speakers.

She told him that two individuals talking to each other in the "Adult" role could socialize easily, but the only proper exchange a parent can have, is with a child. The problem, however, is that humans usually alternate between the three positions. She explained that between the two of them, they were mostly in an adult-to-adult interaction. Still, sometimes, one of them would take charge in some way (become the parent) and the other would slip into the child mode.

She gave the example of an earlier party where she had mistakenly drunk too much punch with alcohol in it (without her knowledge) and Steven protected her and brought her home so she would remain safe. He rose to the occasion and acted like a good "dad" in a position where Lily proved unable to act mature due to her involuntary inebriation.

133

Steven had wondered the point she was trying to make, but soon enough, she arrived at a conclusion: his mother and father always remained stuck in the child mode. They failed to connect to him like an equal, and they certainly never took their responsibilities as parental figures. They demanded respect and admiration without ever offering a justification for that reverence.

Her family, however, acted in such a way that she naturally wanted to honour them. They talked adults to adults with her. Instead of punishing her for bad grades, they would help her prepare for her exams in advance, despite their own lack of high education. Often, she explained, they would just read extracts of her notes and make her complete their sentences. Or they would check her definitions and either ask to guess the word from it, or to perform the opposite. In short, they wanted their daughter to succeed where they didn't have, and they toiled toward that. They even helped Steven on occasion to study for something, or her father would give him some part-time work to gain experience.

George didn't gain much money and the little jobs that Sandra managed to secure barely paid their bills. Yet, they always put food on the table for them for Lily, for Steven and for any of Lily's friends who came by. Often, it centred on a low-cost dish like simple pasta with ordinary sauce and a small volume of actual meat, but inevitably served in a good mood and from the bottom of their hearts. If Steven missed a meal at home, too bad for him. If he did so at the Connoly's, they would whip up something and fill his stomach. In short, they managed to offer a presence in a way his parents never really did, and that provided a massive difference in their daughter's life.

George had often talked about "the Book," capital B, which consisted of a hand-me-down hand-written book of tips and tricks on how to raise a child. It remained surprisingly good considering his grandfather composed it back when "social science barely existed and kids hadn't been invented yet," he used to say, laughing each time. According to him, youngsters constituted a fairly recent discovery, and teenagers came even more later! He claimed that in the past, you had old people, adults and tiny adults who, in short, were kids. One day, a psychologist realized that youngsters weren't just small grownups but instead possessed their own needs and peculiarities.

Later, a mid-stage period was "invented" as something more than just blowing up into a rebellion but rather an important step between childhood and adulthood. "Children can remain carefree in wonderland. Adults are expected to live in the actual world of responsibilities. Adolescents are moving from one to the other. We're required to help them become grounded in reality, while only slowly opening the floodgates of duties. If you don't let reach life on their terms, they revolt. If you give them too much or too little obligation at once, they rebel," he used to say.

The most surprising thing was that Lily never had a tumultuous teenage phase, and Steven's anti-family ideas were stopped dead in their tracks as he spent more time with Lily and thus, with her parents. George lived as a great man, and he missed him a lot more than he missed his own father. It's no wonder he loved Lily that much. She stood on the shoulders of a giant. But George wasn't solely responsible: Sandra raised Lily as a wonderful mother, full of warmth and understanding. Always available for her daughter to talk, play, or just listen.

He remained convinced that Lily, during her future travels, would have visited her parents and her lack of contact disturbed him. He regretted not having noted the date and place of George's funeral to offer him one last respect, but he kept his confidence he would one day have the occasion to do so. Laughing, he realized that even with a time machine, he might not find the opportunity to last say goodbye. Still, he missed Lily so much, but couldn't figure out how to find her. Recognizing how much each time jump proved problematic. It took a while to recharge, he needed transportation, he lacked Sim cards, he required, well, an idea of what to do!

It was impossible to return home at any point before his last stay with his brother, since he mentioned no previous encounters. The same logic applied to block him from meeting Sandra, since she hadn't seen him. Additionally, he couldn't actually visit himself, since the oldest version told him he had talked to him only twice before that. Steven desperately needed a plan, and needed it in the next four days, since after that period, the time machine would have fully charged. But first things first. He needed a Sim card now.

With plenty of time before him, Steven walked to the nearest grocery store, where he once again bought both a prepaid Sim card and a prepaid plan. He also grabbed a pill organizer, some cotton balls and a sharpie. At a local park, he took out the first Sim card he purchased from his wallet and put it with a cotton ball in one of the pill slots. He then wrote the date of activation on it with the sharpie, and repeated it for his current Sim and his original one from 2014. He also reserved already the spot for the Sim he placed in his cellphone. He began to find himself better organized.

Steven decided he would return to his workshop. While walking, a thought came to him. He had observed the future, and so far, everything he had noticed then about previous events, also occurred in the past. He learned of the fire as an historical fact, and lived it. Likewise, he knew he had met his duplicate twice, and despite not wanting to encounter him again, his copy confronted him the night of the arson. He remained bothered by the odd problem of Lily's machine failing to appear to his counterpart. He often thought about why, but ever since he had left his workshop, he couldn't see anything unpredictable. Only the notes from Lily's diary didn't occur, everything else aligned.

He had successfully disposed of the body of his older self using a fire he learned about in the future which, in the end, he became the arsonist behind it. He couldn't understand why his copy attacked him, until he returned to the past and in effect caused him to want to kill him. Steven thus realized that if he decided to break into his workshop when his truck was out, he wouldn't get spotted, in theory at least…

So after fiddling with the Uber app, he caught a ride on his brother's card and saw that the truck proved indeed absent. Sneaking inside constituted just a matter of using his key on the door. Not presuming he possessed plenty of time, he rushed upstairs and looked at the inventory in the apartment. He meticulously ensured not to disturb anything. No one but him had been here, so if he touched something, his future could guess his time travelling previous version would have done it.

He quickly located the parts for his quantum antenna. He would definitely get it. He had regretted failing to bring it with him, and the dust on the cardboard showed that his future self didn't care about it. He left the boxes there, in the same position as they had been, and just grabbed the antenna itself. Checking the apartment didn't reveal much, but he did find an old photo album he had kept.

Flipping through the pages, he once again strolled down memory lane of his life with Lily, so as to prevent the tears from rolling, he tried to think of other things. One of the questions that returned into his mind came from the fire: When he killed his future self, would that constitute a homicide (even if in self-defence) or should he see it as technically a suicide?

Lily's dress at the prom… Her bikini in the Bahamas… Her graduation gown from the University… Steven knew he couldn't keep the picture, but he grabbed his cellphone and photographed some of the best ones for safekeeping. The oddest thing, however, was that he didn't recognize some of them, and he wondered why. He even was in some of them!

Could this travel break the timeline? Was it possible that something occurred when Lily arrived which fractured the timeline in two pieces? So far, everything after he left proved identical, but things before that moment appeared murkier. This left identical things and non-identical events, and the division barely made sense. Going through the photo album had reduced him to tears. He had lost Lily, despite finding the means to prevent her death, but now couldn't think of an idea of when or where to find her.

Wait, he thought, that wasn't technically true. He didn't know where or when she lingered, because he failed to locate her at the various places, she said she visited in the book. Perhaps he could leave her messages. So far, he focused his search on a single direction: try to find her by physically coming in contact with her. What if he could imagine a way to leave her a message? What if he could somehow get her to change her course and set a rendezvous point?

Instead of hoping through time to catch her in each of her destinations, he could leave her notes that would hopefully reach her, travelling by car and bus instead of draining his time machine's batteries. Steven placed back the photo album, grabbed a garbage bag for the antenna parts, and left the workshop and secret apartment as he had found them. Just as he rounded the corner, he heard a noise behind him and saw his truck approaching from the other side. Running away, he turned the corner and wasn't surprised to discover his hands were shaking…

He decided to hurry up and walk three blocks before calling an Uber to get back to his former house. It remained too close for his tastes, but he had succeeded in avoiding detection. And he found a plan once again!

Chapter 3.11—Vague Message

Steven sat at the kitchen table above his time machine, with Lily's notebook, and began creating a list on a loose sheet of paper of destinations which were in his current future. The coordinates were in GPS locations, so he had to enter them in his phone and then, note down the actual physical address of the place.

Many of the coordinates were too far away, including the secluded beach Lily and him had found while canoeing in the Bahamas, a few locations in England and two in Germany. Many, however, seemed relatively close by: either in town, around town or a few hours away. If he could rent or borrow a car, he could most likely visit most of them in the span of perhaps two days, and still would need more time for full reserves. What he needed was to create a good message. What did he want Lily to do? He realized that the shorter and clearer the message, the better it would work.

After going through multiple iterations, he came up with: "Lily, meet me ASAP on your 40th birthday at noon, at the University, in front of our fountain," and it was signed: "Steven who has your quantum machine."

If the message ends up discovered by someone else, they couldn't really decipher it. It lacked last names, dates, and provided no clear idea of which fountain it was. Yet, his Lily would know when and where to meet him. He suspected that even if Sandra or George got a copy of the message, they wouldn't understand it was about time travel.

At first, the ASAP wasn't in it, but he remained afraid she would postpone the trip and that this would delay her significantly, to the point where she would visit the moment she would die. He just hoped her shooting wasn't on her 40th birthday... in front of the fountain.

"Oh shit," he thought... "What if someone else runs after her in a time machine?" So he modified his message.

"Lily, meet me ASAP on the thirtieth birthday of our first kiss, noon, in front of our fountain," and it was signed: "Steven who has your quantum machine." Yeah, that sounded better.

Lily would still know the date, but most people, apart from a few close friends and her parents, wouldn't know when they first kissed. It wasn't on their first date but rather on their second. Most people never heard about that little fact. As for the fountain, it felt now vague enough in his mind. Good. That seemed one thing done.

He wrote the message on a plain sheet of paper and tried to use his best calligraphy. After no fewer than three attempts, he had a message he liked, and he used the couple's all-in-one printer to make copies. If only he had found the computer password, but in reality, he knew almost nothing about them! They would have become so much more advanced than the ones from his era. Now, the big question was: How could he rent a car for two days without a credit card?

That remained something to seriously ponder. Without a stable revenue, he hadn't been able to keep a Visa and instead, had been using his wife's account while they were together. Ironically, a few years earlier, she began by using his, but back then, his card was restricted to a rather small limit. The bank set it to two thousand dollars, so when she got a ten-thousand-dollar gold Visa he cancelled his to avoid the yearly fee, an act he now regretted.

He could visit a few of the spots to drop his letter in town, including two around the city centre, the closest one about a thirty-minute walk away, and the next one barely twenty minutes later. He knew that once again, a walk would help him. While on the way, a new option came to his mind: what if, instead, he bought a rust bucket? Back in the day, you find a used car you can barely drive for less than a thousand dollars. The question was, could he perhaps pound some of the possessions of the new owners to get the missing money and sell back the car after two days to buy them back?

No, he thought. He would never sell it for as much, and the pawnshop must charge interest. He thought about using the time machine to play the lottery, but something Victor had said before dying still resonated with him. He had specifically said that he didn't play the lottery in his defence and as such, he wondered if, perhaps, that consisted of a way to catch rogue time travellers. He certainly didn't want to get caught at this juncture. After all, he technically never signed up for a permit. He therefore ignored the actual rules. Unless that worsened it? What if travelling without a license consisted of the worst offence of all?

He didn't know. Honestly, he didn't care. The old car felt like a bad idea. Using Uber on long distance was bound to cause problems. Perhaps using the buses? Not the mass transit inner-city ones. The ones like Greyhound, but they would surely prove expensive despite Lily's money from the time machine… The rest of the walk, however, he rehearsed his speech. He knew he had to say something about the message, but he couldn't figure out what exactly, and yet, eventually, he was in the shop of an art gallery dealing in old paintings, sculptures and artifacts. He could see some dresses, shows and other clothing accessories which indicated that Lily might have actually purchased some clothes from here in the future.

140

After looking at his notes, he saw that it occurred two years later. The note confirmed she would buy a blue dress on the right side of the store, on February eighteenth of that year.

"Pardon me, Madam," he said to the only employee on the floor. "I have a very odd request... You see, I want to surprise my wife for her birthday in three years and I know she loves your store. I was wondering if I could leave a note for you. She's been looking for a blue dress from the 19th century. I know I don't see one now, but one day, she will come by and buy one. I promise... When you sell such a dress to a woman in the next, say, two years, please ask if her name is Lily and give her this note if it is?"

"Oh my, that's a rather unusual request...", replied the lady.

"I'm trying to be romantic... If I just give her the note, it might ruin the surprise!"

"Romantic. I'd love for my girlfriend to do that, but she isn't into this kind of thing. It would be my pleasure... You say, in two years? I can't promise we'll remain in business that long!" she said, somewhat ashamed.

"Don't worry, I have faith in you...", he said, placing his hand on her hand to reassure her.

He left with a smile, but sadly, the second shop ended up a failure. It wasn't anything related to what she bought, according to her notes: an old purse. The store currently on located offered stuffed animals with little inventory. Seeing the price of the bears, he realized that this might consist of another of those boutique shops for women married to high executives. The schedule on the door certainly seems to fit as it's open less than 30 hours per week, and only Monday to Friday. Already, 50% of his hits ended in failure. Many of the places were apart from each other and would prove ineffective via Uber. Still, he called one to get to the other "cluster" of shops: it was on the other side of town and had three locations, two of which were already in business!

He remembered one as an actual antique shop he had visited in the past with Lily. The owner initially didn't want to deal with the letter, so he had to bribe him with a ten-dollar-bill. He didn't feel good about it… nothing to prevent the guy from just throwing the letter away after his departure and pocketing the ten dollars. More importantly, he wouldn't be able to give money to the majority of the shops. Still, the owner agreed to place the piece of paper on the wall, as if it served as a poster, right behind where the notes said she found the steam governor valve. If she did come seven months later, maybe she would see it.

Walking to the second one, he was already regretting giving the money and promised not to repeat it. The poster idea seemed interesting, since it eliminated the human interaction, but his list still offered dozens of places nearby to visit and didn't have hundreds of dollars to spend.

The third one remains the worst. It occupied a church basement where people could sell their own goods, with the pastor using the rental of tables as revenue to help them survive. Lily would only come six years later, so the chances that someone ran a spot that week remaining there in six years appeared slim. A pegboard for announcements existed, but they seemed rather recent, so the odds of his piece of paper lasting six years neared null. He stopped by a grocery store to buy hotdog sausages and buns, and ubered home. Well, his former home, pretty unhappy with his errands for the day and knowing that the other destinations remained located even further away.

Chapter 3.12—Voltage Check

Steven ate three hotdogs that evening while still thinking about his movement problem. It was already getting late, but he couldn't fall asleep. Opening her diary, he could see Lily travelling over the globe in her search, using longitude and latitude coordinates. He slowly and painfully entered each remaining coordinate one by one in his cellphone's map application and noted on a piece of paper where these other coordinates were. He knew that the diary was now his, but he remained afraid to write in it. To him, it possessed the status of a relic, a talisman, almost an heirloom.

The addresses at the first glimpse appeared to be chaotically ordered, but he figured that with a time travel machine, you could see eras and places in any random sequence. So, she probably noted in the order she visited them, along with the date of arrival, and a brief description of what she managed to retrieve. More importantly, each entry usually had a pair of destination, one directly on a building and the next nearby, either in a storage locker area or somewhere isolated.

While trying to digest his cheap sausages (eating them with high-quality mustard from the new owners of the house), he realized that some of the locations only contained one set of coordinates, and those looked secluded. What if one set of numbers noted where to find what she was looking for and the other was where to park the time machine? He knew of the longitude and latitude dials. He remembered that Lily had materialized at his place, but when he left, he arrived at their home so obviously, the box could also travel on the globe.

Steven had refrained from modifying those settings since he didn't want to land in the middle of nowhere or something, but he thought that now was the right occasion. He would try using only the coordinates found in the notebook, to make sure it would work. He checked, and the machine was now at 74%. He needed to perform a test run. His decision settled on the secluded beach his wife and him had discovered a few years earlier. Taking another picture of the controls with his cellphone before adjusting anything, he carefully changed the location dial to the destination from the diary. Before activation, however, he went upstairs and grabbed a towel... if this worked, he wouldn't skip walking in the warm Bahamas water.

Nervously, after unplugging the machine, he pushed the button and the faint familiar ding resounded, and the reserves counter dropped to 71%. He suddenly recognized how stupid he had been: if the move had emptied his batteries, the island offered no power outlet to recharge! Fortunately, the drain was of only 3%, so he could get back to civilization.

Still, he remained glad to see that the sun still shined in the sky, and he had enough light to check the surroundings for any boats or helicopters who could spot him and found nothing of interest. It's when he was actually swimming on the beach that he realized his mistake: He had forgotten to adjust the temporal control. He thus returned to the moment of his arrival, which was in the morning a few days earlier. The dial didn't work like a clock. It didn't move forward through time, as the time machine stayed motionless.

He dried himself, and realized he still had some water bottles. After drinking half of one, he used the other half to rinse the sand from his body. He had forgotten how it stuck to every part of your skin when it's partially wet! The sun helped him dry up, and after shaking the bottle, it was dry enough to slide one of the notes. He closed the bottle so that he could half bury it near the palm tree where he and Lily had rested on that fateful day.

He knew he had a lot to do, but then again, he had a time machine, so he took time on the beach to relax a little and think back on that wonderful day in the sun. Lily had even tanned topless on her own accord, and about an hour later, both had undressed on the beach and even had consummated their love. Steven laughed as he recalled Lily swearing she would never, ever try sex again on a beach. It's only later, when they were watching South Park, that he finally understood what she had meant. She then made such a good impression of Eric Cartman saying, "So what's the matter, you got sand in your vagina?" that it became a running joke between them until she disappeared a year later.

He found himself delighted to have brought his meal replacement bars. This allowed him to stay longer after the calories of his three hotdogs from... well, a few days into the future, remained memories and his stomach asked for another offering. Still, after a few hours in the hot sun, he re-entered the coordinates for his former basement, and put the target for midnight the evening of his departure for the Bahamas, draining 3% more. After a night of charging and a good sleep, Steven was back at the machine with a plan in mind.

144

He had already discovered that the loss of power increased proportionally to the time "distance" he travelled. He now believed that a small displacement in the temporal domain but a medium one in space affected the batteries a lot less: 3% from the Bahamas with a tiny difference of seconds. What he now hoped to try, consisted of an almost immediate teleportation, but how could he achieve that since the controls stood statically?

In the classic movie "Back to the Future," the De Lorean not only had three digital dials, they moved forward with the real clock. He hadn't understood it then, but could now. If he decided to jump to the same moment as he leaves, he would have to adjust the settings to about one minute into the future, and count down the delay until the present caught up with it. Very annoying… it made Lily's box a challenging to use teleporter… unless you also desired to transition on the temporal place by at least an instant. Even if Steven focused to do it perfectly, he couldn't link his cell with the machine!

Wait, he thought, could he even synchronize it? His phone always connected with the local network and as such would lose its time a few seconds after it arrived at the destination, but that worked only if he travelled within the United States! For the few trips to Europe, he wasn't sure how it would react. Still, for now, he set the longitude and latitude to a location about two hundred miles away, in a clearing in a forest. He didn't plan on actually leaving the machine there. It didn't have a key or anything to lock it, but he needed to test it. The charge rose to eighty percent, so he remained fairly confident.

Adjusting the target to half a minute into the future, he started the chronometer on his cellphone. Exactly at the right moment, he pressed the button and he knew the move occurred after hearing the faint "ding". He waited inside and saw that his cell did change its clock backward by roughly two seconds compared to the app: the jump itself probably took about that period! After validation, he had lost only two percent.

Opening the door, he saw that he was indeed in the clearing in the forest. Good... he thought, everything worked properly. Setting the destination back to his basement and to half a minute into the future, he repeated the operation, this time two seconds before the delay. This allows the chronometer on his watch to remain synced with the new time on his cellphone!

Steven had found a way to travel through space without moving temporally! Sadly on this occasion, the usage increased to three percent, or more than the two from the second attempt. After being confused for a minute or two, he laughed: in both cases, the drain might have been by two and a half percent or something like that, and the meter rounds the values. Plus, it's not as if such meters shined for their accuracy. People always thought that forty-nine percent on their cellphone for sure implied exactly forty-nine percent remained. It's more a measure of the voltage of the power pack which correlates with the theoretical discharge rate. In practice, a drop of one percent might not match the same thing when you're at eighty percent or at forty percent.

In fact, he was increasingly starting to realize that he was putting his life in the hands of a battery meter which might not have even been properly calibrated. Oh snap, a thought suddenly crossed his mind. He had a flashback to a project that Lily had done with him while he was studying. She wanted to build a custom UPS battery backup system powered by boat batteries and needed some meter of capacity. Steven felt happy for her initiative, and they built their UPS with a homemade charger and battery monitor. What this monitor had that he saw as special, rested in its ability to adjust the maximum voltage via both a potentiometer for fine adjustments, and a series of jumpers with increasing resistance for gross adjustments.

They worked for a few weeks calibrating it, making certain that the digital readout put a somewhat accurate percentage of remaining battery. The charger itself was still somewhere in his things, but Lily threw the meter years ago when she realized that a UPS proved more complicated than she thought: you needed an inverter, a system for switching the power, etc.

Steven opened the front panel (which he was now calling the hood) and checked behind the dashboard for the meter. He realized that yes, the machine contained the same battery meter they had built, with wires to interface it with a USB interface. Lily had changed the jumpers to handle the higher voltage. Steven could recognize his work: Lily had indeed built most if not the totality of the components with her bare hands, borrowing his parts she needed.

Looking around, he smiles as some parts reminded him of past projects. A relay system for high voltage, which probably served as the actuator for the time-travel system. He even realized that she rejected his system for generating too much noise for her tastes. She needed it for a project with the university to power animatronic of a fake steam engine, and the "click" was distracting. And yet, he was now able to place where he has heard the faint "ding" when he activated the machine. It ended up a side effect of his crude relay system for ultra-high voltages.

The problem with the voltage is that when the current flows, metal tends to "stick" and causes an arc when separating, which can end up in a catastrophe. This is why most light switches on the wall make a faint click. A lever violently splits apart the metal pieces, forcing the connection apart to prevent the current from arcing. What Steven's system did wrong is that when the violent separation occurred, the plates vibrated, causing the ding.

High-powered current doesn't tend to flow inside the wire, or in his case, metal plates. Rather on the surface, so Steven made them wide and long, as well as sturdy enough for repeated usage, but didn't account for the vibration when rapidly closing. That is, when activating the circuit, or closing it. Oddly enough, when stopping the circuit, (breaking the line or opening it), it didn't create much noise. Only when the system was energized and that caused the small "ding" heard in the cockpit.

Chapter 3.13—Vital protections

Impressed, Steven decided he needed to visit the hardware store. Instead of using the time machine, he let it charge and used an Uber to go buy several locks. He found five he could use and bought the whole lot. He thought about keying them the same, but realized that it would just waste money. Well, he did buy a keychain, a switch, some drill bits, screws and a few pieces of metal, just in case. Back home, well, back to his temporary home, he used the new owner's drill to drill holes slowly in the time machine to install the various locks on the important parts. He put them on the hood, the side door, the back battery hold and two of the side containers. The other two proved empty, so it didn't worry him that much. Maybe in the future?

He did encounter problems with the side containers, but with the metal pieces he managed to secure a latch system to secure them. Someone with an axe or a crowbar would probably pry them open, in fact, they would most likely ruin the metal door to the cockpit effortlessly, but he still figured he felt moderately safe. His "piece de resistance" consisted of the switch. He installed it under the hood, hidden from view, so that the push button which started the trip would be in serial line with it. If he turned off the switch, the machine would stay in place. Now, the machine, if found, would look odd, but would offer some protection against someone just changing the dials and disappearing forever with the machine. If someone stole your car, you could always try to find it by driving around until you see it, but with a time machine, they can go to the far future or disappear on another continent.

Chapter 3.14—Vacation hopping

Steven loaded up more water bottles, more messages, more food, and unplugged the machine. He had messages to leave. That afternoon, he visited North America in record time, especially when he decided to clone himself: by not changing the time destination, he would always arrive at 1:24 PM, the time of his last test. He could explore, find the stores he needed to drop the note, and on the next town, he would once again arrive at 1:24 PM.

148

Most of the areas he would park the machine ended up back alleys, in which he felt relief to have installed the locks. What did Lily do for protection, he wondered? Many of the towns only had one stop, and the "parking space" ending located within a few seconds or minutes of walking away. That helped him because even if time didn't move forward, a reserve reduction occurred.

Two of the antique shops were in rural Québec, and he found problems talking in English with the person on location, but otherwise, he didn't encounter many problems. Roughly half of the stores ended up thrilled to help him, with several of the clerks finding the gesture very romantic. Of the remaining half, many took the note, but Steven wondered perhaps they only humoured him to get rid of someone who obviously wouldn't buy anything.

After having completed the whole list of his destinations in about 16 hours, he returned home (still at 1:24 PM). He went straight to bed after a long day of work, and plugged the machine, which lowered now down to 54%. The next morning, Steven had found the solution to his cellphone problem: GPS satellites! They put GPS in place to provide a positioning system around the world, with four needed to offer a good precision, but they also proved useful for another non-obvious purpose: time synchronization!

Every GPS satellite transmits in its signal its clock so that your GPS receiver could calculate the offset of the milliseconds of difference between each of the signals. When you looked at a GPS map, you generally only cared about the position lock, yet with a special app, you could retrieve the UTC clock and the accurate current one for the city of your choice. This would allow him to find the exact moment precisely regardless of where he was on the globe: in an isolated Bahamas island… to sweeten the deal, he didn't need to wait for a complete GPS lock. As soon as he got reception from a single GPS (or Glonass, the Russian network), he would receive the time.

Steven still had three days in this vacation of the homeowners, so the next morning, he travelled backward to their previous vacation, but not before doing a good cleanup of their house. He didn't want them to suspect he had been there in their absence. That second week of vacation felt like a month to Steven, even if in reality, it only took him about eight days of personal time. He had to leave the machine to charge twice, so he ended up travelling only on two of the six days.

This time, thanks to the GPS trick, he covered Europe, including Great Britain, France and Germany. If he thought he experienced problems with verbal communications in rural Québec, these trips were even worse, and he could barely get 6 places in continental Europe to take the message, compared to over 17 in Great Britain alone! In fact, he spent a whole day just in Great Britain! This country birthed of the Industrial Revolution, after all. No wonder Lily travelled here the most.

This brought a fun memory of his wife: she would often joke or reign outrage using a British accent. He thought it came from her love of British TV shows, from Red Dwarf to classic Doctor Who episodes, but perhaps she simply spent more time than he thought in Great Britain? That reminded him: she had missed the revival of two of her favourite shows! Did she watch them in the future? Did she already know it would come back one day? The new Red Dwarf seasons ended up just fine, but the new Doctor Who proved amazing, at least, the Ecclestone and Tennant years. He had only seen some of the Smith episodes, not enough to form an opinion.

He needed to ask so many questions to Lily, and he felt close to run out of places to visit to leave messages. At least, soon, really soon, he would sit by a fountain waiting for his love to show up. After making one last visit around the house that had once been his, Steven felt confident that it was now in pretty much the same state as it had been when the new homeowners left. Sure, he used some paper and some ink, but that's not something that most people really count before going on vacation. He also tried not put the glasses and plates exactly the same way, but unless they had serious OCD, he doubted they would care.

The time machine showed a charge of 100% for the first time since Lily arrived. He had plenty of water bottles (he bought a 24 pack but previously rarely carried more than perhaps 2 or 3 while travelling), and even still a good reserve of meal replacement bars and snacks. He neglected to shave for a while, but Lily had never really cared about his beard or even his hair. She had always accepted him as he is. She did ask him a few times to put good smelling clothes, so Steven made sure to clean himself up.

Speaking of clothes, he used some of Lily's Euros while in France to buy new clothes. He couldn't use them in his hometown without raising suspicions, but in France, he found plenty of cheap used clothes to fill his wardrobe up. After days of wearing the same pair of jeans and the same worn shirt, it feels good to wear something different. He even borrowed some of the new owner's deodorant. Now was, if his plan worked, the moment he would meet his wife again. He couldn't mess it up. Unplugging the time machine, it's with a heavy heart that he programmed the longitude and latitude of an alley a few blocks from the university, and once on location, made sure that the locks were secured. His cellphone confirmed he arrived at the right place and at the right time: the 30th anniversary of their first kiss, in 2023. Good.

Chapter 3.15—View of the Plaza

Grabbing his bag, he walked until he finally saw the fountain in the distance. He passed by a lot of students buzzing around and even a few teachers, but no traces of Lily yet. It was only 9:47 AM, so he still would wait over two hours for their appointment.

He reached a bench, a new one he never noticed before, probably installed more recently. He found the little plaza to feel both very familiar and very alien from his memories of the past. It felt odd… The fountain persisted there, with the same statue erected decades before he first laid his eyes on it. The architecture around remained similar, but a few had received several updates, such as renovated facing or replaced roofs to a darker colour.

The differences came from the landscaping. The few trees now stood majestically towering over the area, bathing it in a cooling, encompassing shadow. The university placed a modern billboard on the side to advertise to people passing by. But the most significant change centred around the arch. The campus constructed a new arch in front of the plaza, providing a definite separation between the University and the street ahead of it. It provided a more formal look to the place, and it possibly consisted of an attempt by the University to clearly label the zone as being theirs instead of belonging to the city.

With a great view of the plaza, he thought back at why it had become their fountain. When Lily remained a student, most of her classes occurred in the Jackson building, just beyond the plaza, while he could easily park nearby on his lunch break to eat with her on the side of the fountain. He didn't eat there every day since sometimes, work kept him away, but she waited for him in case he came for each of them, or at least, those where the weather allowed it. He regretted not spending more dinners with her, as these were probably the best ordinary moments spent as a couple.

Those years offered a carefree lifestyle for them. They moved into their first apartment, stayed almost debt-free (she did have student debts, but who didn't?) and more importantly, he kept a healthy distance from the influence of his parents. George and Sandra still offered a big presence in their lives, and he really thought that this consisted of the moment when they provided the best models for them. They remained still young enough to do physical activities, but their relationship with Lily really moved from acting as parents to feeling like older friends.

Those dinner pauses thus allowed him and Lily to speak. To fully connect. To truly exchange. They didn't struggle with daily problems to solve. They didn't have parents to manage. They didn't have to discuss money management. They just spoke, soul to soul, without fear, without restraint, without hesitation. It's on the side of this fountain that they made plans on how to raise their kids, which they ended up never having. On which breed of dog they would buy, which they ended up never doing. On how to decorate their house, which they did buy, but never took the opportunity to decorate.

152

They reinvented the world. They solved the problems with the electoral college. They finally discovered the solution to solve racism in America. They planned novels, they quoted from their future plays, they outlined their TV series. They also reframed how to view the past, with Lily sharing her new thoughts on how the Industrial Revolution occurred.

Wait… her ideas were always seen as revolutionary, but by how much? In all honesty, they were book rewriting in substance and star making in style. Lily, one of her teachers used to say, "possessed the uncanny ability to take artifacts and place them in a very vividly described settings thanks to hard work and exceptional research". Steven smiled that Lily, in reality, acted like a great con artist. She didn't succeed via books: she observed them with her own eyes and studied not only their place in their contemporary society but also the people around it.

Lily had visited that era. She had crawled back through the currents of time. That wasn't the analogy she had used… the percolator. No… the colander! That's it. Progress always marched onward and a colander removed most of the jewels deserving of investigation. It kept to itself most of the juicy parts and only a few dropped through the holes and survived thanks to preservations, old antique shops or museums. Lily pretended she managed to locate by pure luck the various pieces she catalogued, but what if she lied?

As a historian, she needed to present receipts and proof of purchases to get her discoveries accepted. She couldn't just show up with artifacts she carried from the past. Even more, they used carbon dating and other techniques to place some of the exhibits on the timeline of the 19th century. Steven thought that most likely, instead of simply bringing these relics with her, she could uncover safe spots where to stash them, perhaps in the odd places where Steven had left notes. Or maybe gifted to a person she learned would give it to their kids until it would find itself in an estate sale, generations later.

That consisted indeed of a great con… she could take a mechanical piece in Great Britain, carry it to, say, South Carolina where no one would search for it or recognize it for what it was. It could make the long trip so that she would know when to pick it up. It would pass any carbon dating, and the chain of custody, or whatever the equivalent is.

That also solved the issue of why she selected the Industrial Revolution as her focus! It was close in time to have a similar English for her to blend properly, and sufficiently far so that few surviving elements would make it to the present in a satisfying condition. Plus, you could find steam engines almost everywhere, until replaced by newer models, often melted for raw metal. Back then, few people cared enough to preserve these machines which started the modern world. Lily picked well.

He thought back to the time when Lily brought him to go to the ancient book library at her university. Oddly enough, it was in the middle of the medical library, itself located in a circular building, where the core, the central room if you'd like, formed its own self-contained three-story structure. Most of the precious old volumes had been published between 1880 and 1920 in low circulation due to the type of publishing fashionable at that era. According to her diary, Lily travelled decades before that, in an epoch that, while within the modern world, wasn't nearly as documented as today, or even 40 years ago.

Steven checked his watch… it showed a quarter to noon. Anyway, where was he? Documentation. He then saw books that made it from the 1800s and even from centuries before that, but it was because they were frequently reprinted, as Lily explained. But the kind of writing she hoped to find included technical manuals created for the contemporary people of that time, not for researchers a century and a half later. When a company sold 100 machines, it might have produced a hundred guides. Eighty of them didn't even survive after the set-up, like those Ikea-instruction manuals discarded on the same day as the furniture had been assembled.

Twenty copies of something wasn't favourable odds for her colleagues… mould will destroy half of them, half of the rest burned to start fires on a cold night. Of the intact five, random basements would swallow three, never to resurface, with the remaining two available for research. Lily possessed a knack for uncovering those books, but any historian with a time machine would too! What she just needed to do was locate a good hiding place and let them age.

Noon had passed while he was lost in his memories. He kept trying to maintain the train of thoughts because he felt, deep within himself, that had Lily spotted his letter, she would have already found him. His wife never remained passive. She acted like a go-getter, and she had the earlier version of his time machine. Had she received his message, she would have known where he would park, she would have realized that he was searching for her.

He couldn't easily send her a note. However, she could reach him anytime she wanted. She only needed to leave a text document on the computer or write something in her diary or even pin a Post-it in the cockpit. He could name numerous methods she could contact him. He now truly possessed no idea how to find her. He was in her future, but despite having a time machine and the list of her steps, he had no way to actually locate her.

Noon did come, and it went. Steve kept this train of thought going, remember back on the best moments spent with Lily: their first kiss, their first trip, their first walk, their last fight… and the great sex afterward. He reminisced over her smile, her hair, and her laugh. He could almost hear it when the sun set over the plaza, and the shadow of the trees left his vision. In its place, he saw the fleeting final glimpses of the anniversary of the beginning of their relationship, slowly losing sight of the fountain where they shared so many meals. He even thought about how they never took a final lunch there. Well, technically they did, but at that moment, they hadn't realized it was the end. Lily graduated a few weeks after they stopped eating there, without knowing the previous time consisted of their last one.

And now, Steven was out of ideas. He had given it all, and he doubted he would even see Lily again.

155

Part 4

Chapter 4.1—Investments

Steven rejoined the time machine with his head down and his tail between his leg. Such a brilliant plan! He travelled the world to leave messages, he left a cryptic meeting that only Lily would get. But he now felt stuck… he couldn't return home. His future self now occupied it, who possessed no idea who he was. With the hardships he went through, he became convinced that something weird occurred and going home wasn't the solution. He could go anywhere and anytime with the machine, but he needed a safe place to recharge, and he needed money, both of which he didn't have anymore.

He could always crash with his brother, at a later date than the last he had seen him, but doing so would be seriously going backward. Not in time, but in personal growth. He successfully broke from his family when he moved with Lily and through hard work managed to become his own person and not another lazy clone of his ancestors like his brother became. Even worse: as technology evolved, how would he keep up with machines of that future? His job consisted of maintaining industrial equipment, and he could perform his job because as new technologies and machinery became the norm, he discovered them in real time. Time travelling cut him off from that exploration, from learning.

Already, before he left, he felt about 15 years out of practice, only servicing machines he already knew by heart. Add a few more years and new clients, and how would he deal with new technology? Granted, it might just consist of anxiety or fear of commitment, or any other such terms Lily used to throw at him when he felt afraid of moving forward. But Lily wasn't here to tell him which. She wasn't here to guide him and tell him which way to go. Lily appeared to remain nowhere, at least, not where he could find her, and that consisted of why he felt so frustrated at fate. Lily acted as his guide and now, he remained alone.

He knew, in the back of his head, that she probably got spoilers. She most likely knew what was supposed to happen and, as such, could give him tips on future events that she knew with the power of hindsight thanks to her time travel machine.

He needed to find her, not just because she completed him. His plan consisted of more than just to save her life, he also required to get serious answers on the truth behind their relationship. He felt that he planted seeds everywhere over the globe, well, at least, over the western hemisphere with the hope of finding her and he failed. Failed, failed, failed.

Damn it, he needed to do something. But what? He returned to his time machine. Ninety-one percent power left, no place to plug other than the last vacation he noted. It ended up his turn to explore, see the future, read newspapers in case they provide any help. Grab lottery numbers, stock charts, anything to help fund him when he could return to the present. He didn't think of a plan, but he possessed a future, and a shortcut to it, a means to get back from it to plan it properly.

With his time machine, he felt the urge to cheat destiny for selfish reasons and who knows! Maybe with enough resources, he would find Lily. First, he required funds. How do you create money when you have a time machine, and you don't want to attract attention? He pondered at his various options. In Back to the Future, one of the props consisted of a sports almanac, but that needed someone going the long way, without a time machine. A person consistently betting on professional games, forging relationships with bookmakers and judging when to fail (so they don't get suspicious) and when to cheat.

The stock market could probably consist of a better option except it required bank accounts with a balance he didn't possess. The lottery was tempting, but Victor had specifically said he hadn't played it, which meant that a time travel authority of some sort observed lottery winners. This made Steven very depressed that even with a time machine, a relatively poor person couldn't expect to generate significant money without a stable home, revenue or presence. Then, he remembered something… He hadn't bought a Sim card for his phone yet, but he was in the middle of a busy area, with the University and all. Walking around, he found a Staples store after a few minutes and went to their copy centre.

"Pardon me, can I print a page from the Internet?" he asked. The reply explained that black and white copies cost twenty cents per sheet, and colour ones cost sixty-five cents each, with no fee for the browsing itself.

In the self-serve section, he brought the page for the Powerball lottery and began looking at the FAQ page. Any prize of up to six hundred dollars could be claimed in cash at any retailer. Matching five balls awarded fifty thousand or one million dollars, depending on if you had the Powerball or not. With a combination of four that always gave one hundred dollars, which you could pay one dollar extra to multiply by two, three, four or sometimes even five, according to the selection made by the authorities.

This meant that he could turn three dollars into two hundred to five hundred dollars cash. Now, most of the weeks listed the two or three bonus factor, but enough revealed a five. He currently had thirty-four dollars left from the bills in Lily's stash and the change he picked up from the older Steven. It remained slim, and after printing the Powerball results of the last year, he at the moment possessed barely more than thirty-three dollars. He found a week when the multiplier showed as five and returned in time to two days before that day.

With four matches to win and thirty-three dollars, he could buy eleven tickets. The jackpot combination consisted of eight, twelve, twenty-one, twenty-four, forty-four, sixty-two, with the Powerball eighteen. Any four of the seven from that drawing would give him five hundred dollars, so he selected eleven groups of four numbers from the list. The first four, the second block of four, the third and the fourth, etc. and filled the rest with the losing options, picked randomly. He grabbed the sheet to purchase at a single place, but only procured one ticket there. Instead, he chose ten other shops in the area to order the remaining ones.

Steven found himself poor, homeless, and only left with a little food, but his situation would soon change. He travelled to five days into the future, and cashed his gains at the stores from which he bought them, giving him five thousand five hundred dollars. It wouldn't serve as a panacea. At least, he wasn't completely destitute anymore...

He went back another six weeks into the past, where the multiplier offered a four, bought twenty tickets for sixty dollars and made another eight thousand dollars. He was now in business, but it proved a risky and time-consuming business: he was boosting the number of winners in his town with time, something even him could find online! Therefore, he would need to travel a lot more in distance and time to collect his prizes to avoid detection. He needed a way to multiply larger amounts of money without leaving a historical proof behind him, and without having to prove his identity at any point in time.

He returned to Staples and, this time, printed the cost of gold over the last 10 years. He found the date where gold ended at the lowest, at $1150 per once, in 2023 or 3 years before his current date, and the highest so far was right now, at $1,543. That's it? Each trip would give him only about 1/3 in return on investment, with a very limited number of places where he could buy and sell gold in cash without eliciting suspicions.

Gold was in an upwards trend, however… so perhaps, just perhaps, in a few years, it would raise higher. With inflation, he believed it would reach over $2,000… If it did, he could double his money and, eventually, be able to buy a small house in cash. It would serve as an anchor point, as a permanent base if you will, maybe somewhere in the great west: it wasn't as if he remained limited in distance! He could even install solar panels to avoid an electrical bill. But Gold needed to be over $2,300, not attractive unless he doubled his investments. Or look at lottery options in other places in the world, where the maximum cash payout would prove higher?

He decided to make a quick trip to the future, say, 2050, to see what the value of gold would be, and if, perhaps, spot better options. The machine did the familiar "ding" when he arrived, and he waited for his cellphone to confirm the GPS time, but instead of 2050, it told February 6, 2037… Oh, oh. Something wrong occurred.

Why?

Chapter 4.2—Intercepted

Steven in slowly panicking: a beacon barred him just as his antenna had blocked Victor and then, Lily. This probably meant he was right next to it, with someone working on it. He listened and couldn't hear anything around him, just faint noises. Nothing showing his presence was discovered. He remembered that when each of the time machines showed up, he failed to hear anything either.

Making as little sound as possible, Steven draws Victor's gun from his bag, and gently opens the door. He sees that he's facing a grey cement wall, the kind you find in old schools. Could this come from a school project? Tip toeing, he exits the time machine, and peaks around the corner. He sees two men in the large room. One sitting at a table with instruments, and the other is working on what looks like his antenna. Both men are showing their back to him and talking to each other. They're wearing lab coats.

"I think the signals stabilized. Are you receiving anything?" said the guy near the antenna. He's holding an advance meter of some sort and receiving measures from it.

"Yeah, I'm getting several carriers, and I think they're where we predicted," said the man at the table.

"I'm getting them now. I think the big one is the moon. I mean, it's almost on one signal… and it's the closest one, so it makes a lot of sense," said the taller man with grey hair hunched over the antenna.

"Then which one is the Sun?" said the one on the table.

"I doubt we'll catch the sun much… it's not moving compared to us. The quantum receiver works like a Doppler radar: it only picks, and amplifies, relative movements. I suspect we only pick the moon because the planet is rotating fast compared to the distance of the moon," said the greying guy.

"So, the one on the right would be Jupiter, and the tiny dots would be its moons?" inquired the sitting one.

"It's possible… it's difficult to tell. And what are the small signals, is that really the noise floor or are we seeing satellites, asteroids? Cars? Planes?"

"Well, the theory is that only big objects or we would find those with a lot of relative velocity. If they aren't big enough, their signal will be weak. If they move slowly, they will remain aligned with the main carrier. I don't think we ever got a theory for the meaning of big." Wondered the scientist sitting at the table, which Steven realized looked much younger than the older one.

Steven slowly stepped forward, with his gun raised.

"Somehow, I fail to think the asteroids would show. Maybe with a better measurement device. I mean, now that we have the device working, perhaps we can find a way to make the signal clearer," said the older researcher, right before turning around and making eye contact with Steven.

"Who are you?" said the elder with fear in his voice. His younger colleague looked at Steven and, when he saw the gun, raised his arms.

"I don't want to shoot any of you, but could you unplug that…", said Steven, with a menacing tone.

"Sure…" replied the junior, as he flipped the power switch off. The display on his monitor turned off.

"Don't hurt us, please… we're just scientists… Wait, how did you get that box in here? Who are you?" said the younger man.

The older man's eyes widened, and he asked, hesitantly.

"Are you Steven Clark? You look like him, but from several decades…", said the senior by the antenna.

Taken surprised, Steven pointed the gun at him. "What? You know me?"

162

"You're the director of this project… this is your quantum telescope that you've been working on for the past what, 20 years?" said the fellow.

Steven was confused. Did he kill his future self? How could it possible that he remained still alive right now?

"What about my wife?" asked Steven.

The older man looked confused… "What about her?" he asked.

"Is she still alive?" Steven inquired.

"Well, yes, I suppose. I mean, you never said otherwise, but I last saw her maybe two years ago…"

Steven held no idea what the hell was happening.

"Where are we?" he asked.

"In your former laboratory… I mean, you retired last month, and we decided to continue your abandoned project."

Laboratory?

"Wait, is this a university, am I a researcher?"

"Are you really Steven Clark? I mean, you're so young, and it doesn't appear that you know much about your own life…", said the older man.

"Yeah, but I can't explain to you why. Can you just answer my questions?" insisted Steven.

The younger man had an epiphany. "It's a time travel machine. You're from the past… that's why you're young and confused. How does it work? Did you build it yourself?"

Steven asked him to shut up. He needed to concentrate, he needed to get out of here. He would need to avoid the antenna's signal, which acted like a beacon which now blocked him from the past.

163

The older man broke his thoughts and began quickly asking questions. "So let me guess, time travel exists, and your antenna blocks it. That's why you always refused to turn it on. You wanted to give yourself room to travel. Let me guess, the machine works at the quantum level. Is time travel common? Are you the only one? When we turn the antenna back on, will this block you here?"

Steven's head was spinning. Someone else now knew his secret... he would be stuck in a future where someone could stop him. He could find Lily, but an old married Lily, not his own Lily. He couldn't do to this future self what he had done earlier. It seems he was unable to cheat using time travel. He was stuck in the present, going the long way, in an era he totally ignored. An era using machines and technologies which he couldn't repair for a living due to the fast evolution in his field, and he became too old to learn again.

The worst is that Victor had implied the presence of a beacon in the future. He had implied it. But Steven hadn't listened, and now, everything was lost. The older scientist saw that Steven felt dizzy and decided to try and plead with him.

"So, I understand that you wish to go back home, but we don't want our past to be altered, " he said.

"What do you mean?" asked Steven, still holding the gun.

"Well, my theory is that anyone who initially gets a time machine will act to change the future to his personal advantage, right?" said the man.

"We could call that the first law of time travel," said the younger assistant.

"Yeah," added the older one. "So, the second law would be, let me think," he said. "If you discover a way to block such travel, you need to apply it as soon as possible to save your own existence from being threatened."

"Believe me, guys, time travel isn't as easy as it sounds. I mean, it's so risky. You don't have your cellphone connection and ignore the new rules, where everyone moves, etc.," said Steven.

"So why take a chance?" said the young assistant.

"In my original past, Lily got shot while travelling, so I have been attempting to find her!"

"Oh, that's like in the classic book. But if she weren't killed, you wouldn't try to avoid it, so she dies. … you can't use time travel to save her!" said the assistant.

"That should actually be the first law," said the older man.

"Nah, not in his case. My goal is to stop her from time travelling. She did it first. So, if I get her to come home directly and stop herself from leaving, won't that restore everything?" said Steven.

"I don't know… it's complicated. A lot of causal looping… Listen, you have the gun, we can't prevent you from fleeing, but we'll turn this back one once you're gone, and if you destroy it, we'll build another one…", said the older man.

"Don't tell him that, or he'll murder us too!" said the young guy.

"Don't worry. I don't intend you any harm. I just want to save Lily, and somehow, she's safe in your timeline. This gives me hope. It means I succeeded. Now, all I want to do is to return to my time. And who knows, maybe at some point, I'll meet you guys, remember you from today and bring you into the project. Perhaps, if you call me once after my departure, I'll confess that I knew this was coming," said Steven with as much confidence as possible.

Yet, he knew he was lying. This consisted of the third future he observed. In one, he killed his future self, a copy that never witnessed Lily appear in his workshop. Someone who possessed no memories of himself when younger. But Steven had been visited by her and in this iteration, Lily hadn't even left.

Could it be that each time travel trip creates a new timeline and that when he catches up to her, they will reach this third one? Did he need this interception by the antenna to join Lily? He had his concentration broken by the older man saying: "I supposed it's possible. Listen, please don't shoot us. We both worked with your future self... I'm even one of our close friends, you just don't know it yet," said the older man.

"And I have a kid... and my wife is pregnant...", said the assistant.

"She is?" said the older man.

"OK, I lied, I do have one... but we're trying to conceive another one... dude, I beg you...", said the assistant.

"Fine, but let me leave, don't interrupt me, or you might break your past...", said Steven. He got reassurances and returns to his time machine.

He entered the date of the last vacation of the new owners, as well as the coordinate of the house, and pressed the go button. Likewise, he heard a faint "ding" following by a weird hum. The battery reserves went down from 91% to 76%, but when he looked outside, he was still in the same place. No move occurred.

"Well?" asked the older man when he saw the door opened.

"I think I might be stuck because of the Antenna...", said Steven. "Let me try something else."

Steven programmed in the alley next to the fountain, and only three days beforehand. He knew that the shorter the distance, the smaller the drop. The faint hum occurred again, after the "ding". The energy pool lowered from seventy-six to sixty-eight percent, or eight percent. Looking at the control panel, he decided to change the last dial, set to 2 since he began his exploration to the highest number, on the flip cards, 79. The batteries dropped down to 42%, and he was still in the lab.

He stayed stuck. Panicking, he saw that the cards had reset to 0 on the next flip, so he cranked it until it went back over 79, and then, again, continuing until it reached #15. With wrapping around 3 times, if his theory proved correct, he was now set to 255, the maximum value you can get with 8 bits of data. It seemed fitting.

He pressed the button, and heard the ding without the hum, with the meter draining down to 1% right before everything powered off. He opened the door and saw that he was now in the alley by the fountain. After turning on his cellphone, and he confirmed that he did arrive at the proper place.

Peaking in the back container, he noticed that two of the batteries were smoking. He not only emptied them, but he also burned a couple of them. Bummer... And he was in a backstreet, with no electric socket. He needed those 2000 volts and remained now 500 volts short, with no way to recharge the remaining 1500 volts. How would he manage to repower and leave this place, assuming those 250-volt batteries even existed? He escaped the beacon, but he stayed in as much of a dire situation. Locking the compartments, he grabbed his supplies and walked into the city.

Chapter 4.3—Improvisation

At first, he walked around the University as if powerless to do anything to help himself, but he realized something very different from a few days earlier. A few days ago, he found himself homeless, timeless, friendless and insolvent. His only asset remained the time machine. Since then, it wasn't even working so he remained left homeless, timeless and friendless. But he's now with money... and plenty to spare.

He first booked a room at the motel near the University. It wasn't a big chain, just a mom-and-pop student place, but it accepted cash payments without any IDs, and he could easily walk to and from his stuck time machine. He felt exhausted, but he needed a plan, and fast. He couldn't remain here. Without any valid identification, he felt unable to do much. He needed to repair his time machine. Plus, 1% meant that just any standby current would drain those reserves up.

167

Wait, he saw plenty of room in that back compartment. Five hundred volts of batteries was roughly. Shit, 38 car ones! They wouldn't offer the same capacity, but it might prove enough to bring him home. He performed a mental calculation in his mind and yes, 38 of them would fit in the back room, if he stacked them properly. He might also be able to take those 38 into two banks of 19 to recharge 2 at a time. Again, a full charge proved out of reach, but that's not what he needed.

He went to the local car shop and bought 20 batteries, and 8 chargers, bit by bit as he remained on foot. That's their full inventory for chargers. Each batterie only came 90% full, and he required more than 20, but he needed to start somewhere. He paid a cab for the delivery and while asking the driver to wait for him, he slowly brought the lot to his room, one item at a time. He picked a few more rooms, as they proved affordable, and plugged the first eight in different outlets of different rooms, hoping he wouldn't bust the breakers, and everything seemed to hold.

The taxi driver helped him find other car shops and auto stores and soon enough, he had rented even more rooms from the motel to plug the 38 batteries and chargers. He also bought basic electronic tools as well as plenty of copper wiring. Steven gave a huge tip, and left smiling. He would now try to work on one of the 250-volt originals. After trying to lift one, he ended up buying a trolley devil from Walmart to carry the lot to his quarters.

He didn't have enough voltage at the inn to connect one of the originals directly. He did possess plenty of those for cars he could link in a row to augment the voltage, and more to wire in parallel to increase power. The good news was that starting at 90%, the new ones soon finished recharging. He made a new circuit and plugged 19 of those from his first purchase into one of those from the time machines to charge it. Then, he repeated the operation on the other one, using a simple current limiter process to prevent overheating anything.

Every few minutes, he would test the voltage of the large batteries and see that it would charge slowly, but surely. It would allow him to charge enough, perhaps just for a single jump. He watched over the circuits the whole night, obsessively checking the temperature of each of them. After draining his thirty-eighth new units, he reconnected them to the power grid, and exchanged his two partially refilled 250 Volt ones with the next pair. With a few hours to kill, Steven took a long nap to rest.

Over the following three days, he alternated between working on the 38 he purchased and employing them to fill the originals until he felt confident he would have plenty of juice for a trip. Now mentally ready to go back home, he waited due to the light rain outside. He didn't want to risk water shorting his batteries in transit. He did check up on the machine, but it was protected sufficiently in the alley and waterproof enough to remain there.

Meanwhile, he used the day to review his timeline at the public library's computer. Lily made the news on several occasions for her excellence in teaching, and Steven had received a grant for research on a project. Unlike his timeline, Lily hadn't discovered artifacts from the past and instead, most of her focus rested in the purely theoretical field. The industrial block where Steven had set up shop was still standing, but the record company had closed much earlier. Maybe Steven had really helped it survive a few more years while he was working there. Steven and Lily, according to the little information he could gather from social media, birthed two kids, a son and a daughter, with no additional data on them.

In short, they seemed happy, at least, from the outside.

The next day, the rain had cleared. The time for the great move arrived! Making several trips early in the morning, he managed slowly to plug his batteries back. He already wired them together for the charging, so he only ensured he would supply the full 2000 volts the system required. When he came into the machine, he noted the meter indicating 67%, but he realized it was lying: two of the batteries consisted of chains of lower capacity car batteries. Nonetheless, he would get his hands on the batteries from Victor's time machine. They were identical after all…

169

He adjusted the time to a few hours after his own departure and specified the coordinates to his shop. He readied to press the button, when he remembered he played with the singular dial he still didn't know which purpose it served. Quickly, he reset it to two, as it previously stood. He glanced one last time at Lily's notebook. Several of the entries in her travels had the number 11 written in the margin, or in a few rare cases, just the number 1. What if these weren't in decimals, but rather, in Roman numerals?

Most of the destinations in other periods had eleven scribbled, while those in his era were mostly just had a one. Others has 111. On a hunch, he set the unknown parameter to one instead of two and pressed the button. "Ding," replied the system, leaving a charge of four percent. Steven slowly exited the cockpit. He was in his workshop, and Victor's time machine was indeed tucked in the corner of the room. The table with his instruments lied there, with the antenna still present roughly in the centre of the room.

He ran upstairs and opened the freezer. Frozen, Lily's body remained there. Steven made it home. The cupboard, the refrigerator, everything lingered exactly as he remembered and even if his truck stayed parked outside.

Steven was back home.

Chapter 4.4—Introspection

The first thing he did was remove two of Victor's batteries and plug them into Lily's time machine. He then realized that for a long time, he thought of the time machine as his own, but that now that he was back home, it returned once again hers in his mind. Odd. Removing the 38 car batteries took longer, but within an hour, he had plugged Victor's batteries and resumed once again charging the time machine, using his own electricity this time around. That reminded him: he plugged back his original Sim card and finally was back on his ordinary cellphone plan. Everything was almost back to the way things had been when he left. He just possessed a lot more money in his bag and lived a lot of interesting experiences.

Instead of living tight with money, he still owned a little over $9,000 left from his winnings after paying for his batteries, chargers and hotel rooms. Carefully, he split his bills into two piles: those printed into the past and which he could use right away, and those from the future, which he could only use when visiting the future. He wouldn't want to attract police attention for paying with fake money! Granted, a few ended up between the two stacks, as they would soon start existing. To his surprise, he could already spend $6,000, a sign that currency needs time to change. He could always take the remaining $3,000 to the future and exchange them for older bills.

Still, he found his way back home. He returned to having no rent or electrical bill to pay thanks to letting the human resources company fund everything. He sat in his comfortable bed and a cozy apartment. Sure, he needed to imagine a way to get rid of Lily's corpse, but now, he knew exactly how. Gently, he wrapped her body in a comforter, and put her in the back container of the time machine. He also grabbed his shovel. Searching on his GPS, he found what he was looking for a deserted atoll in the Pacific. Using its coordinates, he teleported himself there, in the middle of nowhere, and began digging a grave for his loving wife. He knew it wasn't appropriate enough, but at the same time, he knew he would save her. One way or another.

Once the grave felt deep enough, he gently placed her in it and said a prayer for her. He didn't know any. His family hadn't really practised any religion, but he thanked God for giving him the chance to try to save her. By the end of the prayer, he mostly spoke to her, promising her that he could do well by her. With only the sound of the wind and the waves, he put back the sand he removed, but didn't leave any markings. His goal remained to hide her body, not make it obvious where her tomb stood.

He now needed to find the live one in the future, and now, he discovered a new dial to play with to find Lily. He now thought that the number 2 didn't offer a good choice to find her. He dropped almost 50 notes and none of them panned out.

But Steven found a new problem. His sudden interruption in 2037 when his employees will power on his antenna, meant a narrow band of time to explore. He found himself now stuck between 2014 and 2037... He only possessed 23 years in which to find Lily. 2014 was when he turned on his antenna, and the 2037 block occurred when his future/former colleagues turned it on. He no longer disposed of free rein to visit the past and the future. He would forever be stuck between those two dates, stuck and unable to search for Lily outside these bounds. However, he knew she came from the future: she arrived when he powered it off, and Victor materialized from the past, when he turned it on. It thus seems clear that she came from the future, but not more than 23 years away... That gave him less ground to cover.

He thought, what could he do with the remaining dial? What purpose did it serve? Timelines? Could it remain that simple? Could the machine somehow travel through different timelines? That wasn't it, he thought. In theory, each time someone time travelled and inserted a change, it would create a new timeline. Was this something else... new dimensions? That must be it. Lily was travelling in #2 when he activated his antenna, visibly from #1. He had never moved the dial from dimension 2 for any of his travels, which explains why his future self didn't see Lily return. This is why his future lacked memories of his own present: that guy wasn't his future self. It ended up his future self from a parallel dimension, #2.

He didn't know in which dimension the 2037 antenna had been. The machine didn't report the current number and he failed to think of a way to check for that with his GPS. But he needed to be something far because he only managed to put some distance from it when he set the value in the 200s. That one being probably situated far enough to ride around the beacon, and it still burned out two of the batteries doing so. Would he find a way to go around the 2014, dimension 1 antenna via a detour to a high-value dimension? Possibly, but perhaps with even more loss. Unlike the version in the future, powered on for only a few minutes when he tried to cross it, his stayed on for several hours.

Still, Steven felt confident. He now had a whole new pair to explore: #1 and #3... and coordinates of exactly where to find his wife.

Part 5

Chapter 5.1—Notebook

Steven came back home from the atoll and began imagining a plan. If he couldn't travel to the past, neither could Lily. He wouldn't be able to reset his own timeline so that she would just return home. The fact that Lily had disappeared in #2 and not in dimension whatever, meant that somehow, perhaps, in nearby ones, the Lily copies vanished due to his antenna, perhaps collapsing into a single one? Maybe stuck in other dimensions? Or was it just Lily #2 and #1 that left?

He regretted ignoring the number of the dimension where he was stopped in the future, but any in which Lily doesn't vanish means a local Steven and Lily would be living there. What Steven wanted to discover a way for the both of them to experience a legal, fulfilling life. The two of them couldn't just usurp their local version, and even if Lily returned in #1, how would he explain this to the police? How would he justify that his wife was back after 15 years but hadn't aged a day in her life?

How could she assume her previous role without causing newspapers, the media and, well, everyone not to wonder where she had gone? Her job would no longer remain hers, now 15 years outdated with history research, and he doubted she would be able to get tenure a second time around. Even if they managed to make the world accept her disappearance, it didn't mean the problems he accrued over the years since her loss would vanish! What would they do for a living? Where would they stay? His secret apartment functioned for saving money, but would Lily agree to move in such an improvised location?

They would have, in theory, twice the machines, however, so that they could keep on cheating just as he did for the lottery, but would he remember everything if he saved her, or would it reset his life? Because going back to the present of her disappearance might seem to work, he could move around the beacon, again, via a detour. The problem wasn't her, it rather centred on him.

If she returned to 2002, his present self would remain there, unaware she time travelled. It might feel selfish to his past copy, but after over a decade of depression, he now became hopeful and not willing to just give up on everything just to undo her tragedy. He would lose his personal growth. He feared that rescuing her would reset the timeline, or would she possibly arrive at the antenna while alive? Even if she did, that still left their problems unresolved. She would need to explain where she stayed for those missing 15 years. But then, they would have a single time machine, no? Since he wouldn't have travelled back to save her, what would happen to him?

This was giving him a headache, and it wasn't his style to just assume the best would come. He must think of a cleverer plan, so while the machine remained plugged, he began making one. What he needed consisted of a dimension in which he would settle with Lily, with a stable source of income, meaning a world where they could take over the identity of the local Lily and Steven. So, what should he do first once the batteries will finish charging? Should he discover a suitable settling place or locate Lily?

He knew what he wanted to do, more than anything, else… and it consisted of finding his wife. It remained his goal, his purpose. But he knew his wife. Lily liked predictability, stability and confidence. He always thought that his presence constituted her number one source for the three. More and more, he began to see that by living as a time traveller, she probably could find some of that security by herself.

It's something he never fully understood. How could he provide her with a feeling of safety? It's Lily who became the person he relied on for his own security. Before dating her, Steven had always felt empty, alone, distant. He rarely believed that he fitted in with others or even society itself. He came from a rich family of capitalists whose origin of income consisted of using the money they inherited as investment to get more. Furthermore, he wanted to labour with his hands, making him a black sheep within his family and their friends. Yet, at the same time, he lacked the common social skills that ordinary people learned and couldn't relate or connect with them.

Lily knew exactly how to deal with him and help him grow as an adult. She showed the value of his inner being and of his work, instead of only of his investments. She taught him empathy, something he perceived to dwell within him but never truly saw expressed in his presence. He learned respect, for everyone around him, not just those who could one day prove useful.

But Steven had revealed to Lily the importance of taking risks, of leaving the warm comfort of your blanket. He showed her that yes, a few people around her felt indeed very close to her, yet that he and her could go out without them and still enjoy themselves. That she could venture out one night and just waste a pleasant evening on the run. Steven, of course, realized that thanks to his disinterested parents, yet for Lily, it offered a new experience which seemed both exciting and reassuring.

He taught her to have inner self-confidence instead of relying on others to provide it for her. Somehow, he trained her to say no, when appropriate, to take care of herself, and to block a friend who acted abusively toward her. He didn't even know he possessed anything like that within him, but she still revealed it. She allowed him to feel useful to her.

So yeah, maybe he wanted to see her as soon as possible. In reality, he needed a plan, a destination, coordinates for her to put in her own version of the time machine so that she would be able to follow him. He needed to find a base first. A space where Steven and Lily could move after their meeting so that they could have some peace and quiet, and a location to charge their machines.

Steven did have a thought… he picked up the remaining batteries from Victor's time machine and placed them in the back of his machine: that way, if other batteries broke, he could at least replace them! Waiting for the charge, Steven went to the store and purchased his own notebook. He had some travelling to do, he might as well log it.

Chapter 5.2—Nest hunting

The plan felt rather rudimentary. He found an alley near the public library where an unguarded power outlet for a hobby shop allowed him to save his power, in 2036. The shop ended its schedule early on Tuesdays, but the library stays open until 8 p.m. He would simply travel to 2036, on Monday, July 8th, at 6:34 PM, when he felt sure the store was closed. He would plug the time machine, go to the public library and research for a little under 20 minutes on the events of that dimension. Changing to the next one at the same location used a bit under 3% of reserves, and plugging the machine for 20 minutes gave 0.45% of batteries. This signifies that, on average, he could do close to 30 jumps before returning to base and still have over 25% of capacity left. This also meant he would do that in about 13 of his hours, counting occasional pauses.

After 30 trips, he would rest for 3 days of downtime before he could do 30 more.But did he need to lose three? Victor's machine might not possess the right plug, yet it featured an excellent charger. Lily's system, connected serially, simply powered hers in a row. Victor's device used an intelligent parallel one.

Here is the beauty of Victor's design. Wait, he didn't create it himself, but since Steven ignored who did, he called it Victor's. So, as he was thinking, the charm of Victor's pattern is that in a parallel wiring, the charger could more finely control the level of each of the individual units. Lily's version couldn't accommodate different states: they ended connected up at once, and only their internal circuit prevented accidents.

Of course, in theory, Victor's design meant increasing the current, but the voltage also remains lower, so in effect, it didn't change much thanks to it's on board transformer adjusting to the supplied input. Carefully, Steven dismantled Victor's powering circuit and adjusted it to an empty space in Lily's box, fitting it in the existing electrical plugs. He did need to go buy ten rugged relays to enable switching the wiring from serial connection, to supply current to the machine, or parallel mode, to top-up the system. He lost the possibility to do both, since the cables he installed ended up incompatible. Filling up would use a different path from the consumption of the stored energy.

After some testing and playing with his transformer, he raised the input voltage from the hundred and twenty volts to two hundred and forty volts. This allowed to reuse Lily's cable with Victor's charger, enabling him to pull more current than previously and capture more than thirteen and a half amps at once. This increased current and the better optimized charging system heightened the refilling time to two point three percent per hour, or forty-three and a half in total! That meant less than two days!

For the ingenious part of finding those volts, Steven remembered a trick he learned from George. In the USA, the input power to the electrical box is twice the voltage of ordinary sockets, but it splits into two, each offering a hundred and twenty volts. This is why narrow breakers have "a" or "b" next to them, while the electric dryer one take double the size. To deliver the full voltage, you just need to grab two of your halves, an "a" and a "b". Therefore, Steven wired two long cables that when connected to sockets from different sides, would supply the whole spread on Lily's charging cable.

Steven prepared his notebook. He traced a series of the lines, from one to three hundred. He drew vertical lines and left space to put a code in them. His initial visit was to dimension four, the lowest one he hadn't heard of in his travels. The hobby shop and the plug worked, so that ended up his first checkmarks. He left the alley, and now both the library and the street looked identical to how it did in his timeline. That's a second checkmark.

The library let him use the computers for free, and he began his search. Lily did vanish in 2002 and no sign of himself dying or disappearing. That meant placing X marks twice in the next two columns. No worries, he was ahead of schedule and soon enough, was in #5 where he got the same exact result. This was discouraging: he assumed the dimension to look rather different. He expected each one to react as if they owed their existence to shifts in timelines caused by time travel itself, but it seems he anticipated wrongly. If Lily indeed provoked a change in those dimensions, he failed to see a sign of it.

At #11, however, he noticed a notable divergence. Their Steven died in a car accident four years after Lily disappeared. Not something that would help him much, but still a start. He noted it, since it remained the best candidate so far. More interestingly, #12 seemed virtually identical in his criteria as #10. So, #11 sat outside the norm like a freak exception. He just needed another one to differ in a more positive way.

Steven had read the Amber chronicle by Roger Zelazny as a teenager. In it, the royal family of Amber can shadow walk, meaning walk (or drive) through alternate worlds by concentrating on small modifications. Each time they changed course, they would slide into a new dimension. Turn right and the sky shift to a slightly darker colour, go right again and the firmament becomes purple. Pivot left next, and trees replace bushes, etc.

He loved the books not just because they showed a protagonist able to alter his world, but also because his family felt somehow just as dysfunctional as the siblings from Amber. He identified, of course, with Corwin, the prince who decided to rebel and take over Amber, their own kingdom and the only true dimension. The rest were shadows… echoes of the original.

Still, Steven expected these other dimensions to react like in Amber: the further away you travelled, the more variations would you get. Star Trek, after all, only has two: the main and the mirror evil one in which those characters wore a beard! Instead, either Lily left in 2002 or she died even before that. Those which revealed her as alive, showed her married to her Steven. He needed a place to settle down without his counterparts. As the number of dimensions went by, he grew more and more discouraged until he hit #28.

It seems he had finally found the jackpot! It's the first one in which Lily hadn't vanished early, but even more excitedly, both Lily and Steven disappeared while on a cruise in the Bahamas in 2009. What thrilled him the most on that prospect consisted in the fact that his Lily, who would still only be twenty-seven from 2002, could possibly pass for a thirty-four-year-old in 2009. Steven, now thirty-nine, who avoided gaining weight in his thirties, could probably pretend to age badly.

Going past the antenna would mean a trip by a high dimension, but it would remain a one-way jump anyway. Thinking, he realized that since they vanished without a trace during a cruise, it would prove easy for him and Lily to just reappear at the proper rendezvous point and resume their lives.

Reading their eulogy, it seemed like Lily still became a University professor, while the local Steven had a very successful maintenance company. No kids, but a nicer house in the suburbs. It would be difficult to impersonate their current versions with friends and colleagues, but it would become a problem in any dimensions! He still checked #29 and #30, since he was on a roll. In both of them, Lily disappeared in 2002. Only #28 which seemed like a freak exception.

Chapter 5.3—Navigating past the beacon

Steven now knew he could go before turning on the beacon via a long detour, but he was less than enthusiastic about the idea of finding her in the revolution era. He knew nothing about it, and the fear of breaking the present felt even worse. Despite operating a time machine, something nagged at him, telling him that finding Lily before she left wasn't the solution. It wasn't the way to solve the problem.

He felt like the past reacted a little like concrete. The recent past could always change, but could the distant past? Even if only as distant as 2002, that seemed risky. And yet, the past offered something he missed. Someone remained mysteriously absent from his research. Someone who surely knew more answers about some of the details that eluded him. The other person who most likely unwillingly contributed to the time machine construction.

Lily possessed a lot of capacity. He considered her very competent, but she remained just one person. Steven had cut the panels, but he never soldered the seems. He never even helped her hold the panels in place. Sure, maybe she used tools, and rigs, or corner vices. Potentially, she did it completely on her own, but something tells Steven that she asked for help from the other man in Lily's life: her father.

George ran an errant when Steven went to pick up the monitor. He perished due to a car accident when Steven saw his wife again. In the end, George had always been on Steven's mind, but never delivered any answers, and it seemed like the right moment to fix that. He didn't possess any idea when to actually catch George. He knew that two years before turning on the beacon, before George fully retired, he worked at a construction project on the east end, wiring the houses under construction.

He knew because the plumber for that project also executes gig works at DryTek and mentioned that he saw Steven's father-in-law the previous day. This would prove difficult to pin down fully, but he could charge his time machine. He could pick the time, location and dimension. He even fully secured it. The issue now consisted of finding a location near the project. He chose to arrive at night in case his parking stop revealed itself inadequate.

Flipping again to #255, but at the same time destination, he only lost fourteen percent of charge, with no busted batteries. That made a huge difference. Going back to 2012, he entered the location of the project he was working on in dimension one. A little more battery lost, but still only twenty-one percent, and no beacon stopping him.

He arrived finally before the moment he messed everything up. He ended up in a middle of a dirt road with foundations recently poured and with the casings still in place. No one was there, so after a little walk around the neighbourhood, he found a completed house for sale and teleported to park in its basement, locking the machine down as best as he could and turning off the secret switch.

With no power yet in the building, he figured he might stay safe. The home looked ready, but not hooked up yet. Steven landed in the middle of summer, so even strolling around felt comfortable enough in the middle of the night. Walking from lot to lot, he located the one with the only electrical tasks pending. He found a box with switches and outlets, which indicated the one actively being worked on. After eating a meal replacement bar from his bag, he lied down on the floor, next to the boxes, and got himself a nap. When time travelling, he realized, take any opportunity offered to catch up on your sleep.

In the morning, George woke him up.

"Steven? What are you doing here?"

"Hey George. I didn't have any gigs today, and I heard you were working here and thought I could keep you company. We haven't spoken for a while."

"A long while. I always liked you, Son."

"And I liked you too. You were more of a father to me than my own."

"Well, I have a lot of work, if you want us to talk, come back at lunch or follow me around," he says, smiling.

"Or I could carry your tools, like that first day you hired me."

He laughs. Georges possesses a deep grandfather laugh, he always did. Well, as far as Steven knew.

"Sure, but I can't actually pay you."

"If you recall, you didn't actually pay me for that first day," replies Steven.

"I didn't?" he says, confused

"Lily begged you to help me."

"Yeah, when she gets, well got an idea in her mind, she didn't let it sit there."

"Indeed, she didn't"

"So, grab the boxes, I finished the primary wiring yesterday, this morning I install the junction boxes, the switches and the outlets."

"Gotcha. And this afternoon?"

"The ceiling lights, and then, I move to the next house. It's simple work."

182

"I see that."

"How did you figure out I was here? Did you call Sandra?" he says, when they reach the first missing junction box.

"No, it was Allan, the plumber."

"Right, he also works at DryTek. Why they need a plumber, I don't understand."

But Steven knows.

"They have steam to undo the folds on the fabric."

"Right. Not so much water pipes, steam pipes"

"Well, steam is water…", Steven says, which makes George laugh again.

"Is that cranky foreman retired now?"

Steven thinks, this is before his last interaction with him, in a few days, but so long ago from his point of view.

"Yeah, not retired yet. Still going on about Peerless"

"Wow. That was before what, 94, 95? That's a long grudge."

"You know about them?"

"Oh yeah. It was a big deal in town."

"Can you tell me about it? I couldn't find that much information online."

"Right, I suppose it's in the past, forgotten. I'm not a historian, but my daughter is," he says, laughing. "Well, was," he adds, sad, as he wires the first junction box in quick time, and then, moves to place the first switch box, which Steven delivers.

"What happened?" asked Steven.

183

"They made NAFTA in part to kill them after their government basically dumped them."

"Do you know more?"

George looks at Steven.

"Yeah, so in the eighties, the new fad was wool suits, but the high-quality wool was from Italy, which the USA charged a thirty percent import tax on to protect our industry."

"I get that."

"So Peerless wanted to keep importing wool from Italy into Canada without almost no tariff, make suits under the free trade agreement. They then could sell high-quality ones at a fraction of the cost, killing companies like DryTek which supplied business wear makers in the USA."

"They made jackets and pants and such?"

"No, they made wool fabric to make them. We had three suit factories in town, but two closed prior to the trade deal, and the last one nearly shut down, forcing DryTek to pivot when they lost most of their market."

"Wow. And who won?"

"Well, free trade in 1989 was just with Canada, but in ninety-four or ninety-five, they added Mexico. It was out of the question that Peerless, and their competitors could keep going from the USA's point of view, even if Canada promised to protect them."

"So, what happened? We pressured them?" Steven says, as they move to install the outlets in that room.

"I guess. Peerless wanted to import 3 million suits per year, our biggest company, Marx, wanted zero. In the end, they compromised on allowing only one point four million per year. Not even half'

"So, they suffered?"

"Well, they focused on the high-end buyers, and it kept their domination over the US market. Eventually, they even acquired Marx and today, they make most of the best suits, including Calvin Klein, Ralph Lauren, Hugo Boss and so on. I mean, DryTek is doing well right now, but I suppose that for that foreman, he can hold a grudge for decades, it seems."

"Now, he's mostly complaining about China and Bangladesh."

"Makes sense. But see, I have fewer problems with them."

"Why?"

"Canada is a developed country, Peerless was taking advantage of how the USA was keeping some wool out. They didn't do it out of despair, they leveraged our attempts to protect our industry against us. But Bangladesh, God, have you ever heard about them?"

"I can't say I have."

"They got into a brutal war for independence from Pakistan, during which a genocide occurred. It was horrible."

"Oh my, I had no idea."

"Yeah. It was during the Vietnam War. It didn't get that much coverage. Well, on top of that, the monsoon floods most of Bangladesh every few years, plus cyclones, tornadoes and soil erosion as it's trying to develop."

"You seem to know a lot."

"Well, you know our Bengali neighbours, no?"

"Mr. and Mrs. Hasina?" Steven replies, confused.

"Yeah"

"But aren't they from Bengal?"

George laughs.

"Bengali is their language. It's the language of Bangladesh."

"Oh, I didn't know."

"Me neither, but I listen. I get people to talk about them. That's how I learn. I mean, Lily didn't fall far from the tree. Had I been more supported, I might have become a historian, but back in my days, you had to work with your hands, you know?"

"Any particular field of interest?"

"What do you think?" he says while wiring a plug, which reminds Steven how George had a habit of making other talk.

"Electricity"

"Yeah, Son. Electrification. I mean, have you ever seen a house with a knob and tube installation?"

"I have no idea what that is."

"See, the wires, they're in a group of three. Live, neutral and ground. You need two, right, to form a circuit, but the third is to protect against electrocution."

"Yeah," says Steven. He learned all of that in his degree.

"But with knobs and tube, you only pass one wire at a time, and you wrap it in a cloth which isolates it. It doesn't actually touch the walls. Instead, the electrician suspended the raw cooper between them, and where it does touch, little knobs or tubes of ceramic are used to isolate them."

"How is the neutral handled?"

"It's routed back via another path, like water in short. Water comes in one pipe, and leaves in another following a different path."

"And the ground?"

"No ground. Touch a wire and die. Squirrels love to eat the cloths, making the wires bare and then they just became fire hazards."

But Steven sees something in George's eyes.

Sandra offered the main source of Lily's compassion and kindness. Georges could do both, but more importantly, her father clearly stimulated her intellectual curiosity.

George, Steven thought, might just remain an electrician by trade, but he was walking, living encyclopedia of personal histories.

And not just about the past. He could tell you about the new public library building, for which he did the electricity, but not just from the perspective of the building. Also, how it came into being, how it was financed, why that location ended up picked.

"I have a question for you, George."

"Shoot, Son"

"I did some panels for Lily a while ago. Like, when I was in trade school. Big ones, like minivan size, and I didn't help her assemble them. Weren't you the one who did?"

"Oh boy, that takes me way back. Was that for the train exposition that got cancelled?"

"I don't recall," says Steven, lying. He never heard of a train exposition.

"She wanted to make a train simulator, but it had to run on batteries because it would be outside. I helped her build it, with the storage bins for the teaching materials, but then, it got cancelled, and she got a mover to put it in storage."

"Were the batteries installed?"

"Now that I think about it, no. I did racks for them, but she ended up not buying them. Why?"

"Oh, I found the system at a metal recycler when I went to pick up scraps with GTW."

"I guess the college got rid of it. It wasn't small."

Steven laughed. "It wasn't. Did it use huge gauge wires by chance?"

"Hell no. Why?"

"Some were in there."

"I guess they put her projects together when she disappeared. Those wires were for her Tesla coil project. Didn't you help her with that?"

Steven had no memory of such a project.

"I don't think so. I think it never really left the ground?"

"I suppose not. Tesla coils are cool," George replied. Steven agreed. What's not to be cool about a small tower which delivers electric arcs while making musical sounds?

So, it's not just to him that Lily lied. Also, to her father.

Steven helped George until the patriarch called time out for lunch.

George could talk for hours, and listen for days, but Steve wasn't much into the mood of talking. Instead, he let his father-in-law talk, mainly about his friends, about the state of the town, which entered a decline, about politics.

At lunch, Steven said his goodbyes, but he knew, in his heart, that it would remain the last time he would speak with the great man. It brought him no comfort, but now, Steven received some answers. He programmed the time to return to one of the vacation days, not thinking about the dimension number and landing in 2015.

Chapter 5.4—Not going back

To his surprise, he crosses the beacon in 2012 without getting caught. He needed a few minutes to realize the mistake he made, the risk he took. So, he could go from 2009 to 2015 over the antenna he turned on, despite the fact that it caught both Lily and Victor.

Steven opens his notes and pencils a timeline, and write on it "2009", "2014" and "2015". Above the line, he draws a short one, and on the left, scribbles "Victor" and on the right "Lily." Victor had come back from visiting his daughter in the past. He was grabbed when they installed the beacon in 2037, but couldn't return home after they unplugged it: he remained on the other side.

Lily, when she died, came from the future, and she arrived when he shut down his antenna. Now, he was able to navigate from before, to after the cycling on and off in dimension 1. Could this mean that since he powered it on and off only once, it wouldn't be impassible anymore, now that he got two boxes caught?

He thought of two ways to test it. He could turn on his antenna again, on this occasion utilizing Lily's ride to validate his hypothesis, or he could just jump from the future to the past of it. He decided to try both, but scientifically. First, he travelled back to his shop, in dimension 1, from the vacation period of the new owners of his house in dimension 2, soon after his last visit.

Victor's black rental was still there, but so was the beacon. He carefully picked it up, and brought it inside his temporal vehicle, setting the destination to one of their absences before 2014, back in 2013. Nervous, he pressed the button, and checked his phone, confirming he was in the right time. Opening the door, he recognized the small storage space in his former basement. Gently, he went and notice the lack of the new owner's car.

Good, he thought.

Installing the antenna in the main area downstairs, he placed the furniture aside to make enough clearance for Lily's box. He then plugged it in, powered it on and looking around, he spotted a duplicate of Lily's device appear next to him.

The door opened, and he saw himself get out to say, "From an hour ago." And about 30 seconds later, he vanished. He waited a minute and immediately pulled the power cable. In the corner, the machine returned. "From just now. Leave, just now," says his new copy. Quickly, he jumped into his ride, still in the small locker, setting the destination to 60 minutes earlier, and after travelling, arrived at the point of removing the power from the beacon, in the living room. After opening the door, he sees himself and the still there copy of the machine, and repeats what he just heard "From just now. Leave, just now"

But Steven looks at the time. This trip took him to the moment after he turned off the beacon, and one machine was already trapped. This means that he was in the future. He didn't even change the time destination, and when he pressed, actually made it this time. So, each turn-off could only grab a time machine once. What about a power on sequence? After seeing himself leave, he set the destination to two hours later, and the beacon caught him. Leaving, he just says to his previous self, "from an hour ago," but once inside, the machine couldn't start.

The beacon remains still on, but if he stays, the future machine won't find a place to land as the basement lacks the space for it, with two already there. He knows that within those 30 seconds, he manages to leave, so he flips, as fast as possible the dimension to 255 and goes. This time, no battery blows up, but the power meter goes from 93% to 21%. Is it because the beacon was only on for about a minute? Was it because he wasn't fighting against it since he was already caught in one direction, while in 2037, he was trying to go back?

He couldn't tell, but he had to charge, and he could hear the residents upstairs. Visibly, the dimension 255 people who owned his house didn't leave for a vacation. Not risking opening the door, he plugged in, and waited for what felt like an eternity for the percentage to get back to 30%, after which, he returned to dimension 1, with 11% left. Now, he knew. Finally, he understood how the antenna worked, and he flipped the switch off and disassembled it. He would never power it in anymore. The copy in 2037 would be on beyond his control, but now, 2014 and 2013, for that matter, seemed to feel safe again.

190

He closed the holes by only turning it on once. Well, twice, but behind the first one. This target range for discovering Lily now stood between 2014 and 2037, since she obviously came from the future, from that point of view, without having crossed 2037. Still the same 23 years, but not because he trapped both of them in that era, but because he has narrowed the search period. He would now focus on that period, without looking back to the past. It became time to find Lily, and create a future for both of them.

Chapter 5.5—New Attempt of Finding Her

Back in his workshop, Steven couldn't wait any longer. A recharge, a shave, a shower, enough sleep and he would see Lily! Steven looked at himself in the mirror. He used to keep a stubble looking older but considering that he was 12 years older than the last time he saw his wife, he had decided to get a clean shave for the first time in almost 20 years! He actually went to the barber shop to get a professional shave, a clean young haircut. Steven felt that he had truly lost almost 10 years! That didn't mean much, but it constitutes a start. Who knows how Lily would react to an old buffoon like him…

With a clear blue checkered shirt, and a fresh pair of jeans, he felt that he had lifted a few years from his old, battered clothes. Fresh cologne and deodorants really helped him smell good, which gave a lot of pep in his step. Steven knew he wanted his Lily, that is, the one he knew a few hours before he left. He could pick her up at any point in time, but doing so would mean getting a younger, less mature version of Lily. Granted, even as a teenager she seemed mature, but he certainly didn't want to get a Lily say, from before their experience owning a house, or a still studying Lily.

His only bet remained that entry he had first searched. The one where she had bought the steam governor piece. The place he had stalked for the full day the first time around. This was where he would grab her, as she left the store with the piece, as this lead probably soon before the moment of her demise. He knew she held the piece; he knew she needed time to store it in the storage area. Had she met her fate while buying it, it would have stayed in the store. If she met it while putting it in the time machine, it would have been lying on the floor: You don't store something when a bullet pierced in your heart.

She likely had another stop, and the murder on that other stop… He simply needed to prevent her from going there, and he would save her life! Perhaps he would cease to exist after his success, since his younger self would erase his timeline. Still, his last decade provided to leave him miserable without her. If he ended up vanishing, so be it. He made his peace with it. At least, at this point.

On this round, he didn't have to steal his truck or pay a cab. He used a clearing in the forest nearby and simply materialized (in the proper dimension, #3) on the morning of the day she bought the piece. He took a calm, relaxing walk with his bag toward the antique shop. He already knew the place, he already knew the owner, he already knew exactly where the part was. This time, however, he wasn't in the wrong timeline. He previously checked the coordinates of the location where Lily would park: he found it just around the corner, in a small alley. The stroll to the store took about a minute.

Steven began, of course, by the alley. Not only did he want to spot if Lily preceded him, but he also needed to visualize the area for himself. It was opened on both ends, so he decided to sit on a park bench on the other side of the alley, the side away from the antique shop. From his vantage point, he could see the other opening, but not the little corners and nooks and crannies. Lily might be able to park her time machine somewhere hidden, but he would see her exit from the other side.

His next destination led, of course, to the antique shop. He browsed and saw the part: Lily hadn't come yet. Looking over, he also spotted some binoculars that were at a very reasonable price and bought them. The owner stayed the same, his expressions looked the same, his newspaper spread on the counter seemed identical. Walking gently, he returned to his bench and sat with the binoculars around his neck. He confirmed that without them, he could see the alley rather well, and that with them, he could see plenty of details. He estimated the minimum trip to last four minutes: two for travelling, the delay wasted to find the item, and the chattiness and arthritis-stricken fingers of the shopkeeper taking at least the rest. Likewise, he couldn't imagine Lily staying less than five, from her arrival to her departure.

He set his cellphone to notify him every four minutes and began waiting. He regretted not buying a book, but he had mourned 12 years, he could certainly locate some patience for a few hours. Well, or so he thought. On each alarm, Steven rose, took a short walk, checked the Alley and returned to sit just in time for the alert to ring again and bring him back on the tour. He kept telling himself to remain seated, but he couldn't. He just couldn't. A little before noon, he ate a replacement bar, the last he hoped... it would leave him with two, but they tasted bland and honestly, didn't feel like a meal.

He did go buy a cold bottle of water in others to use the restroom at the convenience store (and get a cold bottle of water). He checked the alley, and that the part was still there, much to the surprise of the owner who inquired if he liked the binoculars. Steven tried to keep the chit-chat to a minimum, but it's the four-minute alarm on his cellphone which served as the proverbial bell to save him. He returned to his seat by passing through the alley and saw nothing of interest. He vowed to remain seated, and managed to last a good twenty minutes before he once again stretched his legs.

The lunch hour provided much more agitation: he saw three people pass by on foot, and later, two of them returned the other way: probably people working close on a lunch break. None went through the alley itself, but one of them, the lady, gave him a dirty look both times she passed by. Maybe she thought he was peeping Tom. Around one PM, he began to get tired of waiting, and by one thirty p.m., he had stopped even going into the alley. At two PM, Steven just about only looked when his cellphone rang and instead, would look around the area at the stores, at the cars passing by, at the few birds flying around.

At two twenty-four a.m., he saw that something new stood in the alley. He hadn't seen at two twenty a.m. He hadn't noticed anything. It just appeared there. He stood up and ran toward the alley. Near the machine, he listened and couldn't hear anything. Did Lily already leave for the store? Was she still in the machine? Steven decided to wait for a good minute, and during that minute, he stopped his alarm.

At two twenty-five a.m., he opened the door of the time machine, finding it empty, and the dials set for a few minutes earlier. Good, she hadn't set her destination yet... He entered and closed the door behind him.

Inside the machine, he realized how vulnerable he stood: he couldn't see outside. This version still didn't possess locks. He grabbed Victor's gun, and put it on his side, away from the door. His heart was beating too hard, his hands felt moist, and his brain kept playing in a loop the words he wanted to say to her. His breath becomes shallower, to the point where he almost forgot how to breathe.

He kept listening, but couldn't hear anything at all. Nothing. Not even the birds or the wind. Was the machine that sound proof? He didn't recall heating much from inside the cockpit. He wondered how long it would take, when suddenly, the dashboard filled with light, and he realized that the door opened, with Lily standing right in front of him.

"Stevie? What are you doing here?" she asked, puzzled.

Part 6

Chapter 6.1—Glorious Meeting

Steven felt breath taken. The last time he saw Lily, she was dying in his arms, with her skin already fading away, with her life draining from her body. The Lily that was standing now in front of him was a live breathing, feeling woman, which he hadn't put his eyes on in fifteen years. Here stood the woman he had fallen in love with, married, and lost.

"Lily, I'm so happy to have finally found you," he said, standing up and grabbing her little body to hold close to his. Lily instantly reciprocated her hug, which turned into a kiss, only interrupted by her pushing him away.

"Steven, I'm not your Lily... I have to explain something to you...", but Steven put his finger on her lips.

"You're my Lily. At least, if you arrived from dimension number one. I know, this is the dimension number three. I know you came from 2002, and that you time travelled using this machine to come here and buy that piece of a steam controller. I know you probably hid it somewhere close after travelling back to the nineteenth century to find it. I know because I have your time machine. This very one you're operating right now, but the later version. I'm using it after you left it behind."

Steven stopped, not because he was out of things to say, but because of how winded he became. Lily took the opportunity to talk.

"Wait, so you're my Steven, but I see that you're older than I am, so you found me in a previous timeline. You probably last spoke to me something like ten years into my future. You caught me in an earlier time. Sorry, I'm not yet your Lily," she said.

"No, you are. I have to tell you something," she said. She interrupted him.

"No, don't bother... I won't let you break my timeline. I'll continue on my way, and I'll contact you when I catch up to you," she said.

"You die in my arms on your way back to 2002. This is your final trip. I'm here to save your life. I don't have a current Lily because you will perish soon unless I stop you." Lily looked shocked, gently pushed him aside, and collapsed on the chair.

"But I have notes from the future!" she said.

Steven pulled out both of his diaries.

"Wait, you have my diary twice," she said, puzzled.

"I have this one," he said, showing one of the two, "from when you arrived in my workshop, bleeding. The other copy is the one I packed when I sold our house and which was in your papers."

"But that's not possible. It can't be both in storage and on me when I die… I didn't bring it with me today. Oh… Steven, you handed it to me. You took the version from my parents, eventually deliver it to me, and it's that one you found. That means that you probably ended up provoking my demise… If I have it when I perish, it implies that I get it after meeting you. Don't you see? You're causing a self-fulfilling prophecy. You're solving a paradox. Now, I need to die… or you won't come searching for me to give me my diary." Steven become the one despaired.

"Oh shit… I didn't think of that! So how can I save you then?"

"I guess we need to figure that out now."

"I do have a question that's been burning my mind. How could you write entries in there, from a time after you died?" Steven asks.

"Oh. That is a great question. How is that possible? Wait, that means I won't perish right away. We have some time between you finding me, and me dying in your arms. The way I use my diary is this. I describe in it what happens in my life, right? But then, I bring it back to a trip to the past, and leave it for my past self. That way, I know my future."

"But that leave you with two copies?"

197

"Indeed. But the thing is, I keep writing in my newer copy, but here is the thing that can screw with your head. If I write, and I accidentally slip my pen while writing, I realize that the slip was already there when I held the one from the future. So if I know of a slip, will I lose sleep because I know of it? Well, the way I solve it, is by cheating as little as possible, and it works out. I write my diary without looking at the one from the future, and instead, when I get it, I transfer the notes from it, in summary, into a computer document."

"Weird."

"But only when I need to keep notes."

"Like the cold you noted, you would have transcribed it."

"No, unless later I realize that it's important."

"This is super weird to me," he says.

"I bet. But it's like, second nature for me."

"I have so many questions."

"Sure, but first, let's get out of here, I don't like staying in a single open place like this for too long," she said.

"I have the coordinates of my copy of the time machine. Let me offset them by a few feet"…

"No need, the machine can only materialize if it has enough clearance," she added nonchalantly.

Steven was impressed. He programmed the numbers, and a "ding" later, the two machines sat side by side, with a few feet between them.

Chapter 6.2—Gloomy thoughts

Lily inspected his machine.

"Locks? Brilliant! Why didn't I think of that?"

Steven unlocked the main door.

"Hey, that's a new keyboard? And a new monitor?" she inquired.

"Yeah."

"What happened? Be honest, please…", said Lily.

"Aren't you afraid of knowing your future?" asked Steven.

"Steven, I've understood my life since I was 11. I'm not scared of spoilers. I just don't want it to change! We had a very bright destiny, and you just about ruined it by breaking the timeline."

"Wait, what do you mean you've understood since you were 11?" asked Steven.

Lily blushed. Steven thought she looked so cute when she did.

"When I was eleven, this woman came to see me. She said she was my future me, and she gave me a manual explaining it. It showed another dimension. She's the one who supplied me with the first version of this book, with the notes on how to build my time machine, how to find you, how we could be happy together. How to become a university professor, the idea is to study steam governors, everything. It was almost that diary, but she made a mistake. Her trips were only in her own dimension. She only understood dimensional travel when she was much older, and it was too late for her to repair anything."

"So, from which one is she?"

"It's #0 with my machine. She made me promise to never visit her, so I put her at #0, and the two of us at #1. The numbers don't matter, but somehow, there remains some logic."

"Let's back up, you had this diary since you were 11?" he asked.

She blushed again. He wanted her so much, despite a little rage rising at the possibility that she duped him.

"Yeah Stevie. When I initially met you, I had been dreaming of you for years. I knew exactly where you would be at the fair. But please don't think I really manipulated you. In the original dimension, the first Lily did go out with the first Steven. It just didn't last. She couldn't make it work. Your family…"

"They pulled him apart from her?"

Lily grabbed his hand.

"He killed himself. Committed suicide when he reached 22. The first Lily managed to prevent the suicide when she invented the time machine, but not repair his deep depression. He unalived himself half a dozen more times. Don't you see… how bad used to be your life? I didn't manipulate you to make you fall in love with me for selfish reasons. I did so because it was the only way to save you."

"According to her… in another dimension…", added Steven, in a stern tone.

"Steven, search in your heart. You were in a dark place when I met you. Didn't you feel your life turn around when I arrived?"

"So, you didn't just use me?"

"Of course not, I love you, from the bottom to the top of my heart. Even since before I even met you. The other Lily didn't just give her diary. That diary was just to warn me of future events. She would frequently come to visit me, and we spent hundreds of hours during which she tutored me on many subjects, including electronics, time travel, your family, and so on."

200

"I was stuck. I couldn't make the quantum modules work. The other Lily had stopped visiting me and my module didn't work despite her notes. You were always good with these things, so I invented a fictive use and made you debug it. Wait, did you complete it?"

"Yeah, like 12 years after you disappeared. I could receive signals thought…"

"Oh, Steven. It's a quantum module for time travel. Those signals, quantum interferences, like the movement of the moon, the planets, remain relative to the module. But it's an interference itself! That's why we call that a quantum beacon. It lights up across multiple dimensions."

"That's what happened, Lily. When I turned it off, your time machine appeared, and I found you dying in my arms."

"So that's why you're older. And that means we can't go back to earlier…"

"I know, I was stuck in the future too…", Steven replied.

"Then how are you alive?"

"What do you mean?"

"Every time travellers are aware of the 2037 trap. The quantum beacon pulsing there which captures the time travellers crossing it. It turns on and off on a cycle to catch everyone. We never see people from after 2037 anymore, and that's the furthest we can move. One of us managed to infiltrate the base by arriving a few weeks before it came online and brought pictures of the construction: it's a massive metallic cage with the beacon in the middle. It's in a Faraday mesh and they were installing huge Tesla coils, as well as machine gun turrets. We think it's a foolproof plan to kill anyone caught. Sadly, she failed to tell us the dimension number, but we never travel past #76 for that reason."

"For me, the device was in a laboratory. In that one, both of us lived to retirement without turning on the antenna, and one of my colleagues did and captured me. I managed to escape…"

"Stevie… that's probably the same as the beacon. It's yours which is at the centre of that trap."

"Are you serious? Do you mean to say that I'm the person who put restrictions to those 23 years? I didn't even realize it!" added Steven.

"You aren't. That was another dimension, Stevie. If you assembled your copy in #1, your clone could create it in theirs as an echo. Decisions don't always ripple but if I failed the construction, and you succeeded, our duplicates most likely did the same, based on your work."

"Right, you also vanished in most of the low-numbered ones."

"Makes sense" says Lily.

"She didn't in the 2037 beacon dimension, and I still built the antenna."

"Well, we know it's a far away one, above 73, and the further they are, the more deviation they form. But how did you even break free?"

"I kept switching dimensions until it let me leave, even going past the limit of the flip cards, to what I estimated was dimension 255."

She looked at him, dubious. "What?"

"I think that once you get to 79, the next display is 0, but it's now 80, and after another round it's 160, and then 240. I went to 15, so 255."

"Stevie, the universe consists of only 80 dimensions, from 0 to 79. Lily 0 mapped them."

Steven ponders. "I bet it only formed 80 back then too! But perhaps when you travelled, you manifested 81, and when the one from, let's say, #6 built hers, the limit increased to 86."

Lily gasps. "But 255, that means the existence of people with a copy of my machine that we never met."

"Or potentially it's my fault by going there, or maybe each one of us create 80."

"Right, it's not necessary to know for us to get out of our mess."

"But I did burn two batteries and drains most of the energy from the reserves, I barely made it out."

"I'm shocked you even made it. Happy you did, but surprised," she says, hugging him again.

"It doesn't bother you that I'm older?"

"Why would I? And I guess you won't mind that I remain young," she says, smiling. But then, her mouth turns into a frown, not giving sufficient time for Steven to reply.

"So, what happened to the keyboard and monitor, Steven? I think you've avoided the subject long enough," Lily said, with both of them clearly realizing that need an answer. Steven always demonstrated a habit of feeling overly guilty of things for which he sometimes remained only partially responsible. Lily helped him a lot by preventing him from lingering on his perceived errors.

"When you arrived at my workshop, you were wounded, from a bullet in your heart. Your blood ended up over the console. You died in my arms, without saying anything really coherent, but I needed to replace the keyboard and the monitor."

Lily was starting straight in front of her, with wide-opened eyes. Tears were pooling around them.

"What did you do with my body?" she asked to avoid sobbing from exploding.

"At first, I placed you in my freezer. I know, but the police thought I was the number one suspect in your disappearance, so I didn't want your corpse to decompose or something. Later, when I returned from searching for you, I found an isolated atoll in the Pacific Ocean and buried you there."

Lily held him in her arms.

"Good. You did well. Stevie, you have no idea what it's like to really time travel. You probably only did a few trips and haven't encountered any travellers, but I did, and it's terrifying. Coming face to face with a copy of you that thinks entirely differently," she says, shivering a little.

"I sadly intercepted a man from Hong Kong and accidentally killed him when he was trying to murder me. Oh, now I know why he feared the beacon! It's because of the trap you mentioned."

"Wait, did you meet another one, in 2014?"

"Yeah, a Victor something. He had a permit for time travel."

"Oh, yeah. These guys are from the 2030s. Dimension seventy-six. Their Lily decided not to journey for a history degree, but instead, she refined the interface and opened a rental shop, with a kind of police she founded to monitor the multiverse, as she calls it. I met her… she's mostly crazy. She thinks it's her job to maintain the temporal continuum or something. I managed to convince her to stay out of number one, two and three, which is why I only operate in these. She refers to our little deal as time accords, and made it formal," Lily explained, laughing.

"Why three dimensions?"

"To prevent accidental changes… I keep #3 for when I bury items for later retrieval. I visit #2 for any research work. #1 is our home, so I leave my time travel to a minimum…".

It felt logical to him… but he had a burning question…

"Wait, you arrived with the dial placed to #2. We're in #3. You would have wanted to go home to #1. It doesn't make sense," he kind of asked… but realized with shame that he had just stated facts.

"Who knows, maybe when I was bleeding out, I thought I had selected #1?" she said.

"But you programmed the coordinates and the time properly?"

"They could have been adjusted before the shooting. Listen, Steven, I'm more preoccupied by another problem. I can't go home because of you. If we save me, you're reset and lose your progress. I couldn't do that to you."

"Oh, I have a solution for that! Dimension twenty-eight!"

"Twenty-eight? What's there?" she asked, puzzled.

"The Lily and Steven from that dimension disappeared on a vacation in the Bahamas in 2009, probably drowned, and neither resurfaced. It's a few years after you left, in theory, we could just resume their lives which are nice and comfy. You will just be younger than you used to, and I will look older, but most people shouldn't be too concerned."

"But we can't go to pre-2014… your antenna blocks us."

"We can, because I only turned it on twice. The passage is safe travel to us without problems, it caught the time machines it would stop and is now free for us."

"Really? That's a relief, do we just move to #28? Without knowing much about them?"

205

Steven looks at her.

"I figured as much, and they vanish while on their trip, we could research their home during their vacation," he says.

"You fully planned everything with very limited information. I remember why I married you," she says, smiling. "Let's try your solution… people think I'm dead in our dimension, so yeah, maybe it's time to pay #28 a visit, to scope it out?"

"That seems like a good idea."

Lily kissed him passionately. "Let's go to the Bahamas!"

Chapter 6.3—General explanations

Having two time machines meant more coordination between them. First, they both travelled to the same alley behind the public library Steven had parked behind earlier in others to visit it together. They selected a month later to avoid anyone remembering him.

To Steven, going somewhere with Lily felt like heaven on earth, yet he noticed that Lily wasn't her usual cheerful self. She didn't present a bad mood per se, but she remained far from the bundle of joy she used to be. He tried to reassure her that she wouldn't die. She still kept looking around her as if she were about to get shot.

Steven and Lily searched for a specific information that Steven hadn't bothered to retrieve yet: the house address of this dimension's Lily and Steven's home. With two time machines, they required a safe place where to park them. They would also need to find a bearing on their lives: they would have to impersonate a couple they didn't even know and interact with their friends.

"Lily," asked Steven, "how does the multiple dimensions actually work? And what about Time Travel itself?"

Lily seemed suddenly more at ease.

"So, imagine that life is like a CD. Normally, you listen to a CD from the first song to the last one, but with a machine such as mine, you can skip tracks and move anywhere on the disk. Now, in theory, any changes that you make are propagated into the future, altering the timeline. What we discovered is that if you only remain in a single dimension, you can't break anything because whatever you do in the past, already occurred, like a self-fulfilling prophecy."

"Wait, I saw that!" said Steven.

"You did?"

"In #2, I found a fire of unknown criminal origin, and I decided to use that event to dispose of something. Doesn't matter what. When I was on the site, I expected the arsonist to arrive, only to realize that I'm the guy who started the fire."

"Exactly. Now, what will really keep you up at night is, who thought of the fire? You became the arsonist only because you read about it in the future, so it's a convenient location to get rid of that something. But without the initial one, you wouldn't have gone there at all. As such, you couldn't have created the fire in the first place. It couldn't exist without you initiating it, and you travelled there before you lit it. Well, that's a paradox right there! And you know what? No time traveller in a single dimension can really cause a paradox. It's impossible. You can't go in the past and break something unless doing so is what caused the break. You couldn't have started that fire with time travel, even if you wanted to do so. The universe prevents you from doing it," Lily explained, with an ominous tone at the end.

"But I did start it…"

"Yes, you did. But not in your home dimension. You did that in #2. See, the Universe of #2 will preserve the causality of its members, but it had no grasps on you since you're under the authority of Dimension #1, your home one. You can wreck any other dimension that you please without causing a paradox because those events aren't your past, they're the past of your local self. That universe keeps you in line: it has no idea where you're from, what you did, how you grew up."

"So, is it only #1 that I can't alter? But I made some alterations. I stole batteries from Victor's time machine," he said, confused.

"OK, so this is where it gets complicated. Victor's time machine is from #76, so right off the bat, any time traveller who stayed in #1 can alter it. But you had probably explored #2 In the meantime. You didn't return to your past in #1, or visit your future in #1. When you came back to #1, you weren't really a time traveller. Imagine that your CD is in a multi-CD player. You paused your own CD, and played with another one, but when you came back to ours, you continued more or less on the same track, right?"

"Yes"

"So, Universe 1 only lost track of you while you were away, but you didn't break causality. I never did either. I always returned to our dimension less than 30 seconds after I left it. No time travel."

"But I thought Lily from dimension 0 broke her timeline?"

"Ah yes. That, she did. You see, previously, we knew of time travellers from the future, like from far eras. We've seen people from thousands of years from now, and we've discovered that other machines are variations of hers. Not a single exception. In the whole history, past and future, only one design ever emerged, the one Lily #0 invented."

"Wait, I thought the beacon from 2037 blocked them…"

"I'm getting to that…", said Lily.

"Lily zero, created the time machine, and kind of broke something. We don't know what. She can break her dimension and no one else can. It's as if it was a childhood disease the multiverse had never seen, and after it did, it protected itself and prevented someone else from discovering time travel again and breaking their timeline. Or maybe Lily #0 found the only way to do it, with the quantum modules she invented and didn't tell us who to override the protection. Lily #76, you know, the one who thinks she's the police of time travel, she believes in the vaccine theory and, as such, is convinced the Universe has tasked her with protecting it from abuse."

"But you don't?"

"The Universe isn't an entity. It's not alive. It's the laws of physics trying to reconcile quantum time displacement with the regular universe outside time travel."

"So what are dimensions?"

"Some liken them to echoes, created automatically. Others think that their creation occurs when we bend the quantum transportation in such a way as to create a new universe. Lily zero firmly believed she created the dimensions, perhaps she has a God complex. Lily 76 thinks that they already existed, are limited to 80 in total, and, as such, need to be protected. Lily 28 was against time travel and refused to build her time machine."

"Wait, you know this Lily?"

"Yeah, not the whole set, but when you said #28, I knew exactly who you're talked about. I know a few of the Lily. I was the first one to build her machine from the plans from Lily zero, so I helped a few others build their own."

"What happened to the Lily from #2?"

"I suspect your beacon blocked her just as I will be when I return to die."

"Wait, but I was here to prevent it."

"You don't get it, do you? You got my body. It already occurred. I'm from #1, you're from #1. We can change some of the future, you buried my body in #1. We can plan somewhat of a future together, we can try to avoid this ending, but it will occur."

"It's inevitable?"

"If you're really my Steven, and if I die in your arms, nothing we do can allow us to prevent it. Even if we never return to our dimension."

"And for the disappearance of the other copies of you, I only saw one time machine and one Lily?"

"Yeah, we never figured that one out. Each beacon only grabs one machine, the one from the lowest numbered dimension. The others just vanish. We have no idea where or when. We're safe because #1 is the lowest active one, it's probably why Lily 76 is so worried. Being so far means her time machines have no chance against almost anyone around a beacon."

"That's scary…"

"Yeah, we only understood this later. Guess which dimension we helped next after discovering this?"

"28?"

"Exactly! We caused her to reject time travel. It's us who modified her timeline by warning her of a danger the lower dimensions previously ignored."

Chapter 6.4—Games?

After having found what they felt was enough details about the Steven and Lily of #28, the couple decided to travel to the house of their alter ego. They choose the day after they left for the Bahamas, going through #255 to avoid the antenna in case they could get stuck again.

"How does the time machine really know to go in the basement?" asked Steven when they arrived downstairs of their new home.

"Lily 0 told me that since the machine doesn't have an altitude dial, it takes the lowest eligible location above the sea floor. Just pay attention in cities with a subway or near shallow mines, or you might appear somewhere underground. Also, don't go in the Netherlands", she says, smiling. "For most places, however, the machine remains too big for sewers, so you appear either outside or in a cellar," she replied.

"So that's how you could park your machine in the storage area in our house without me noticing it. It fitted quite snugly in there...", he said.

"Yeah, honestly, that's why I wanted that house. I measure the room so I could leave it there. But this one is nice... a large enough basement for both of our machines. Can you imagine? The two of us time travellers?" Lily replied.

"Until you have to go back to die...", said Steven.

"I've been thinking about that. The only thing we know is that a Lily died in your arms. It might have been Lily 2 or Lily 3... maybe it wasn't me...", she replied.

"Do you think so? Can we tell if my time machine is the future of yours?" Steven asked.

Lily thought, and returned to her time machine. She created a file in the "My Document" folder called "test-steven.txt," and typed in it "this is a test from Lily 1."

211

"There, go to your machine, if the file is there, it's me who dies, if the file isn't, it's another one," she said. Fully reassured.

Steven hesitated, but went to look. Sure enough, the file was there, exactly as she had typed it. Her face returned to white, and she almost fainted.

"I was sure…", she managed to express.

"Don't worry. We'll find a way," he said, holding her in his arms.

After a few minutes, they began exploring the house. It felt much nicer than their old one, with several years of decoration made, and the home picked for comfort instead of having as a priority to hide a time machine from their Steven.

Lily located extensive notes about her classes and research, as well as details on her professional plans. Spending a few hours looking over these, Steven managed to access both of their Facebook accounts on their respective computers. As it turns out, they use the same passwords as Lily and him do.

He attempted getting a picture in his mind of their actual Facebook friends. This was 2008, in the early years of Facebook, so it wasn't reliable yet as most relationships compare to analog signals. The binary friend or not format of Facebook fell short. He figured, at worst, they would wait for phone calls from friends and try to pick it up.

His own epiphany came when he found the file cabinet with both invoices to his clients and the user manuals for some of the machines. He saw that DryTek textiles were still using the same machine he had to recalibrate, but he had hundreds of other clients, giving him a lucrative business. He even had an employee, Tom!

In the closet, he uncovered birthday and Christmas cards and several personal items from friends and family which helped him describe in more detail the relationships they had. In the living room, he discovered things that puzzled him: this Lily and Steven were into board games, apparently.

A few boxes displayed *Ticket to Ride, Carcassonne, Catan, Alhambra, Race for the Galaxy*, and even one still wrapped up: *Stone Age.*

.Steven had grown up with classic (and usually boring) ones like *Risk, Monopoly* and *Uno* and didn't even know there existed that many board games. What a world! He wondered if they got only popular in this dimension, or if he missed that whole fad while hiding from the universe in his workshop. Lily eventually joined him while he was looking at the Ticket to Ride board game. It seemed simple enough and made a note to try it one day.

"I think I should be able to teach her class. I have her notes. It will need some adjustments, but I should be able to myself. At worst, I'll explain at first, I'm still dizzy from vacation. What's that?" she asked.

"Apparently, they're into board games, and new ones," he said.

"Hey, this one appears to be about trains. You know me and steam engines," she said, laughing.

Just as in the past, her sunny laugh was contagious. It wasn't long before both of them were kissing passionately and a few minutes later, the Lily and Steven of this universe had one less condom in their reserve as their counterpart consecrated their marriage once more.

"Is it me, or it was better than usual?" she asked.

"It's been 15 years for me," he said.

"I last had sex with your two days ago, but that wasn't this. Maybe it's true that men are like wine, they get better with age," she said.

Steven blushed, and kissed his wife, happy to have found her again, but still worried about possibly losing her once more.

"So do we just stay here?" she asked.

"No, we need to return via the cruise ship. Otherwise, we will receive too many questions," he explained.

"My time machine or yours?" she said, flirting with him.

"I'd say mine. It's lockable. We'll need to leave it somewhere in the Caribbean and come pick it up later when we come back home."

"Ooh... are you taking me on a cruise?" she said...

"Yes Milady. Now, if you excuse me, we need to plan our trip!"

Chapter 6.5—Grounded

Steven and Lily ended up just changing into Bermuda shorts and a Hawaiian shirt and a sundress, respectively. He carried his bag. Before leaving, Lily inspected the changes he made.

"I love the new charge module. The time it took to charge the batteries was really my number one problem. This new charger is so much faster!" she said.

"You should have brought me into the loop years ago...", he grumbled.

"Lily 0 warned it was a terrible idea."

"Maybe her Steven was a jerk, but I'm not. Like you said, you helped me a lot to get over the problems with my family," he said. She kissed him on the cheek.

"The locks are really a good addition," She reaffirmed.

"You haven't seen my anti-ignition lock," he said, proudly.

"What? That's cool... where is it?"

He showed her the switch under the control board. She laughed. It seemed so simple and yet so ingenious, she

Soon enough, they left. One moment in the basement of their bathroom, a "ding" later on a beach, on a deserted island he had already visited.

When they left the time machine, the glaring sun temporarily blinded them, but Steven noticed a big black object on the beach, further away, and that he wasn't parked in the same place as his previous visit. Instead, they were on the other side of the coconut tree where he had hidden the bottle on his previous visit, in another dimension. They could both hear shouting, and their eyes focused on the action occurring.

It took Steven only a second to understand the scene, but Lily was still trying to figure it out. Steven took out Victor's gun and shot it once in the air. Steven remained calmed and focused, but the three women standing up on the island were instantly frozen in fear. Next to him was his Lily, Lily 1, who hadn't really registered that her Steven wore a weapon until now. He had been carrying the gun when she first saw him in her time machine, but she had been too overwhelmed to note it as important.

In front of him, with her back turned to him, was a second unknown Lily, who was holding a massive bloody shovel in her arms. She was wearing ordinary day clothes, which made Steven realize that she probably operated the time machine. The time machine possessed black paint, not unlike Victor's. He wondered if this Lily was #76. No, apparently, she looked a little older… this one appeared visibly young.

Standing in front of that unknown Lily lied, what Steven thought, Lily 28, in a bikini, in her thirties, with a gaping wound in her stomach and a leaking head. Standing wasn't the right word. Wobbling felt probably more appropriate. At her feet lied Steven 28, also wearing a bathing suit, on a towel, with blood draining from multiple wounds. By the time it took to register the scene, the dressed Lily had turned and was swinging the shovel as hard as she could before realizing she stood too far away.

Lily 1 had grabbed a coconut from the ground and then threw it as hard as she could at the unknown Lily. Trying to hit the projectile to avoid getting hit, she dropped the shovel as her swing made her lose her balance and the coconut made her lose her grip.

"Who the hell are you?" she said

"Raise your hand, don't move," ordered Steven.

Just as she complied, Lily 28 fell on the ground. Lily 1 rushed to her side.

"Which dimension are you from?" asked Steven.

"How the hell should I know? A girl arrived in this time machine and tried to kill me. Then, a psycho-bitch tried to stop me. I've been on the run ever since. Are you with psycho-bitch?"

"No," replied Steven. "Why did you murder them?"

"D'uh, to take their place. I mean, I only wanted to eliminate this one, but her Steven refused to let me replace her. I'm her younger self, for crying out loud!"

"What happened to your Steven?" Steven asked.

"Murdered by the asshole who attempted to assassinate me. I did everything to save him, but every time I tried, I failed."

Lily 1 replied from the other side. "You can't change the past from your own dimension…"

Steven was now focusing on his wife, who was speaking with the dying Lily in her arms.

"So, are you going to kill me?" asked the unknown Lily who used to have the shovel.

"This one just died. We have to get rid of these bodies…", said Lily 1.

"Wait, are you trying to take their place too? Take me with you… hide me… I don't want the psycho-bitch to kill me…"

"We can't trust her…", said Lily 1, to Steven. "She's probably from a far dimension. I can't predict what she'll do."

"Oh, I understand that," says Steven.

"Steven, let's get rid of the bodies first… do we have something to tie her?"

"I don't want to be tied up," says the intruder.

"You just killed this couple. We don't know you. Give us time to trust you."

"And why should I listen?" she says, definitely

"Because we'll protect you from the psycho-bitch, and we have a gun," she Steven, pointing the gun at this copy of his wife.

"Fine," she says.

Lily 1 grabbed a bag next to Lily 28, who has a string she unties and as Steven got closer to the intruding Lily, his wife tied her doppelgänger's wrists. Using the unlucky couple's towel, she also tied the murderer's legs, after forcing her to sit on the hot sand.

"What do we do?" asked Lily.

"Put both bodies in my time machine, we'll bury them on the same island where I had buried you, but in another dimension…"

"Good idea, go to number 3."

Lily struggled to drag both bodies into the time machine and the shovel.

"You stay here with the gun?" he asked, when she returned.

"Just do it quickly, I don't want it…", she said, kissing him

"I'll do better, I'll come back five seconds later."

Steven programmed the destination, but before leaving, he made sure nothing had changed. Digging both graves took a lot longer than he expected. He was hurrying in the hot sun to come back to his wife earlier, when he realized two important things: he possessed all the time in the world, since the time spent digging meant nothing.

Second, nothing forced him to dig in the hot sun… so he travelled, with the body, to later in the evening when the cool afternoon breeze felt now stronger than the hot midday sun. He managed to finish the job after the run had set, but the moonlight still allowed him to see enough. Grabbing the shovel, he programmed his destination to five seconds after his departure and pressed the button.

Chapter 6.6—Grievances

Steven didn't come back to the same location he had left. He was now on a different island and could barely see the other one. Remembering they were still in his bag, he grabbed his binoculars and looked. Several new time machines were now on the tiny island, some of which stood half in the water, half on the beach. He could see several people in big black uniforms in the middle of it all, but they obstructed his view.

Looking around him, he saw a big log lying on the beach near him. He grabbed the shovel, pushed the log and used it as a makeshift canoe, using the shovel as a paddle. Many times he risked flipping over, but his wife's life was in danger. Only one thing gave him hope: his Lily wasn't wearing the same clothes as she had been when she died in his arms. Still, his heart filled with courage once more. He would avoid failure, since once again, he had secured the knowledge that he was going to save her. He knew it consisted of a lie: he could die trying, she could die after he did, but those reassuring thoughts helped him paddle more.

As he grew nearer, he could hear arguing. "But I'm Lily from Dimension 1. We have a truce between you and me… don't you forget it, or I'll get Lily prime to rescind the help she gave you."

218

The response, alas, sounded inaudible to him. He did hear some garbled sounds like "responsibility," "authority" and something about "punish" or "punishment." The waves weren't collaborating with him, but Steven wanted to keep Victor's gun dry until he would reach his wife.

He heard a gun shot, lunged forward, and his left feet felt the sand under it. Steven jumped off the log and rand up the beach until he was going around the corner and saw the scene. One of the guards held the murdering Lily in front of her time machine.

Close by was his Lily, who had her hands up. In front of her stood an older copy of his wife, probably Lily 76. Armed men surrounded them in black suits, with guns either pointing at his wife, or the tied up, Lily. A guard in front of him, on the other side of the scene, yelled "Intruder," and a guard next to Steven turned around and took aim at Steven with his gun, yelling, "Drop your weapon!"

His wife, Lily 1 yelled, "That's my husband! Steven 1, according to the dimensional accord, he has immunity too."

"DROP YOUR WEAPON!" repeated the soldier who was closing in on him.

"Do I have immunity?" said Steven, while keeping the barrel pointed to the ground and raising his left hand in submission.

Steven received an identical order from the same person, who clearly won't answer his question.

"Only if I have guarantees…", he said.

"Inspector General Lily… the accords cover him too…", mentioned his wife.

Lie 76, apparently titled Inspector General, nodded and her subordinate backed off.

"I still need you to drop your gun," said the soldier with a calmer tone.

Steven let of the weapon, which fell quickly on the ground, and put his bag on top of it. "It's in the sand it, but it remains mine," he added. The soldier nodded.

"What's going on, Lily?" he asked his wife. It's the inspector general that replied.

"That was a fugitive from dimension 64 had been on the run for a few weeks, while I have been trying to arrest and execute her for crimes against the multiverse. We just tracked her here with a stolen rental time machine which was hacked to allow travel to any dimension or timeline. Fortunately, she didn't alter the tracker."

"Wait, I received a visitor, Victor something. Was the tracker active?"

"Yes, we realized he arrived in Dimension 1, which officially stays off-limits to us from the accords, and noted that you disposed of him. Well done. If you're ever keen to join the agency, we have an officer position opened for you. We've seen your work in dimension 2. You broke a few rules, as expected, but otherwise respected the timeline. We would have closed his eyes even without the accords," Lily 76 explained.

Lily 1 took charge, and with panache and confidence. "As per article 17, I'm hereby extending the accords to this dimension as my Steven and I lay claim to it."

Lily 76 replied, amused. "Article 17 deals with crimes committed by people with impunity in virgin timelines."

Lily 1 sighed. "Number 18, then?"

"Perfect, in accordance to the accords, dimension 28 is now protected from his date forward, and from the actions of Lily and Steven from dimension 1 into the past. But I still need to execute Lily 64."

She didn't want to go this easy, so she kicks her guard and slips behind him. He starts to turn, but she jumps into her time machine, which soon vanished.

Lily 76 sighs. "Here we go again!"

"You really will catch her and terminate her, right?" says Steven.

"Yes. She began killing her clones in other dimensions to find a place to settle. We've been trying to stop her for a while."

So, Lily 76 is the psycho-bitch, realized Steven.

"You wanted to make me an agent. Can I get a method to track her, and my Lily and I will handle her?"

"Why?"

"She seemed more responsive to us, it might be easier for me to eliminate her."

"She might kill again."

"She might. But if you help us with a way to track her, we might stop her from murdering other people," Steven says.

"Sure, but I wouldn't let you undo your Lily's disappearance. That would be a crime against the multiverse. If you return to dimension 1 to prevent the current timeline, the accords are off."

"Why?" Says your Lily

"I won't answer that. Rest assured we wouldn't take this action lightly," says Lily 76.

"When we catch the renegade, what do I do?"

Lily 76 replied. "We'll give you a stun gun to use until we can confirm it was really her. We'll execute her before she regains consciousness."

"Great, can you delay a few minutes and let me specify how to execute her?" asked Steven.

"It's disintegration. It's always disintegration," she replied. "We can't have any traces of her body, and frankly Steven, we're tired of digging up your corpses and disintegrating them. Your disposal ideas aren't as genius as you think they are. We just clean up after you. The time accords don't cover buried bodies."

"Oh," he replied. Hurt.

"What did you have in mind, Stevie?" says his Lily.

"I'll explain later, until then, Inspector General, can I have more latitude with the fugitive? Once I find her, I will stun her and let you retrieve her time machine. But I want to handle her personally. Give me some time"

"Will you cause her harm?"

"What? No, why would I? She's a dimension clone of my wife."

"Not every copy of Steven loves their Elizabeth."

"Well, I'm not them. But I have a plan, and I think you will like it."

"Why?"

"Because it preserves the timeline integrity."

"Fine. But we still need to find her."

"Lend me a tracker, and I will."

"Lieutenant, hand him one."

One of the guards supplied Steven with a box with an LCD panel on top. It lists a dimension number, coordinates and a time, which moves forward each second.

"That tracks the time machine itself?"

She nods and then gives you a USB stick from her pockets.

"This is a recall program. Plug it in the USB drive, and 10 seconds later, the rental will return to our hangar. Don't stay in it."

"I don't plan to risk it. Thank you," he says.

"And this is a stun gun. It sends an impulsion which makes the victim pass out. You only have four charges, but it should be enough. It's a cone effect and the range is about 16 to 18 feet."

"Good to know," says Steven, taking it.

His wife and him each take their time machines, and leave the beach, appearing in the basement of the house owned by the couple they would be replacing.

Chapter 6.7: Grinding for a fugitive

By the time they arrived at the house, the fugitive already moved to another location, still in Dimension #29. Unfettered, Lily sat on her husband's lap and quickly adjusted the coordinates.

"I just did it more often."

"And it's a train simulator, one of your specialties."

"What?"

"I spoke to your dad."

"How is he doing?"

"Want the truth?"

"Always"

"Died in a car accident after retiring. But I travelled before that to know how you built this machine."

"Right, it's the explanation I gave him. Should I feel guilty of not having considered my parents earlier?" Steven ponders. This reminds him of the kind of question she uses to help him figure out things. So, he thinks about him, not about her. This felt like the perfect opportunity for the other way around.

"They were always close to your heart, so regardless of where they are, they will always remain with you."

"Aww, Stevie. Years of isolation didn't make you jaded."

"It did, but the last few weeks walking in your shoes brought me back to life."

Lily turns around enough to kiss him, and with her left arm, pressed the button.

"Is that a stun gun in your pants or are you happy to see me," she says, laughing.

"Both actually"

"Nice," she says, as they find the other machine in an alley, next to theirs, but with no traces of the fugitive. It's in the middle of the night.

"Perhaps you can recall it," says Lily But Steven thinks of a new plan.

"We can track the machine, but we can't do so with her. If she moves with it, we can find her again," he explains.

"If we wait, she will kill another Lily. I know the one in this dimension. She's nice."

"Perhaps, but do you have a bearing on her destination?"

Lily looks around. "Yeah, two blocks from here. Let's go"

Steven locks their time machine and follows his wife down the street.

"This Lily bought a house after her divorce."

"We separate here?"

"We don't always work out. These are echoes of us."

"Shouldn't she go see this Steven to get him? That's what she wants. To settle down"

"She's not aware they split, and intends to kill the Lily to take her place," says Lily.

When they reach the house, they spot two cars in the driveway.

"Two cars?"

"She found someone."

"Oh"

"She isn't me. She's far removed from me."

"You met her new spouse?"

"Yes, I visited them. And the others. She's the only one who got remarried, but Steven, it means nothing to me."

He sighs. "I know that"

She points to his head. "You know that here," she says. "But you don't know that there," he says, pointing to his heart. The front door remained partially open. They hear a scream and run inside.

"Stop it," yells someone with Elizabeth's voice, but older.

"Where is Steven?" says another voice, younger, also sounding like Elizabeth.

225

"How the hell should I know? He moved on with his life. I did too. Can you put down the knife?"

"Fine."

But as Steven and Lily get upstairs, they spot the fugitive leaving a bedroom, with a kitchen knife in her hand. She grabs Lily, twists her arm and puts the knife under her chin.

"Let me go or I kill her."

"I can stun you both and take you."

"I'll slice her throat before you take out your gun."

"Fine, I'll move out of the way, but let her go."

"Which ones are you?"

"The same from the beach, we want to help you."

"Yeah right. I'll take my chances," and on that, she lets go of Lily, and pushes her into Steven's arms, before running down the stairs, still holding the knife. Steven pulls his wife up and looks at her.

"Are you OK?"

"I am. Got a scare, but I'm OK."

The resident Lily and her spouse leave the bedroom, wearing night gowns.

"Did she leave?" asks Lily

"Gwen?" says Steven, recognizing his wife's former coordinator.

"I told you. She isn't me."

"That's an understatement. Are you Lily #1? The one who came to help her?" says Gwen.

"Yeah. That was a fugitive. Lily #64. Bent on killing one of us to settle with her husband."

"Thank you for helping us. Go get her," says the older Lily.

"Do you really not know where Steven is?"

"I do, but I wasn't going to tell her."

"We need to warn him."

"Darn, he's at his parents' house."

"With my brother?" says Steven

"What? No, your brother moved to New York."

"So who he got the house?" asks Steven

"Yes, when his brother moved away."

"Oh, OK, let's go, thank you for your cooperation, and sorry for the trouble," says Steven.

"But I have a ton of questions," says the resident Lily, but Steven, dragging his wife, already flew halfway down the stairs.

The murderer left in the black machine, predictably. After unlocking just the side door, they check the tracker, which slowly calibrated itself.

"So, Gwen?"

"Didn't I tell you she was gay?"

"You didn't…"

"Must have slipped my mind. Well, I guess this Lily found comfort in her arms…"

"Did you ever get feelings for her?"

"Me? No. I only ever had eyes for you, big dummy," she says, kissing her husband.

"We have a lock," he soon says. The fugitive barely travelled geographically and didn't temporally.

It takes about 20 seconds for Lily to set the coordinates and, as expected, they find themselves in the backyard of the Clark mansion. Everything looks good in the back, so the couple, after locking their time machine and disabling it, run to the front where, Steven sees how broken the fountain was before the repairs.

His brother having moved to New York means he never fixed it to please their father. He guesses that his counterpart didn't bother with it. After all, he did see the damage. This time, the door was closed, but not locked and right on the other side, they find Steven arguing with the fugitive, who still has the kitchen knife.

Next to Steven is Susan, from GTW, in a big pajama, while the resident Steven is in boxers. Both Lily and Steven are shocked to find her there, as in their original timeline, Susan happily married another man, and Steven even knows she's a mother.

"Woah, this is freaky," says Susan. "My best friend, twice?"

"Wait, you're sleeping with her husband and still call her your best friend?" says the fugitive.

"Hey, they got a divorce. I didn't cause it. I also got one. And I'm not sleeping with him. I'm dating him."

"Elizabeth," says the newly arrived Steven, holding the stun gun, pointing to the fugitive.

"Will you just leave me the hell alone?"

"No. You can't just kill people to get your way."

"Can someone explain to me what is going on?" asks the boxers wearing Steven, but everyone ignores him.

"Well, find me a Steven who is available, and I will stop killing people. I didn't kill mine. He died on his own and left me alone."

"That's no reason to kill other copies of you in other dimensions. Well, I know a Steven who is available: me. We can work something out."

"You already have your Lily."

"Yeah, but displaced. We can leave for dimension 28, and you can go fetch me in the past."

"As if this could work."

"It can," says the Lily holding Steven's free hand.

"Bullshit," and suddenly, she darts away, and Steven fires the stun gun, but misses. That's one less charge.

They want to run after her, but the resident Steven stops them.

"Someone, please tell me what the hell is going on."

"We're from other dimensions, in which I invented a time machine. This Lily lost her Steven, and thought that since you divorced, she could settle here. In other dimensions, she killed our copy to replace her," explains Lily.

"Shit, and my ex-wife?"

"She's fine, we saved her," says Steven.

"Good. Just because we split doesn't mean I want her dead. I found my happiness, she's allowed to find hers," he says, kissing Susan. The two-time travellers rush in pursuit, but of course, Lily left with the black machine.

"So, Susan," says Lily, teasing him.

"I never saw her as a potential girlfriend."

"Did you really never see it? I did. Did you see how she looked at you back then?" says Lily.

"At me? She's basically in love with you. Even in the future. Can't stop talking about you," says Steven. Which makes Lily laugh, as the tracker stabilizes.

"Same location, but dimension 24."

"Good, Steven won't be here. I think it's time to recall her machine. It's enough, we risk her wising up and going back and doing real damage."

"Like what?"

"Like killing someone as soon as she steps out of her time machine, or going to our dimension to wreak havoc. Or finding some explosives to blow up our machine," she says.

"Wait, we could pull a Back to the Future Finale," Steven proposes.

"What do you mean?"

"Arrive five minutes before her?"

Lily smiles and changes the arrival time. On location, they're still in the backyard, and Steven is holding the stun gun.

"Five minutes is way too long," he complains.

"I know, still four minutes left," says Lily.

"Speaking of Susan, can you tell me the truth?"

"About what?"

"The picture, in their office. In black and white, it's you, isn't it?"

"What do you think?"

"I think it is."

"Think harder"

"Huh?"

"We're in dimensions #1, I only time travel in #2 and #3. Echoes, move outward, so it's not possible for such a picture to go from #2 or #3 back to #1."

"Are you telling me, seriously, that they own a picture of a woman who looks almost like you in the office of one of my clients?"

"Hey, stranger things can occur. I met a guy who looks just like you in #3 while hiding a steam governor."

"You did?"

"And his last name was Clark. He might have been one of your ancestors."

"So, it's not that strange."

"Who says that she isn't one of mine?"

But then, the black box materializes, and Steven runs to where the door is. When it's open, he fires the stun gun, and the fugitives drop the knife on the ground, and falls slowly on top of it, unconscious.

"Shit," says Lily. The knife fell flat, and as such, didn't cut the clone.

The time machine is searched, and when they find nothing, they plug the USB recall stick, and they put the tracker on the floor. They close the door and as promised, the machine returns to wherever it was supposed to go.Lily put the knife in one of the storage bays of the remaining time machine, and both help the now unconscious Lily into the machine, to be sent to dimension 28.

231

Chapter 6.8—Glimpses of normality

A long and sturdy chain is bought, and solidly anchored in the basement, close to the restroom, and long enough to make it to the sofa, but not long enough to reach the two parked time machines. The bring the still stunned fugitive, downstairs and get her ankle tied to the chain, using a heavy-duty padlock.

Lily decides to survey the house for the first time as a possible resident. She pays more attention than when she only tried to find a destination. Meanwhile, Steven waits patiently for their prisoner to wake up. Often, he goes to take her pulse, to ensure she's still alive. It's not like the Inspector general offered any instructions about the effects of the stun gun. He did try some cold water on her face, but when she didn't wake up, he dried it up. He tried talking to her, shaking her gently, nothing occurred.

And so, taking his distance, he waited. Lily was back to his side, cuddling him on the sofa.

"Despite my travels, I never saw a clone of me sleeping. Weird, isn't it?"

"It's not that weird. When you visit people, you don't typically visit them sleeping."

"I know, but sometimes I spent a few days."

"And you went to your room, and they went to their room," Steven added.

"When did you become the reasonable one with answers?"

"I did spend over a decade alone."

"Right. Now you're the mature one. I like that," she says, kissing him.

A good 10 minutes later, the prisoner began to move, and a few minutes later, woke up.

"Where am I?"

"We chained you to the basement in our new houses," says Steven.

She looks at the chain.

"Are you insane? You can't keep me chained like this."

"It's only until we get a good understanding. Just a few days and we will let you go back to 2002 to live with me, assuming the role of my wife."

"This will break everything."

"No, because in 2014, I will leave you to come to this dimension."

"And I will be alone."

"You will have 12 good years with me. That's 12 more years than if we deliver you to the Inspector General."

"And what do I do after you leave?"

"Continue your life or find one of the widowed Stevens. We'll even help you. You'll know our dimension. Hey, maybe it will be me. Or maybe we can right away find you a new dimension. We haven't fully decided yet."

"Or perhaps we can share him," says Lily, next to her man.

"I'd like that. And I will be safe from the bitch?" says the prisoner.

"She can't act in my dimensions. We have an accord."

"Fine. So, what do I do, in the meantime?"

"You have a restroom, a television, I can bring you books, we will bring you food, and keep you company. It's only for a few days to get things ready," says Steven.

"Fine"

The couple gets upstairs.

"Share me?" he says, teasing his wife.

"Hey, anything to reassure her."

"So, what do we do now?"

"Well, you have a technical manual to learn, I have some time travelling to do."

"What? You will go again?"

"I'm safe out there."

"You disappeared."

"You don't get it, do you?"

"What?"

"I never disappeared. Never."

"You vanished for 12 years."

"You still don't get it. So, I left for a simple run. In the middle of that run, you found me with your modified time travel machine. In the process, we realized I couldn't go back, so we picked a dimension you scoped where we could move. We found… my clone, now downstairs, and chased her, and now, we're here. But had you never travelled and found me, I would have made it back to 2002. We would have never met the woman downstairs. We would have never moved to this dimension. The only reason we're moving here, and you thought I was lost earlier, was because you didn't know I was a time traveller. Now you do, and you will have your own. '

"But I only built the quantum antenna."

"Beacon"

"Fine, the quantum beacon because you didn't show up."

"Right, each of the occasions in which one of us jumped dimension, ours kept running. It only gets reset when we come back. I never did because in that loose end, you also changed dimension. But normally, you wouldn't be able to do so."

"I see. What's the purpose of the beacon, you said something about navigation?"

"Yes, the positioning process uses it to steer while travelling. Not only does the Earth is in orbit around the Sun, but the Sun moves in the galaxy, so the system needs it to locate where the Earth is, and then, close in on our coordinates."

"So, what makes it a beacon?"

"Your emitter. In a time machine, it's passive, in your setup, it's actively sending pulses and interfering with navigation, pulling us in across dimensions."

"Thank you for explaining. So, am I being the only idiot dumb enough to turn an antenna into a beacon?"

"Twice, it seems," she says, smiling.

"Still, are you sure you will return?"

"Well, you will know where I'm going, and when. And from now on, I will tell you why I leave and whom I see, which is oddly not many people. I usually pick up antiquities at night, and bury them elsewhere also under the cover of darkness."

"So why risk it now?"

"You still don't get it. Because of the diary"

"Huh?"

"It contains trips and events I haven't done, but need to occur by the time the book makes it back to you."

"Can't you just copy them over?"

"For some, sure. Like the sickness and my periods, we don't care. By dying, I interrupted them. By the way, you do know why I logged them, right?"

"No?"

"Do you recall I had an irregular cycle?"

"That, I do"

"Well, it's not. It's just that the cycle follows my body, and not the calendar on my wall. Sometimes, my 29 days occurred in only 20 because I spent 9 time travelling."

"Oh"

"But the steam governors and the interviews, I still need to do them, since I picked up and delivered to the college museum some of the pieces that I hadn't picked up yet. I never needed to do them in chronological order, but now, I must complete the process."

"How long will it take?"

"For me? Maybe a year? For you? A day or two, and only because I will return here to recharge with your new hyper speed charging circuit and spend time with you. I could do it at once, if I could fit multiple copies and charge them side by side. In reality, I will never actually leave your side. I will charge 100% of the time here, coming back seconds after leaving."

"Nice"

"But I will need to plan my travels. I won't be fully available to you when I'm here."

"So, what do I do, in the meantime?"

"As I said, review your company paperwork, talk to our prisoner. Reassure her"

"As if that were easy."

"Then review your paperwork next to her, but don't bring the keys. At worse, I will have the time machine without the hidden switch, so I can come back earlier and solve any issues, including if she chokes you with the chain," says Lily.

"Don't joke with that."

"I'm not joking. This isn't our dimension. We can do whatever we want with the timeline."

"When do you leave?"

"Well, I need to copy some content, maybe you can try to make us supper or something?"

"Sure. I saw pasta and some canned sauce."

"At worst, you have two time travel machines to get to a fast food joint," she says, laughing.

Steven felt good to have his wife back, and the next few days weren't that bad. They slept in the same bed, often ate in the basement with their prisoner, who was getting more positive. Almost remorseful. The trio even watched a few movies, including a comedy which made everyone laugh.

A few times, the chain was unhooked for the prisoner to change her clothes or take a bath, but when she wasn't watched, she would often lock her ankle on her own. To prove Steven could trust her. Steven and Lily played a few board games at the kitchen table, but the chained dimension clone wasn't interested. Things were getting back to normal, and fast. Only two days had gone by.

Chapter 6.9—Globe Trotting

Steven first went to buy supplies at the hardware store. Easily, he added a new one hundred amps and two-hundred-and-forty-volt breaker in the electrical panel in the basement, and then ran a thick wire from the panel to the parking space for Lily's time machine. It felt weird for him to refer to the other one as his, but he had modified it.

At first, he wanted to run two wires, but Lily explained that she would take no pauses in her travelling: she would be charging a hundred percent of the time, and once done, would leave. Previously, since the upgrade to two hundred and forty volts using Victor's system, the process was operating at two hundred and forty volts, thirteen and a half amps, or three thousand two hundred and forty watts. It means forty-three and a half hours to power the time machine fully.

The new cable was able to deliver at a peak of twenty-two thousand, but Steven kept it at twenty thousand watts. That's a sixfold improvement, so that a full cycle lasts about seven hours. In reality, Steven had spare batteries from Victor's box, so he hooked up chargers to do hot swaps. It wouldn't help much, according to Lily, but the practicality is that they could add more watts in them.

Considering that in each loop, Lily never spent more than fifty percent of her power, it means that with the swap and the plugged in delays, she only wasted four hours before departing again. Not that she left for long! As soon as the machine vanished, it came back within two seconds, a window small enough for Steven not even worry if she returned.

Lily would have rested, eaten, her hair would have grown, her clothes would change. She might disappear for a blink, but sometimes days or weeks elapsed on her side. "You're older, so it makes sense for me to spend that time away from your timeline, I age, you don't", she explained. And moreover, she would charge, albeit slowly, while sleeping on location. Not when spending the night in the eighteen hundred.

But when in the late nineties or early two thousand, a few percent felt better than nothing. Once, she even filled to 100% while on a complicated planning task. Her goal was to do as much as possible on each trip so that she would reduce their quantity.

The weird part is, the sequence sort of fit. She copied the original notes, and she noticed that the blocks appear organized in a structured way, but with a different launch place. It's on her second trip that she realized she had it wrong. Instead of coming from #28 and travelling to the first destination in one go, she began by just moving to the proper dimension, at the indicated starting spatial-time coordinates.

Each jump saves more batteries than deviating from the plan. The reason remains simple: she takes items from the Industrial Revolution, hides them, and retrieves them in the modern era. The order of the trip minimizes the frequency of going from the past to when she buries them. Rather from a far period and the last few years, she chained them so that she journeys from 1804 to 1805, and to 1807, before doing 1980, 1981 and 1983. It helps move them to places she picked or bought them, in the timeline before her disappearance.

"Dimension travel's cost increases by the number you crosse, but time travel also drains more than teleporting."

"I witnessed that in action," replied Steven.

But even if she did everything she could while away, Lily still had some preparation to do in the present.

"If I have to just plan, I might as well come back and see you," she says.

Steven didn't mind, it gave him the occasion to review the schematic while talking to their prisoner. She expressed more optimism. He even made her understand that until she settled in her new life, he needed to keep her restrained or the Inspector General wouldn't trust him.

"But how will you avoid her?" she repeated.

And once more, he lied, explaining that his wife's dimensions remained off-limits to the Inspector General. That she would stay safe and happy. The accord were extended to #28, but Steven kept no illusion that #76 wouldn't just snatch #64 if she lost trust in him.

"How will I even do her job?"

"That's the neat thing, she already did it."

"Huh?"

"The only task for you is to show up at the college with the lesson plan and give it to students. Plus, my Lily will be returning sometimes to guide you, so you can leave questions, and she will pick them from you, reply to them, and send them back."

"Why can't she just take that place herself?"

"Because her goal is to be with me. If she goes instead, my timeline gets wiped out, but since you're from another dimension, so it doesn't reset mine." He explained confidently. Yet, he saw no way to judge how much he was unwillingly lying.

Still, it reassured her. It made her calm. It's not that he wanted to befriend her, if he stays honest. He just needed her not to turn homicidal again, to make her belong somewhere, and it tore his heart in two when he peeked in her eyes aware of his lie. Was he as cold as his father? How could he do this? He knew why. She remained physically identical to his soulmate, she possessed the same eyes, but she still wasn't his wife.

She decided on the path of a killer, willing to assassinate her copies just to find a way to steal their Steven. Back to him. But… he wasn't her husband. She never previously met him when she first spotted him on the beach. In his mind, he perceived her as a criminal, but presenting herself this sweet and calm, he couldn't resign himself to judging her.

She appeared to look just like his Lily. She has the same body, how could he think that she would always remain that foreign? Sure, it was easy to see that #64 is so far from his. He met a Lily from just twelve dimensions later, and she's cold, unwavering and willing to kill anyone in her way, animated by an almost religious fervour.

He realized that this dimension laid only twenty-seven steps from his origin, and he could notice so many discrepancies from his own life. This Steven felt mentally healthier, with friends and a business which bloomed. This Lily grew more reserved and refused to time travel. The prisoner in front of him was over twice further, and the few talks with her show considerable differences.

For example, she left her parent's home when she turned eighteen, rebelling against them and not going to college. Instead, she ran away with her Steven, managed to keep the flow of money from his father, and it's while on a trip that he died. Both seemed to have histories more like Michael and Camille, in the shadow of his family. In fact, Camille isn't even known to this Lily, with Michael assuming the role of the black sheep in her story. Perhaps that's why she didn't build her time machine? Maybe she lives too much in the present.

The little attention that his Lily gave him, such as reminding him that he possessed value, only his wife could provide that. This stranger would fail to do so, because she never received this reassurance herself. His Lily got it from the precursor Lily, the one who cracked the code of time travel early, but of dimension jumping too late.

"You told me you helped a few dimensions, right?"

"I made it to thirty-four," explained Lily. His Lily.

Maybe that explained it. Number twenty-eight refused time travel, but still spent some weeks with the original. Perhaps her interventions offered more than just to set up the machinery. Potentially, she would also support her counterpart emotionally in the same way she guided him. This broken Lily didn't get that chance and now, an even more deranged Lily had condemned her for her crimes.

But then again, Steven didn't decide to murder anyone, and both Victor and his dimension clone from Dimension 2 stayed at the forefront of his reflections. He had killed them, but it consisted of self-defence. That wouldn't lead to prison, right? Surely, it must not. But Lily interrupted his thoughts by leaving once more, and soon after, returning with even longer hair, and wearing one of the old-looking dress he had spotted in the time machine.

"I should get them cut."

"I love them this way."

"I have to live like this dimension's Lily."

"She grew a lengthier pony tail than when you arrived."

"OK, but mine grew since, so can you trim them now? My next trip is just a few days."

"Me?"

"You used to cut them when I was in college."

"Sure"

Steven found a pair of professional hairdresser scissors, and soon enough, Steven felt like back in college, shortening his then girlfriend's ponytail.

"Where did you get your dresses in the time machine?"

"From the past! I have this tailor who made me a few. I can't show them anywhere. He created them for me in the 1800s, but they didn't make the long way around."

"Why?"

"I'm a steam machine historian, not a clothing one, dummy."

"You look good in them,"

"Thanks," she says, smiling and taking a bow, ironically.

"The children you described in your thesis, and when telling your stories."

"Yeah, I met them."

"And those who died accidentally?"

"I couldn't help them, Steven. Can you imagine if I had made a major variation in the history? A kid I save might become parents. If they do, their offsprings will compete with existing ones."

"Even if it was in an alternate dimension?"

"What does it change, in the end? To them, that's their own home. I won't play God with the others just because I can."

And that was what Steven needed to reassure himself. Their prisoner did try to play God. She attempted to replace her counterparts. He was only hoping to restore what he lost, but not at the cost of anyone else. Not on purpose. She had stolen a time machine, she had killed people to impersonate their lives. He only defended his.

After cutting his wife's hair, they shared a meal. Not with their prisoner. Upstairs, like the married couple, they are. It was mostly in silence. They had a lot on their mind. But it felt like a pleasant silence. They were in good company. Soon enough, after some planning, Lily left again.

Chapter 6.10—Going back

"It's time," said Lily as soon as she returned, a second or two later.

"You think so?"

"I feel guilty of sending her to her death."

"I know, and she's my twin, in a way, but let's not forget that she murdered the Lily and Steven we're taking over," says Lily, pausing. "And that she assassinated many other dimension clones and only failed to kill more because we stopped her."

"I'm not claiming she deserves to live, but who are we to decide?" says Steven.

"That's the great dilemma, isn't it? If we hadn't intervened, if you hadn't intervened, Lily 76 would have disintegrated her. She wouldn't have found any peace at all, and we gave her some."

"Knowing she was going to die."

"Sure, I don't like it, but the universe wants a Lily to die. We don't have a choice, it's settled. It's me, or her. Because number twenty-eight died, and remain too old anyway," says Lily.

"What about the other Lily who vanished?"

"If we spare this Lily, as soon as Inspector General Lily finds out that #64 remains alive, and she will, she will disintegrate her. Our plan is to redirect her demise."

"Fine. But I don't want any mistakes, so just to keep ourselves a hundred percent certain, lend me your hand."

"My hand?"

"Steven grabs a sharpie from the desk, and writes, 'Lily #1" on her arm, just above her left wrist, so that when her blouse sleeve falls on her wrist, it's hidden, but he can easily inspect it.

"You don't trust me?"

"I don't trust her."

"Rhetorical question, how do you know we didn't switch?"

"Last time I spoke to her in the basement, she admitted to being number sixty-four, and only I ever had the key to her chain. Plus, you worry about her. She wouldn't worry about you."

"She doesn't know anything about steam governors, you could ask us questions to quiz us."

"Lily, I understand next to nothing about steam governors. I couldn't check on you."

"Really? I would bore you to death with facts."

"Yeah, fifteen years ago?"

"Right, it was the last few years for me. Sorry"

"I'll pick up the clothes and tell her to change."

"Unlock her, but don't let her leave."

"The basement only has one door, and the first owners secured the windows with bars, you'll be upstairs until it's time to leave."

"Steven?"

"Yes?"

"She isn't your wife, you realize that, right?"

"Yeah, I know she isn't you."

"So, leave her some privacy to change."

"Lily, give me some credit. It's not as if she had anything new. I didn't even undress her body after she died."

"That's not the point. It's not that I mind. Honestly, I don't. It's that she might."

"I know"

Steven picked up the clothes and headed downstairs.

"Hey, how are you today?" says the prisoner, cheerfully.

"I'm good, Elizabeth. And I have good news for you."

"You do?"

"I'll get you out of here. We're going on a trip, and I'm removing that chain from your ankle."

"Oh, so do you believe me now? The only thing I wanted was a place to live."

"Hey, it doesn't matter to me. I needed was to let things calm down."

"Is your Lily fine with that? I mean, she would have to share her husband with me."

"Hey, she chose when you would be let out of the basement," said Steven, technically telling the truth.

"You haven't answered my question."

"She won't share with her husband. We found a dimension with a young Steven, well, your age, willing to take you. He will think you're his Lily, but won't be in your way. What you need to do is pretend to be her, and you will have your place. And my wife's accord protects it."

"And I won't have to run?"

Steven must swallow hard.

"You will never have to run again."

"Nice. I'm tired of running."

"I have a change of clothes for you. I will first unlock you, and let you go to the restroom to change."

The fugitive nods, and soon enough, is unlocked, and spends a few minutes in the restroom. When she comes back, Steven has his heart tighten in him. But at the same time, the sleeves remained short enough to show her skin fully devoid of writing. Is that how governors feel when they send death row prisoners to their last walk? At least, they get a last meal of their choice. This killer didn't.

His Lily is called and says hello to her clone, who requests and gets a thank-you hug, which Steven knows will leave a bad memory in his wife's mind. Steven almost to left in his own machine when he realized his mistake and used Lily's. Checking around, he made sure he configured everything correctly. Soon enough, they boarded it, while his Lily placed the diary where he had found it, so long ago.

Steven, his wife and the fugitive get cramped into the unmodified time machine, and he simply pressed the go button, as they set everything earlier. Within two seconds, Steven and the two dimensions clones were back on the island where everything occurred.

"Where and when are we?" says the fugitive, way too close to him and his wife. Lily made this cockpit for only two people, and three felt cramped.

"We're back at the beach. It's complicated, but we had to route there before going because we needed a lift to get back home."

"Right, I will keep your time machine."

"Exactly, but I programmed it to return it to us once you leave it. You'll have a few minutes," says Steven lying as the time machine isn't even connected to the computer on Lily's machine. Rental is, but this version of his wife never built her own machine.

"I don't care. The only thing I ever wanted was a place to live, and a husband to love."

247

"You'll be with a younger copy of me, in 2002."

"That's perfect"

"Stay here, we will leave for a minute, don't touch anything," says Steven.

But as she looks at him, he zaps the fugitive with the stun gun he had tucked in his pants. She slouches over the keyboard, unconscious. He leaves with his wife to go back to the beach they left so long ago now, and barely left.

In local time, they left for less than five seconds. In fact, they didn't even leave the Inspector General an opportunity to look up the travels of the fugitive. Steven gets to her. "I caught her. She's in our time machine, stunned, I have a plan," he says, handing her the stun gun while keeping it pointed at the sand.

"So, what do you have in mind, Mr. Clark?" asked the matriarch, giving the stun gun to one of her men.

"It's simple. This began when I saw my wife die in my arms. So, we now need to shoot her in the heart, send her in the future, and then, back, to get stuck in my quantum antenna and perish in my arms to preserve her corpse."

"You want us to kill your wife?" asked Lily seventy-six.

"No,", replied his Lily. "He wants the method of execution of Lily sixty-four to be by gun so he can send her back in time in my place. So, she dies in his shop."

Lily 76 sighed. "Another body to vaporize...", she lamented.

"You already did! She's the first one I buried in the Pacific," he replied.

248

"No, that's your Lily. Lily one," said the Inspector general.

"How can you tell?" Steven asked.

"It was her box!" she said.

"Yes, we send her back with Lily's machine… as such, we preserve the timeline, the criminal executed, my wife gets to live on."

"What about the Lily and Steven of this dimension?" she asked.

"They were always going to die anyway… we'll just take their place," Lily one added.

"We don't use guns."

"I had one, it should be on the beach that way."

The inspector sighs, and picks it up, as she's coming back, Steven says to Lily seventy-six, "So, you want to shoot her directly into the heart, so it matched what I saw."

"I got that."

But she seems uncomfortable holding the gun. Suddenly, Steven realizes what he must do. The self-proclaimed Inspector General remained the one who condemned this clone of his wife to die, but he's the one who gained her trust to play a role. He couldn't ask someone else to do it for him. He felt unable to remove this guilt from his mind.

"I'll do it."

"You're sure?" asks his wife.

"It's my responsibility."

The inspector hands him the gun, and Steven opens the door to his wife's time machine. He lifts the unconscious Lily's head and places it strategically, pointed his gun at her chest from outside the machine, and fired. He closed the door and heard a small "thump" as the criminal fell forward. Steven changes the destination from 2002 to 2016. And sends her.

"Just locate the machine in my basement in #2 and send her back to 2002 as soon as she arrives", says Steven.

Lily 76 replied. "Sure, but it's stupid. You're stuck here without a time machine…"

"Well, we're not. We have a pedal boat to take us back to our cruise. My wife and I are on vacation, I'll let you know. Well, our now dead copies we're replacing were. We're on vacation from our work, from troubles, and now, we're on vacation from time travel. If you excuse me, I plan to continue what our counterparts from his dimension were doing when they were killed: spending an afternoon of sex on the beach." Steven watched Lily seventy-six nod and leave with her soldier. When he turned around, his Lily was untying her sundress.

www.ingramcontent.com/pod-product-compliance
Lightning Source LLC
Chambersburg PA
CBHW060913250626
47159CB00008B/2989